Ever Since

by

Dorothy Callahan

Copyright Page

ISBN-13: 978-1544963136
ISBN-10: 1544963130

This is a work of fiction. Names, characters, corporations, institutions, organizations, events, or locales in this novel are either the product of the author's imagination or, if real, used fictitiously. The resemblance of any character to actual persons (living or dead) is entirely coincidental.

Published by:
Somerwynd Services

Cover By:
SelfPubBookCovers.com

Artist:
Shardel_18574

Dedication

To Carissa, LVT Extraordinaire!

And to all the LVTs who work their butts off every day in demanding and life-saving situations: you pour your heart and soul into your job and get bitten and scratched in return. You give blood, sweat and tears while juggling multiple cases and trying to simultaneously placate doctors, owners, and receptionists. You are awesome!

Acknowledgements

Special thanks to NY Officer Rod Gifford for the detailed information on police procedurals regarding Matty's accident. I would have hated to spring my hero from prison before the story even started... even though that could have made things interesting!

To my critique partners, Laurie Gifford Adams and Lorraine Lander, who kept this story on track. I'd never be able to finish a book without your amazing input!

Last, but not least, to my amazing husband, Craig, who always understands when I need to hide behind my keyboard all day. I'd never have this career without you!

Other books by Dorothy Callahan

Taming the Stallion: *How does a girl arrest the most perfect man?*

"A strong debut novel!" USA Today Bestselling author Mary Buckham

"A book that touches the heart of Animal lovers." Ria Donée Waters, author of *Raven's Heart* and *Lube Job*

"Pick up this book today and enjoy." CozyReader, TheRomanceReviews.com

"A great book. I couldn't put it down. The plot was well thought out, and the characters were well developed." A western fan

"Wow, what a great read. One of the best books I have read in a long time." Love My Puggle

Loving out of Time: *Do you sacrifice the family you have, or the one you want to start?*

"If you haven't read a time travel I would recommend this one." KindleCoffee

"Romance. Time travel. Adventure. What more could you want?" Print & Film Fan

"The story line and characters are engaging. The book kept me up all night. I look forward to reading more from this author!" Ria Donée Waters, author of *Lube Job* and *Raven's Heart*

Third Eye's a Charm: *Lies. Deceit. Denial. A ghost. Must be Wednesday morning.*

"The details give the story such imagery that it's easy to lose yourself in this book."
Heather Ladue, Online Customer

"Dorothy Callahan's books remind me of Jill Shalvis' books in that they are a sexy, fun read with a great storyline built in!" Stephanie Coffee, Online Customer

"There are days when you just want a story that is easy to read, makes you feel good and reassures you that all is right with the world. This is one of those books."
USA Today Bestselling author Mary Buckham

"Dorothy Callahan's sense of humor reminds me of Janet Evanovich's. I could not put it down." Carissa, Online Customer

"Callahan does a great job of keeping readers on the edge of their seats with this book." Lorraine Lander, author of *The Color Chronicles* Series

"Adorable story with just enough twists to keep it interesting!" Elegantly Evil

A Decade for Darius: a girl never forgets her first kiss

"I've never read a romance where the two main characters were more perfect for each other. As always, Mrs.

Callahan's writing is full of wit & charm. You won't be able to put it down." Print and Film Fan

"The characters absolutely leapt off the pages. Ms. Callahan integrated humor, wit, and a quiet intelligence in all of the characters and in the writing itself. The story was engaging, complicated enough to keep me guessing, and passionate enough to have me fanning myself and thinking back to that first love." Online Customer

"Author Dorothy Callahan gets top marks for her second chance at love romance in A Decade for Darius. It was a beautiful story featuring interesting characters with a strong emphasis on antiques. It strongly reinforced the idea that love can conquer anything, even the passage of time."
Romancing the Book

"I have read this book twice and am on my third time. It is filled with romance, mystery, action, and Dorothy Callahan's usual sense of humor/wit. As always, I can't wait for the next book!" Lisa, Online Customer

Chapter 1

If there was anything worse than being completely alone at Christmastime, Cora didn't know what it was.

Oh, wait, yeah, she did. It was being completely alone because she was suddenly unemployed and stranded five hours from her family with a major Nor'easter blowing in that would keep her isolated from the people she desperately needed to see. *That* was worse than being alone at Christmastime.

Unfortunately, the realization of her situation didn't improve her mood. Her grandparents would be clearing up the breakfast table right about now, so it wasn't like she stood a risk of waking them. She dialed and heard a child pick up. "Hello?"

She had so many cousins she hadn't seen in three years that she couldn't place the voice. "Hi, who's this?"

"I'm Babycakes. Who are you?"

Ah, Bobbie, the firstborn and therefore angel of her cousin, Jemma. She smiled. "Hi, Babycakes. This is your cousin, Cora. Is Nana there?"

She heard the girl scream for her grandma, and with a resigned chuckle her Nana picked up. "Cora?"

She forced joyfulness into her voice. "Nana! Merry Christmas!"

"Oh, sweetie, I'm so glad to hear from you! Does this mean you're coming for the New Year's Eve bash? You're the only one not here, you know."

She jolted. "What do you mean?"

"Well, your brother just got here, Sherry's coming today, and—"

"Wait, wait, wait. Peter's there?"

"Oh, yes!"

"He actually closed the shop?"

"Can you believe for the entire week? Your cousin Dale and his family came in from Georgia. Randy's here, too. My sisters both made it, and of course, everyone else. It's a full house this year."

God, when was the last time she'd seen her siblings? Or her cousins? Aunts, uncles, grandparents? Damn it, she needed to start pinching pennies, but *the whole family was there.* "Damn it!"

She didn't mean to say it out loud, but Nana heard. "Cora, you and your filthy mouth."

"Sorry. Slipped out." But then she realized what else Nana had said. "Wait. Did you say Sherry's home?"

"Yup! Your mother talked to her last night. She said she's coming."

She heard Nana tell whoever was nearby that she was on the phone with Cora, and then the chatter in the background swelled. "Dear, everyone wants to know when you're going to be here."

Fuck! She considered how much was in her bank account, how much gas she'd have to buy to get there. She'd be fed and housed, so it would only be the gas money.

Money she couldn't really afford to spend right now.

But the whole family was there!

"Cora?"

"Yeah, I'm here." Cora worried her lip and looked down at the rummaging at her feet. Herbie nosed her sneaker and then tugged on the lace, untying the knot. She made her decision, consequences be damned. "Do you still have the crate for my rabbit? Or do I need to pack his playpen?"

"No, it's still here, I think in the barn. I'll have your brother get it out."

"That would be great." Cora found her head tipping back as she closed her eyes. It would be hard to admit to everyone that she lost her great job of six years, but if she ever needed to be surrounded by her loving family, it was today. "It will be great to be home." She meant it, too. Skaneateles, the most beautiful and cleanest of the New York Finger Lakes, was her stomping grounds, and today it called her back.

"Obviously, space at the inn is limited, so don't be surprised when you see I had to crowbar a few more people into every room."

She forced out a laugh. "No, I understand. Have you resorted to mangers in the barn, yet?"

"Cora, don't you blaspheme!"

A chuckle. "Can't wait to see everyone again. Man, the foals must be all grown up now."

"Oh, they are. Your mother is very proud of this crop. She's been doing ground work on them all summer. You'll see."

"I can't believe you still host every year, Nana."

She chuckled. "Soon, you're going to have to do it. You or Sherry."

"The cooking gene stopped at you, Nana. Have you ever tasted anything Sherry cooked? It's awful. I'm surprised I survived with her feeding us. Even her after-school snacks were atrocious."

Cora loved Nana's joyous laugh on the other end. "I'll tell your sister how you feel."

"Don't bother," Cora interjected. "I don't hold back. You know that."

"Every time you open your mouth." That comment was followed by a happy sigh, though. "Well, dear, you better get moving. That storm is coming in from Pennsylvania by evening. How long, again, to get here?"

"From Long Island?" She racked her brain from former travel times. "Five hours, tops. If I'm not there by dinner, send out the search party."

"Can't wait to see you, Cora." And then she

laughed. "I just knew this would be a fantastic Christmas. Just you wait. It's going to be the most perfect New Year's, too."

Cora loved how much faith her Nana had. Maybe Cora needed a little more of that, too. After all, her veterinarian boss/friend said she was going to do everything in her power to get Cora's position reinstated as a licensed veterinary technician, so maybe she really *was* on vacation this week and not unemployed. She couldn't worry about it. Not today. Not this week. She trusted Carla to make everything okay. It *would* be okay. Even if she had to get another job, it would all work out. Somehow. "I want a tenth of your faith, Nana, but I'm going to let your positive thoughts ride shotgun on the drive up. Especially as I trudge through the City. How's that sound?"

"Perfect, dear. Absolutely perfect. In fact, I can think of only one thing that would make this week any better."

"Oh, yeah? What's that?"

"You'll see when you get here. Love you."

Before Cora could even frown, her Nana hung up the phone.

Chapter 2

Most of the congregation had left by the time Matty folded up his bagpipes and settled them into their hard shell case, making sure the African blackwood drones didn't rub and chip as he pressed them into storage. His Da waited for him outside, ready to drive him and his Highland cousin Davey, already seated in the car, back to their home in the Finger Lakes. The pastor came up and thumped him thrice on the back. "Great seeing you again, Matty."

"Thank ye. It was fun to play at ma old church, see everyone again."

"I could tell people missed you. I'm glad to hear you're doing so well."

Aya, as well as a man with a damaged heart could do, but Matty wasna in any mood to correct the man. Freshly returned from the Highlands had made his accent return, and traveling with his cousin, who'd never left his village before Matty dragged him about, ensured that his accent stayed fresh.

Funny, really. He didna care much for the way he once spoke, but he knew Cora had adored it.

Cora.

He forced himself to reply to the pastor. "Aya. It's the first break I've had from touring in nigh six months."

The pastor smiled kindly at him. "How long will you be home?"

However long it took to win Cora back, but he didna want to admit to such fanciful ideas. "I doona know. Mayhap a week or two? By mid-January, I'll need to be back on the road." He grinned. "Canna have the Bagpipe Barons on tour without their master piper, now, can they?"

"I'd wager not. Merry Christmas to you."

"And ye." They shook hands as the pastor headed to the back of the church.

As Matty smoothed out his kilt and collected his case, he heard a woman's challenging voice call out, "Matteu MacKenzie."

Cold swept his spine at the familiar voice, and he looked up into the familiar eyes, not prepared for facing Cora's family just yet. Grandmamma Foote didna seem ready to tear him apart with her teeth, based on the gentleness in her eyes, which frankly surprised him. What *did* surprise him was that she seemed to have forgiven him for walking away from her granddaughter. After all, not a one of them had contacted him in the fourteen months he'd been gone. He stood and affected a neutral pose, summoned a wee smile to his lips. "Grandmamma Foote, ye look well."

"I look old; you can say it. I'm in my eighties, after all." She swung her arms open to him, and Matty stepped into her warm embrace, relieved she didna shoot him down.

"What brings ye here, Grandmamma?"

"Oh." She waved off the question. "I wanted to hear you play, of course. And, your father told me last week that you'd be home for Christmas."

"Aya, first time in two years. The pipe tours are most popular in winter."

"Really?"

Matty found her interest too pointed. "Aya."

"Then, how about playing for the family for New Year's Eve? I'll pay you, of course." Grandmamma handed him a sealed white envelope.

He stepped away from her offer. "I'd never charge ye, Grandmamma, ye know that." He opted for frank honesty. "I canna tell ye how happy I am for the offer, though." He raised his brows to her, wondering what her game was.

She waved off his unspoken question. "Matty, I barely remember a Christmas when you weren't here. It's not the same without a Scotsman around." She shoved the envelope at him again.

Matty grinned but refused to take her money. “Ye should know ye get ma services for free. I will, however, be happy to take a meal at your table. Me and ma cousin, Davey, that is. He’s a bangin’ player; simply needs more stage experience. But, ye’ll get us both for free.”

With a sniff of acknowledgement in how he maneuvered her, Grandmamma stuffed the money back into her pocket. “As you wish. So! Your father says you’ve been overseas for the last fourteen months, and I haven’t seen you in two years. It’s been too dull at home, and if feeding a set of master pipers through the holidays is all I have to do to enliven things, so be it.”

Feeling as a bug under a microscope, Matty found himself shuffling under her gaze. Finally, he addressed the elephant in the room. “Ye know I didna bring Cora with me overseas.”

She inhaled a deep breath, standing taller as she studied him. “Yeah, I do.”

“Yet still ye want me there?”

She smiled. “Our door is always open to you.”

He blinked and looked down, away from the never-ending love he saw in Grandmamma’s eyes. She had always acted so kindly to him, taking care of him on long summers when his own parents worked away their days. He’d come back from Scotland fully intending to make everything aright with Cora, and spending the holidays with the Foote-Steppe family served his purposes perfectly. Finally he said, “I’ve missed ye. All of ye.”

“Missed you, too.”

He’d fix this. He’d use this chance to make it work this time, beg Cora to join him on the road. He’d worked hard to become the man she deserved, so this would be the perfect chance for her to forgive him. He looked down the nave at the toot of the car horn outside and smiled back at Grandmamma. “When do ye want us there?”

"Will three hours give you enough time?"

He cocked his head. "Ye want us there today?"

"Is that a problem?"

No, but he desperately wanted to ask, wanted to know if Cora would be there, but the words faltered on his tongue. He owed her family this much, anyway, and Davey could use the experience. He wasna about to let his motives or fear show, though, so he smiled. "We can be there in three hours."

"Storm's blowing in. You might want to bring a change of clothes. Maybe even a week's worth."

He held her eyes, cocked his head. Was this Grandmamma Foote's method of asking him to stay? Days before the party, too, so did that mean Cora would be there? His mouth dried. "I'll keep my luggage packed."

With a smile, Grandmamma reached up and buzzed his cheek. "Welcome home."

Two hours later, Matty rolled his eyes at Davey, barely a year younger in age but a full ten in spirit, as evidenced by the fact he couldna get his arse moving. "Have ye na packed yet, ye lazy bugger?"

"Bugger off, coz. Ye know I got all I need right here." And he grabbed his bollocks through his kilt and gave a rogue grin.

"Ye'll no be causing mischief at the Foote house. That woman raised me as kith and kin."

"Then she should know ye got naught but tuppin' on the brain."

Nah. Matty hadna been with a woman since the day he made the biggest mistake of his life. "Doona confuse yer actions with mine, ye blighter. I've a heart o' pure gold."

He got a scoff and smile in reply.

Matty grinned in turn and gently double-checked his suitcase and pipes, making sure he had all he needed.

His Da and Mum knew Matty wanted to rectify things with Cora so they let him go with little fuss. The problem was, Grandmamma Foote said nothing of Cora being home this week.

Home.

Matt wasna sure if any place would be *home* again if he couldna win Cora back.

Baby steps, Grandmamma Foote would say. Start with baby steps.

With Davey finally packed and loaded, Matty drove the eight miles to the Foote home in the fading light of early afternoon, listening to Christmas carols on the radio and feeling more nervous as he passed each street closer to his destination.

"I willna get used to driving on the wrong side of the road."

The innocent comment made Matty grin. "Yer in America now. They do things a wee bit different here."

"Fair enough." Davey seemed in fine spirits when he added, "I canna believe yer taking such a tiny gig."

"It's na a gig." Matty slowed down to bear right on the snow-covered road. When he no longer felt the wheels sliding, he settled back into the seat. "Da told Grandmamma Foote last week I was coming home. She must have decided then to put us as part of the entertainment."

"Fancies ye, does she?" He gave a bawdy wink.

"Loves me as her own son." The truth of that statement physically hurt to admit. "Well, grandson, that is. She's the loveliest of ladies. Ye'll like her."

"I'd like her more if she paid me."

"Yer na to take money from Grandmamma Foote. I mean it. Nary a dime."

"Then what's the point?"

Cora was the point, but Matty hadna shared the truth of his failings or feelings yet. "To see if ye can finally play a Throw on D as good as mine."

"Ma Throws on D lure the mockingbirds straight down from the branches, they do."

"Aya, right."

The gentle banter continued as the sun slipped below the horizon, leaving a purple sky overhead. When the farmhouse came into view, both he and Davey caught their breath, Davey most likely in awe of the scope and glitter, Matty in tentative hope.

He didna see Cora's car, but who was to say she hadna upgraded?

He hoped she hadna upgraded to a new lover. He didna think he could stomach watching her cozy up to another man, even if Matty had deserted her at the lowest time of her life.

He was naught more than a buggered rat bastard. Would serve him right should Cora's belly be rounded with another man's child.

Only one way to tell.

Since the weeklong party was well underway, they had to pass both the house and the barn to find a space to park in the U-shaped drive. They got out and trudged over the crunching snow, aiming for the wide plank steps.

"I thought ye said she lived in a farmhouse, na a mansion." Davey stopped, mouth opened, looking up at the scope.

Instead of answering straightaway, Matty drank in the view. Colonial by design, the front had a deep porch festooned with swags of bulb-lit garland, garland that he and Cora hung most years. Detailed scrollwork topped each column, and the swing where he and Cora would snuggle on long summer nights no longer hung from the rafters. Shutters that he had painted black still flanked each wreathed window on both floors. One of the two dormers peeking from underneath the roof drew his gaze, reminding him of the day he and Cora had sat in that window seat, drinking hot chocolate and making out instead of studying for finals.

His eyes climbed to the two red brick chimneys, standing like disapproving sentinels against his nostalgic thoughts. Yellow candles glowed in every window like a thousand watchful eyes, waiting for him to slip up.

Davey stood oblivious to his inner turmoil. "Never seen a house so perfectly symmetrical. Except for the offshoot on the left."

He nodded. "That's where the library and additional bedrooms above had been added." He glanced to Davey and added, "Her grandda managed the peppermint-oil factory in Lyons. Moved his family here after he retired." He raised his chin to point. "Wait 'til you see the back of the house. Both floors have walk-out sleeping porches, and the whole right corner of the house is rounded with windows, both floors."

Wryly, Davey said, "I thought the only money in oil was petrol, not peppermint."

"Factory's now closed." Matt shrugged as he climbed the steps and rang the bell. A small child tugged open the door, two wagging, barking dogs flanking her. By her frown and the way she looked him over, Matty could tell she'd never seen kilts before. "Why are you in a dress?"

He smiled down at her. "Babycakes, do ye na remember me?"

She shook her head, but before she could answer, Cora's brother Peter shooed the massive yellow Lab and ancient Bichon Frise aside and flung open the door. "Matty! Come in, come in. Kilts? Isn't that a summer festival thing?"

Before Matt could even reply, people swarmed him, drew him in, hugged him, slapped his back in hearty welcome.

They didna know.

It was too fine of a welcome, too open.

Grandmamma Foote parted the sea of people and wrapped her arms about his neck. "Matty! So glad you made it. How was the drive in?"

Had no one here been told the truth? He glanced about the smiling faces for a moment and said, "Na bad, yet. Give her a good hour and ask me again." He turned to introduce his cousin. "Ma cousin, Davey. He plays ma second."

"I've as good a march as this one—" Davey cocked his head at Matt as he took her hand to shake— "but his fingers are a wee bit faster'n mine."

Matty grinned. "That's as close to a compliment as I've ever heard from him."

The banter made Grandmamma smile. "Welcome, welcome. Come in." She looked over her shoulder. "Oh, Peter, take their bags, won't you? Put Matty in the back bedroom upstairs, and Davey in the gathering spot upstairs. Hope you don't mind, Davey. Full house this year."

"We doona mind," Matt sent a glance to his cousin as they followed the woman into the kitchen, where she led them to the counter filled with appetizers.

"As promised, all the food you can eat."

The noise from Davey spoke his appreciation, but Matty only laughed. "Na exactly what I requested, Grandmamma. Only a meal at yer board."

"Stuff it, coz. The woman wishes to feed us, so dig in."

With a sigh of exasperation, Matty faced his hostess. "Apologies. Turns out ma uncle never fed him much. I feel like I took in a manner-less stray dog."

The comment made Grandmamma laugh and swat his arm. "Eat! Eat!"

"Aya, I see your homemade guacamole dip taunting me over there."

Another laugh, then Grandmamma kissed his cheek and shoved a brass key in his hand. "You must be cold in those kilts. Grandpa's got some scotch in the library if you need a quick warm up. Otherwise, the lasagna will be ready by five."

He placed a hand on his stomach. "Aya, ye make the best lasagna, Grandmamma."

She grinned and turned toward the sound of something breaking, followed by children screaming their accusations. "See? Things are already getting lively. Welcome home. Love the accent," she tossed over her shoulder as she hastened around the corner.

"Scotch?" Davey prompted as he shoveled pepperoni and cheese slices off his plate, and Matty nodded.

"I'll show ye." He crossed from the kitchen, back to the living room, then unlocked the double glass doors to the library. The thick carpet, heavy drapes, and hundreds of tomes muffled the ruckus from the next room.

"Nice." Davey nodded in appreciation as he scanned the area.

"Aya, I know."

A female squeal. "Matty?"

He recognized Sherry's voice and turned, bracing for—

She launched against him, throwing her arms about his neck and moving him a good step backwards. "Oh, my God, I can't believe you're here!"

He gave her a brotherly hug and eased her away from him before she started rubbing suggestively up against him, like usual. He didna want Cora's sister flirting with him. It was her standard treatment, benign, except for the fact she always pinkened his cheeks with her bawdy suggestions. Nothing had ever transpired between them, and nothing ever would, but he figured Cora never much cared for the interaction, even if she waved it off. So today he would set a new precedent. He turned Sherry to face Davey and said, "This here is ma cousin, Davey. This bonny lass is Sherry Foote-Steppe, and she has been trying to get under a MacKenzie kilt for as long as I've known her."

She gasped, mouth open and everything as she stared at him. "I have not."

Davey raised a speculative brow at the introduction. "Foote-Steppe? For certain?"

Matty lowered his voice to a stage whisper. "Aya, and doona be buggering the Foote-Steppe children of their surname if ye know what's best for ye. I once witnessed them tear apart a child with their teeth for the mockery."

Sherry rolled her eyes. "We were *all* children at the time. And even though he was a total snot, we never resorted to savagery."

"Bloodied his nose, she did."

"He fell."

"*Assisted* fall."

"Nope. He fell. Running away screaming like a girl because I said I was gonna kill him."

To Davey he added, "Savages, the lot of them."

"It's the truth. You were too busy serenading my sister to really notice."

"And then ye tried to seduce me, did ye na?"

"Flirting is far from seduction, Matty."

"Hardly, lass. But ye never did stop trying." Now Matty grinned and raised a taunting brow to his cousin. "Now, Davey, if ye think ye can manage a wee cockstand, I bet this lass would be verra happy to straddle ye."

She gasped again and Matty braced for the two fists flying into his stomach, one hard and one manicured. Dryly he asked, "Break yer hands?"

"Doona speak to the lady like that."

Aya, he'd made Davey scowl, for certain.

He watched Sherry shake her wrist. "Ow. Maybe." Her eyes locked on his. For the first time in memory, he'd made *her* cheeks pinken. "Matteu MacKenzie, I didn't think you had it in you. To fight back."

"Fighting? Who's fighting? Thought if ye needed a good tupping, I found ye the perfect man." He accompanied this with a hearty pounding on Davey's back.

Her eyes darted to Davey's and back to his. "You know I only flirt with men I can't have, and you, Matteu MacKenzie, as are unattainable as ever."

The admission made Davey step close and claim her hand. He pressed a kiss on the back of it and held her eyes as he said, "Then please, keep flirting with this bugger, but doona say a word to me. I'll na have ye flirting with me and fouling up ma chances."

She blushed again. "Wretched. That's what you two are." She backed up, a begrudging smile on her face. "Where's my sister?"

Aya, none of them knew. Did Cora na tell anyone, either? Nah, she couldna have kept such pain inside. She wasna the type to cry, but she certainly wasna the type to lie, especially after everything that had happened between them. Their families went back far too long for nothing to have been said. He didna know if she was here and couldna say anything without arousing suspicion, so he shrugged and told Sherry, "We'll be in here if ye see her."

"Okay. See ya," she said as she headed out.

Matty sipped his scotch and noticed Davey followed her to the doorway, leaning along the jamb to watch her go. "A looker, that one."

"Aya, she is right bonny. I've never seen her so tanned in December, though."

"And ye never took her up on her offer?"

He shook his head and took a longer sip. "I had already given ma heart to another when we met. I wouldna and willna cheat. Ye, however, doona have to live up to ma high standards."

A narrowed glare came from Davey. "*A wee cockstand*, eh? Is that what ye think I've got swinging low?"

Matty could only chuckle as he leaned along the desk. "Took ye long enough. Wouldna want Sherry to be disappointed after lusting after a MacKenzie for so long."

"I doona disappoint." But then the front door opened in the living room and the adults and barking dogs swarmed around the newcomer. The cries and exclamations made Matty move toward Davey at the library door to see who came in.

"Whoa. Will ye look at that," Davey said, and Matty rolled his eyes as his cousin adjusted himself under his kilt. "It's a mighty cockstand I've got working, I tell ye."

"Whoever she is, I'm sure she didna plan on getting tupped at the holiday family gathering, Davey."

"She's no family to me," he said.

With a groan, Matty stopped at Davey's side and peeked to see who had arrived and subsequently caught his cousin's interest so keenly.

His breath caught as he took her in. She hadna aged a day. Straight dark brown hair spilled from underneath her dark knit cap, her eyes still as gray as the snow clouds churning outside. Her chin tapered to a fine point, and her skin looked too pale, even for wintertime. He noted dark circles and thought she needed a good night's sleep. He saw no joy in her eyes despite smiling at her family. Perhaps the drive in had been perilous, but she looked weary to his eyes. Weary and sad.

Damn. He did that to her. He knew it, deep in his bones.

Davey set his glass on the nearest shelf and straightened and took one decisive step toward her. Without conscious thought, Matty slammed his hand on Davey's shoulder to stop him. "Not her."

He shrugged off the grip. "I've na had a good tupping in months, coz. She'll do just fine."

Anger and protectiveness surged in his blood, and Matty gripped his cousin's shoulder again, this time harder. "If it's death ye seek, ye'll be finding it at ma own hands if ye so much as lay a finger on that one."

Perhaps the fire in his words stopped him, because Davey actually met his eyes. "Is that so, coz? Why? Who is she?"

"Cora MacKenzie."

"MacKenzie?"

"Aya. Ma wife."

Chapter 3

She had barely hugged her brother before he leaned over to gather her belongings. He glanced at her Nana pointing up the stairs and said, "I know, I know. Back bedroom. I got her bags."

Cora shoved the rambunctious yellow Lab away from the carrier and then grabbed his collar to haul him off of it. "It's not a bag. It's my rabbit, Herbie."

The children nearest her squealed and circled around, and Cora knew her little bun would be in his glory once he settled in and the dog was put away. Most rabbits merely tolerated young children—mostly because children insisted on picking them up—but Herbie never minded. He even liked well-behaved pooches, like Nana's Bichon, Faberge. "Oh, crap. Peter, before you head up, can you grab my duffle bag from the car? Eight hours traveling in this weather and my mind is shot."

Her brother nodded and stuffed his feet into Gramps' rubber waders and trudged out to the car for the rest of her belongings.

A firm hand on her elbow spun her around, and Carla found herself facing her sister. "Oh, my God! Sherry!" They squealed and tossed their arms around one another. "You're so tan! And so... blonde!"

"The Sahara sun will do that."

"You've got to tell me about Africa."

"You bet."

Cora waved and smiled at everyone and headed upstairs with her bunny, both siblings helping her carry the load while she fended off the bounding yellow beast. When she opened the door to the back bedroom, she braced. "Holy shit, it's freezing in here." She noticed the metal dog crate and told Peter, "Oh, thanks for bringing this in for me."

Her brother snorted and offered the helpful comment of, "You've brought enough shit to make someone think you've got a baby and not a stupid rabbit."

It felt like a punch straight to her gut, so Cora lashed out. "He's smarter than any kid you'd ever make, Diesel-for-brains."

Sherry jumped in with, "Modern people have pets first to make sure their parenting styles are compatible. If you ever spent time with anything that didn't need a battery, perhaps you'd know this."

"You still think you know everything about men," he said.

"And you still know nothing about women," Sherry replied.

Despite the fact she still reeled from his comment, Cora smiled sweetly at him and added, "And you're still a jerk. But a handsome one, if that helps. Thanks for doing the heavy lifting."

He extended a middle finger to both of them before bowing and closing the door behind him.

"Holy shit, my bunny's going to freeze his buns off, especially—" she jacked her thumb at the dog nosing outside her door and then dumped her duffle on the bed—"if I have to keep the door closed because of Dozer." Someone else had already claimed the other side of the mattress. Oh well. Nana did warn her that she'd be crowbarred in with others, so hopefully whoever it was would be okay with Herbie sharing the room. Finally, she'd get to catch up with one of her cousins!

"Oh, I saw Ol' Red in the closet in my room. Let me get him."

While Sherry went after the plug-in heater, Cora busied herself setting up Herbie's crate. She lined his blanket on the bottom and added his litter box, then set out his dish of pellets. She'd grabbed all of his treats from home, including his canister of raisins and pouches of yogurt treats and honey snacks, but only brought enough pellets to get her through her stay. She stacked all of his consumables on top of her dresser, right next to the cage. She could hear Sherry struggling with the machine in the hallway so she held open the door and sighed. "Oh, my dear Ol' Red. How I've missed you."

"He's practically a fixture," she said as she lowered the ancient plug-in heater to the carpet. "Or a legend. Hang on. I want to watch the lights dim when you plug him in."

She laughed at the family joke. "I think Ol' Red predates Christianity." The unit gave off a decent amount of heat, but wasn't energy efficient by any stretch of the imagination... unless one counted the dimming of the lights. "Okay, here goes."

They both playfully made a descending "*Wooommmm*" noise as Cora turned up the dial, a sci-fi sound indicating a loss of power as the heat coils glowed to bright red.

"Still working. Maybe Nana upgraded the fuse box?"

"But not Ol' Red?"

They laughed and sat on the bed, eager to catch up. As soon as Herbie's carrier opened, he sniffed along the carpet, then stretched up to the bed for attention. Cora scooped him up and set him beside her, where he flopped along her thigh for a cuddle.

"What a sweet rabbit."

With a wry grin, Cora said, "He's Herbie, the love bug. Mom called him that when I told her he always hunkered down for loving; she said it was some VW Bug from a 70s movie."

The comment made Sherry laugh. "Yeah! I remember."

Somehow, Cora didn't think a white velvety-soft Rex rabbit with tan spots resembled a VW Bug, but she made no comment as she stroked his amazing coat. "So, Africa?"

Like she was lit from within, Sherry gazed at the ceiling and leaned back against the headboard, beaming. "It was transcendental. Reading and seeing the need on TV is nothing like standing there helping people who desperately need and seek medical attention. The hardest part of being there was not getting caught up in the wars."

"Wars?"

She nodded. "Constantly. We moved our hospitals all the time. Didn't stop the GSWs and bombing victims from finding us."

"My God, Sherry, gunshot wounds? Bombing? That's awful! Weren't you scared?"

She shrugged. "We made sure to never leave singly and always had an armed guard escort us. Oh, yeah, and this." She peeled down her pants to show the layer of chain link underneath. "A lot of us women wore them."

Cora raised a brow. "Is that... a chastity belt?"

A nod. "I was working in the rape capital of the world."

"Okay... so why are you still wearing it?"

Now Sherry grimaced. "Lost the stupid keys." She leaned forward. "On a scale of one to ten, how weird would it be to ask Pete to hack it off?"

"Seventy."

A sigh. "He's got the tools, though."

"And a burning need to hold something over your head, for, maybe, eternity."

"That's what I thought. Maybe I can raid Grandpa's tool kit for wire snips?"

"He'd never know unless you woke him to ask."

Sherry grinned and looked to the door. "I think you're right." She leaned forward again and lowered her voice. "So, speaking of chastity belts." Sherry got comfortable and her eyes glowed. "I can't believe he finally put an end to my over-the-top flirting. I mean, it's like he's a different person. Or maybe I am. Maybe my blonde tanness totally shocked him. I mean, I barely recognize myself in the mirror these days, so maybe I did kind of shock him? Anyway, how long has Davey been here? I mean, is he staying? He's quite a cutie!"

Through all of this, Cora tried to follow her sister's rambling but only wound up frowning and getting confused.

"Seriously, were you going to keep both of them to yourself? Greedy, sis. Totally greedy."

Her frown and confusion grew, so Cora asked, "What the hell are you talking about?"

The comment prompted Sherry to sit up and smack her arm. "Matty's cousin! When did he get here? He has the most awesome accent. And the kilt is way hot. Way."

"Matty's cousin."

"Yeah. Earth to sis. Where've you been hiding him?"

The prolonged stare didn't clarify anything. "I have no idea what you're talking about."

Now she got The Sigh. Complete with Big-Sister Eye Roll. "Some days I swear I want to wring your neck. Didn't you all come here together?"

Perhaps Herbie sensed Cora's frustration, because he jumped off the bed and ran into his crate, where he thumped his hind feet to warn of danger.

"Sherry, for the love of God, what the hell are you talking about?"

The question earned her two hard hands gripping her wrists, as well as a level stare. "Who. The. Hell. Came. Here. With. Matty?"

Perhaps her lungs collapsed. At least, that's what it felt like. When Cora finally managed to suck in her breath she asked, "Matty's here?"

"Duh."

“Who the fuck let him in the door?”

Like Ol’ Red set her on fire, Sherry flung off her grip and leaned back. “He’s your husband.”

“Like hell he is.” And then, sensing a matchmaking event in progress, Cora turned to look at the duffle bag on the far side of the bed and growled.

Chapter 4

When a large male hand thumped along Matty's shoulder, he turned to look into a cold and calculating pair of gray eyes.

"Matty."

Finally, one person who knew the truth and wished him dead. Fighting relief that at least he could be honest with someone, Matty faced Cora's father and offered him his hand. "Mr. Steppe. Ye look well."

For a long second, Papa Bear glared at his hand, and when he didna take it, Matty knew in no uncertain terms that he wasna welcome here. Mr. Steppe made no comment but indicated the library with his chin. "Come with me."

Although Matty had wanted—even sought—a reckoning, now that Mr. Steppe found him, he didna feel quite so brave. Still, he would swallow his due penance like a man. Chew on some humble pie. Quaff it down with a wee pint of humiliation. Aya. He would. He'd worked hard this past year, and now he was ready to do anything to win Cora back.

The door closed harder than necessary, and Mr. Steppe circled him like a hungry predator before taking the leather seat behind the desk. For a moment, Matty didna know if he should sit. He hadna been asked. So he stood. And waited.

"Why are you here?"

Aya, the anger behind the question gripped his heart in fierce talons. He looked to his feet. No point mentioning the invite. Or the gig. "I wish to fix things with Cora."

"And you think you're still welcome here; is that it?"

Thankful for the scotch that warmed him, Matty crossed the floor and took a seat to face his father-in-law. "I wasna expecting the warm welcome, for truth. I assumed your wife or even Grandmamma would have told everyone what happened by now."

"You mean, when you abandoned my daughter."

Aya, it hurt like hell to hear it. He had, but na like a coward, intent on putting his guilt behind him. No. Matty had had to take the bull by the horns, grab the offer before it expired. He'd needed to prove himself to Cora, and he'd done just that. But now, now he felt her absence, needed her at his side. "Aya, I did, but it wasna to be cruel. I left her a note, telling her I had to audition for the only open spot on the Barons. But I swear to you I've grown up. I am na that man who needs to prove himself to anyone. Na anymore."

The scoff spoke volumes. "Does Cora even know you're here?"

He shook his head. "I doona know. I havena seen her."

"If she doesn't kick you out on your ass, I will."

He raised one hand in supplication. "Please. I want to make it right with her."

"You wouldn't have to if you hadn't run away like a pouting teenager."

No, he hadna run away, but obviously her family didna know the truth. Na by the welcome he received. Certainly na from Sherry. She would never take sides with an in-law over her sister. Odds were only a few people knew the truth, Papa Bear being one of them. But he wasna going to be cowed away from his wife. "With all due respect, sir, Cora is ma legal wife. Ye canna prevent me from trying ma best to win her back."

He stood abruptly. "Actually, yes, I can."

Perhaps the Matty from two years ago would be cowed, but this Matty wasna. "I was invited by Grandmamma Foote to stay until New Year's Eve, when I'm expected to play. Ye willna be getting rid of me by then."

“I can try.”

“Aya. Ye can. But I’m expected to perform, and I willna let Grandmamma down.”

“Because you’re so good at sticking ‘round when the going gets tough?”

He lifted his chin. For the past year, he’d done exactly that. “Aya. I am.”

He let Mr. Steppe scrutinize him for a good, long minute. “You get one week. And then I will not be responsible for my actions.”

“Yes, sir. I willna let ye down.”

The comment made Mr. Steppe blast around the desk, sticking a giant finger into Matty’s face. “You think I give a damn about me? This is about Cora. Don’t you ever forget that.”

He leaned away from the fury he saw in his father-in-law’s eyes. Forced his heart to calm itself in the face of the man intent on wringing his neck. “Every moment away from her has killed me.”

“And yet, she was the one who almost died.”

Died? He didna think her stint in the hospital had been so dire as that, and neither had the doctor who had treated her. Aya, he failed her, miserably and completely, and if Cora had succumbed to her fate that night, Matty wouldna have been able to face his reflection ever again. But he had been assured she would recover with no permanent injuries, which was why he had sent her the note with the flowers, explaining his actions. He held his father-in-law’s eyes. “The doctor assured me they kept her only as a precaution. He said her health was sound.”

“But you didn’t stay to find out.”

No. He hadna. The offer was about to expire, and in a moment of cold logic, he had elected to grasp the brass ring, Cora’s blessing or no, and once he boarded that plane, he considered his life a do-over.

And now, he needed to rewind, erase his fame, his notoriety.

Nothing mattered to him if he couldna get his wife back.

He held those cold eyes and bit back a rejoinder, expending enormous self-control to prevent snapping to his feet and yelling at his in-law. Instead, he tempered his tone. "Aya, the fault in that is mine. But I'm here to remedy my sins, be the man your daughter deserves."

"She *deserves* a man who works to support her. She *deserves* a man who won't walk out. Tell me, how do you fit into that equation?"

The question made him blink. "I make money enough to well support us."

"Musicians don't make good money."

"With all due respect, sir, I'm na just *a musician*; I'm the master piper in Bagpipe Barons. The leader. I'm on tour in some of the biggest venues in Europe. I write and play tunes for the show. I can both make and repair bagpipes. *Rolling Stone Magazine* interviewed me last week." He held his eyes and added, "I've made enough money these last fourteen months to pay cash for a house on the lake. This lake."

That statement of fact made Mr. Steppe blink and stand a wee bit straighter. Matty and he both knew damned well the price of lakefront property in Skaneateles. His tone and eyes filled with doubt. "Really."

He nodded. "I've always been serious about ma music, sir." For a moment, neither said anything. "I know ye never much liked me, but I've never stopped loving yer daughter."

The man grumbled and moved behind the desk to shove the chair back in. "My daughter doesn't care what you make in a year. What she cares about is how she's treated. And you failed."

Failed? Matty considered the last year of his life a

bloody financial success. "I will never fail her again."

Those cold eyes held his in a silent dare, coupled with a faint sniff of disdain. "Don't make promises you aren't fit to keep. You fail her, I'll break those damned pipes of yours over your head. Now get out of my sight."

Chapter 5

Without preamble, Cora yanked open the duffle bag on the far end of the bed and saw men's clothing. She pulled up something woolen from the bottom and recognized the green plaid kilt before she had even yanked the length of it free. "God damn it!" She stuffed the items back in and saw the hard-shell suitcase on the floor. His pipes. She'd know that black box anywhere. She yanked that one off the ground and stomped to her door, her hands full.

"Cora, for the love of—"

She dumped both items in the hall and slammed her door shut.

"What the hell is wrong with you?"

Now she looked for a lock, ignoring the thumping coming from Herbie's cage as she dropped back onto her bed. Damn it! No locks, only a glass doorknob with a keyhole. "Wrong with me? Absolutely nothing a divorce won't fix."

"Cora! Don't say such things!"

The D word was not spoken in her family. Her parents survived job loss, a miscarriage, even having their car repossessed, long ago. But they stuck it out. Her grandparents endured an overseas boat trip just to fend off disease, near starvation, and poverty level wages before Gramps got into the factory.

No. Her family believed in "'til death," and right up until Matty pulled his stunt, so had Cora. But since Matty had kind of left her to die, she figured she'd satisfied that requirement.

"Talk to me. What happened?"

The tone her sister used had turned soft, melodic. Like she snapped into work persona and affected her doctor voice. It screamed, "Trust me to make everything okay." She got that talent from Nana. All the women did. Healers ran in the family. And now she unleashed it on Cora, who refused to be lured by it. "Mom didn't tell you?"

She shook her head. "Tell me what?"

All she could do was suck in a shocked breath. "I told her to tell you. How many times have you two talked over the last two years?"

"I don't know." She shook her head in thought. "Every month or so?"

"Son of a bitch. Mom knew he left me, and Dad, of course. And I told Nana. How come they didn't tell anyone else?"

Now Sherry's hand landed on her wrist. "Left you? It probably comes back to the D word again. I don't know what's going on, but I have to ask: is it something you think I wouldn't understand?"

After heaving a breath, Cora rested her hand on her sister's. "No. I knew you'd understand perfectly. It's why I asked Mom to tell you."

"What is it, sis? What happened?"

Where to start? She met the concerned eyes of her sister, equally gray, but filled with compassion, the compassion Cora usually reserved for animals and not people. So she drew in a fortifying breath and asked, "Did you know I was in an accident?"

She waited while Sherry studied her, her eyes flicking from one to the other as she searched her memory. "Yeah. You got into a multi-vehicle accident. They admitted you for a day to monitor for internal bleeding, right?"

Oh, God, it hurt to swallow. Hurt to remember. Her chin dropped in a slight nod as she tried to find the starting point. "Matty was driving us here, home."

"Yeah. And somebody died, right?"

Cora would never forget. She wished to feel

anything besides the anger she still carried from that day. Sorrow, compassion, regret, anything. But all that churned in her gut was anger. Sheer, total, all-encompassing anger. "We weren't seeing eye-to-eye about careers. I heard from one of my coworkers that a night-shift job was hiring. It had a great starting pay and awesome medical, and we'd both be working nights if he took it. But he was adamant that he wanted to play pipes, so he'd been taking all these weekend gigs, which hardly paid. But suddenly he'd gotten this chance to interview with Bagpipe Barons— you know, the Celtic song/dance troop? Anyway, it was going to have a brutal tour schedule. If he got accepted, I wouldn't see him for almost a year."

She'd been so mad at him. She hadn't asked him to give up playing; only to man up and get a normal day job like the rest of America. Anything to keep their heads above water. They weren't kids anymore living with their folks, but grownups with rent and financial responsibilities. But to take this offer? He'd only be making a touch more than the night shift job, with no medical benefits and little chance of getting a raise. She'd be screwed if he took it, relying on him to send money if and when he made it to a bank, and they were already at risk of getting evicted.

She'd actually put her foot down.

"So, it was dusk, and since I told him to get his head out of his ass— maybe I said clouds— and apply for the night job, Matty only got madder. We were outright fighting when the deer came out of nowhere, charged up the embankment and bounced off the hood into oncoming traffic."

"The motorcyclist."

Cora nodded, couldn't swallow. "She never had a chance."

The event played out in slow motion like it always did. The buck's eye locking on hers through the windshield, the slamming of the brakes after impact, the carcass flying across the road and the sound of the motorcycle pedals screeching sparks down the pavement. They stopped and raced out, and Cora knew at one glance the biker had been killed.

Matty didn't have the experience with death that she did. He wasn't used to being there at the end, when frantic owners raced in with their dying pets and had to make that final decision. He didn't know the signs, the look, the scent like she did.

He tried to drag the buck off the woman only to watch in horror as her body came up with the deer, the antlers lodged into her torso.

Gruesome. No other word for it.

Even Cora felt nauseous at the sight. She'd been to a wake before, but she'd never watched a person die. Her hand had landed on her stomach, feeling ill.

"Then what happened?"

At Sherry's question, Cora looked up, not realizing she'd been recounting the events of that night aloud. She even had her hand on her stomach.

She stared at Herbie, hoping for strength to continue. "Matty looked horror-stricken. I could tell he didn't know what to do. So I called 911."

Her sister blinked with sudden comprehension. "He ran away, didn't he? Joined the Bagpipe Barons overseas where he wouldn't have to look you in the eyes. He couldn't handle it. Now he's back. That's why you didn't know he was even here."

"Yeah." But really, it was *no*. Once Cora got out of the car, Matty had turned, paled, and pointed at her lap, and that was when she saw the blood. Her blood. That was when Cora realized *three* lives ended that day. She had been eleven weeks into her pregnancy, and they had been heading to her parents' house to share the good news.

Good news they never got to share.

The expression in her sister's eyes filled with love

and compassion. Mostly love. She tugged Cora in for a hug and held her tight. “I didn’t know you two were estranged. I’m sorry I got mad at you.”

Nobody knew the full truth. Cora had insisted that Matty not share the news, and once he abandoned her, she felt no time was the right time to share. He was gone, wasn’t he? Nothing she could say or do would bring back either Matty or her unborn child. “I’m not mad at you. Just... shocked. And now I’m angry, actually. Just thinking about seeing him right now feels like ripping a stitch out of a healing wound, over and over again.”

She grimaced. “I’ll try to run interference.”

Her fingers clenched the comforter as her lips twisted. “The EMTs rushed me in since...” –she grappled for a logical medical reason—“the deer hit my side, and Matty stayed for questioning and would come to the hospital once they cleared him of wrongdoing. And that’s where he left me, Sher. I called and called, but he never came to pick me up. Of course, all I’m thinking is that he had a concussion and was lying dead at the side of the road somewhere, and when they released me and I still couldn’t reach him, Mom and Dad had to come get me. I asked one of my neighbors to stop home and see if he was okay, and she informed me that Matty had asked her husband to take him to the airport the day before.”

“Oh, God, Cora. I’m so sorry.”

She managed to unclench her fingers and smooth out the creases in the material. “I waited for him to come back to me. For months. Finally I filed for divorce and got nowhere. So I tried with a different lawyer. Then a third. No one could track him down or reach him on tour. I was abandoned and alone and struggling, paying off debts we incurred that I couldn’t afford, and nobody on this goddamned planet could serve the bastard or grant me a reprieve.”

“No wonder you’re angry.”

"Wouldn't you be?"

She only got a shrug. "I guess. I don't know. I don't have time for relationships."

"At least you'll never have to deal with the shit I'm going through."

Her words made Sherry bow her head. "I always thought you two were the perfect couple. He always watched you, watched over you. Took care of you when you couldn't take care of yourself. Even stood up for you against Mom when she asked too much of you."

"Not Dad, though."

"No?"

Cora shook her head. Dad had always hated Matty, ever since they started getting serious.

"Well, he never let Mom push you around, and I've seen that woman drive her techs to insanity. God, I would've given anything to land a guy who looked at me the way Matty did you. It's why I always had so much fun tormenting him; he was safe. He'd never waver, never take me up on my outrageous offers."

"Yeah, thanks for throwing yourself at my husband all those years."

"I was never interested in Matty."

"Moot point, now. Have at him."

"No way. Never."

As reassuring as Sherry's words were, Cora's unease only grew. "Why didn't Mom tell you? And why didn't Nana kick him out?"

A considering sigh met her question. "They might have been respecting your privacy. But, knowing this family the way I do, I sense a matchmaking scheme in the works."

"Yeah. Me, too. What the hell am I going to do?"

Her question made Sherry grab a pillow to hug. "No one knows he left you, Cor. Everybody flocked him, hugged him like they were glad to see him."

"Fuck."

"Yeah." Now her sis leaned forward. "Are you going to play along?"

A long sigh. "If I don't, people are going to think I'm a raving psycho-bitch."

"What if they already do?"

The tease made Cora curl her lips. "I'm sure some of you are onto me by now, but not the little ones. Not the aunts and uncles. Fuck. I'm going to have to play nice, aren't I?"

"Ugh. I'm sorry."

But now Cora smiled in truth. "Not as sorry as he's going to be. In fact, I'm thinking I might need to catch you throwing yourself at my rat bastard of a husband."

"I'll drink to that!"

And they raised pretend glasses and toasted the death of her marriage.

Chapter 6

When Cora made her way downstairs, drawn by hunger and the tantalizing aroma of Nana's lasagna, she found her fingers clenching into Sherry's elbow. She didn't want to see him. Scratch that; she did. She wanted to stab him in the eye with a candy cane, string him up on the mantle by a necklace of garland, stick him in the snow and hose him down until he became an ice sculpture. Or scream and rant and rave, and maybe even get in a few good punches.

She might even do the same for Nana, for forcing her to bunk with him!

Why did he have to come back to America? Why, why, why? As if losing her job wasn't bad enough, eventually now she'd have to talk to him. Eventually she was going to come face to face with the only man she'd ever loved, the only one who knew her inside and out.

The only one capable of breaking her into a thousand pieces all over again, and right now so little held her together.

Now that she knew he was here, Cora couldn't stop searching for him. Not in the living room. Not in the library. She found the other Scotsman seated in the far corner, surrounded by ten kids all asking him about his clothes, his accent, and did he live in a hut like the movies? Steering Sherry past the gathering, she peeked into the sunroom.

There he was. Leaning on the glass, looking out over the snowscape where the horse barn floodlights fanned their warm beams onto the unspoiled mounds, turning everything into soft shades of gold and gray-blue. He spoke with one of her male cousins, talking cars, but she could tell his attention was elsewhere. He wore his full Scottish regalia, complete with *sporran*, that round male purse hanging low from his hips. She hadn't seen him dressed like this in years and took a moment to absorb the sight. His white button-up came crisply to his neck, held tight by a black bowtie and matching vest and jacket. His family tartan of blue and green striped plaid came almost to his knees, with little matching flags called flashes tucked under the hem of his tall white socks. His *sgian dubh*, the small decorative knife, peeked out over the flashes on his right calf.

He'd trimmed down since she last saw him. Started growing a shadow beard. He looked more focused, more determined, and Cora wondered how she'd come to that conclusion when he barely paid attention to his own conversation. His raven-black had grown longer, but even from this angle she could see his eyes glowed with their usual jade-green intensity.

She took in the measure of his shoulders, the small span of his waist, the muscles flexing under his white hose as he tapped his foot to a beat he probably heard in his head. He always did that. As a teenager, she used to think him impatient, but now she knew everything with Matty was music. Her eyes flew to his fingers and noticed they didn't tap, but fingered notes as they rapped away on the wooden window muntins.

Was it possible for a man to get more gorgeous as he aged? Was that even fair? Or allowed?

She must have made a small noise, possibly of despair, or even desire, because Sherry yanked her out of the doorway just as Matty must have sensed her staring and started to turn around. But Sherry sauntered in and draped herself along Matt's side, purring away her string of sexual promises.

Cora couldn't believe it when Matty grew impatient and placed her sister off to the side with a firm but gentle reprimand.

In a cloud of disbelief, Cora spun out of the doorway and leaned against the wall, out of sight. It was true, then; Matty wasn't putting up with Sherry's flirting.

She was secretly glad, even though this would complicate the whole *jealous wife* charade she thought would work so nicely. After all, even though Sherry was stuck with her unwelcomed chastity belt and nothing could physically transpire between them, Cora had to admit—even to herself—that she'd grown weary of Matty tolerating/enjoying all of Sherry's attention.

She'd never worry about Sherry; she was all flirt and zero action.

Caught in her ruminations, Cora startled to hear Matty's heavy heels cross the floor, and she peeked in and saw her sister's wrist gripped fast in his hand. "Davey! Where are ye, lad? I've a woman seeking some alone time with a MacKenzie!"

At the same time Sherry turned beet red, Matty saw Cora lurking behind the wall. His eyes riveted directly to hers, and she watched him take a deep breath, like one of awe. But when he opened his mouth to speak, Cora reached in and yanked Sherry out of his grip and wove through the living room and into the kitchen, where Nana shoved plates at them. "Dinner time. Go sit down, while the food's still hot."

Now was probably not the best time to give Nana a piece of her mind; not when a MacKenzie might be hot on her heels.

Although... he wouldn't even be here had Nana not invited him....

The youngest kids had their own table where they shoveled into mac 'n cheese and snuck bits of their meal to the overbearing circling Lab, so Cora maneuvered Sherry into the only two vacant seats in the dining room, ensuring Matty couldn't sit beside them.

Didn't matter, because she could tell the exact

second he entered the room. Like a planet, she felt the gravitational pull towards him but resisted looking over. Thank God her younger cousin beside her had just started his meal! That gave her a good twenty minutes of reprieve.

Matty accepted a plate from Nana and scooped up his slice of lasagna, his full attention on Cora, though she thought she did a credible job of pretending he didn't exist, even going as far as to suggest some great colleges for her younger cousin to consider, throwing herself fully into the conversation.

But her cousin took one look at Matty's glower and pushed out of his seat. "Uncle Matty! Here, take my seat. I'll go sit with my brother."

"How verra kind of ye, lad." He set down his plate to her right and almost sat before stepping back into the kitchen.

The sisters exchanged glances. Cora whispered, "Was it something I said?"

They chuckled and focused on their meal when Matty returned to her side, holding a sandwich plate with two slices of bread, one lightly buttered and one heavily.

"With a sprinkle of sugar, just the way ye like it," he said, pointing to the barely-buttered one as he placed it between them.

Sherry audibly sighed.

Cora impaled her with a deadly stare. Not a peep for fourteen months, and his first words to her were about sprinkled sugar? No greeting, no apology, just a snippet that would ensure any of her family would believe he'd never left her side.

Cora seethed at his assumption that she'd blindly play along.

That first tantalizing bite of Nana's lasagna was almost to her lips when the wind gusted against the house and the lights flickered. A handful of children shrieked.

"Thar she blows!" Gramps announced, pointing out

the window, and Cora looked behind her to see the Nor'easter blowing in, pelting the window and obscuring the landscape.

In the doorway, Nana shook her head like she always did when Gramps pretended he was a sea captain. Another gust rattled the panes, and as Cora managed her first delicious mouthful of the meal, Nana said, "Oh, dear. Cora, would you mind bringing in the horses?"

She looked at Sherry, then her piping hot food. Then Nana. Swallowed. "Now?"

Her query earned her a raised brow. "Your mother turned them out this morning and I forgot about bringing them in with the chaos. There are ten of them to be brought in."

Matty lowered his fork. "Where's Dr. Foote?"

"Emergency call." That expectant eyebrow hadn't lowered, and Cora knew there was no point in mentioning how if her mom turned them out, she might want them out, so she heaved a resigned breath and bowed *adieu* to her meal. Damn it all; she should have chewed Nana out when she had the chance, because now she definitely couldn't do it. "Until we meet again." The second she reached the dining room door, Nana said, "Matty, why don't you go help her?"

Shit. A definite set up. She glared and said, "Nana, Matty doesn't know diddly-shit about horses."

"Language!" Nana scolded her as a few kids gasped.

"Actually, I do," Matty added as he stood. "I've been learning about their care."

Under her breath she said, "Of course you have." She glared at him but managed something resembling a smile to Nana. "Fine. We'll be right back." She stalked to the front door and rummaged through the hooks for her coat. She donned her hat and gloves and headed out into the storm without waiting for Matty.

He raced out after her, tugging his arms into his sleeves as he caught up and zipped his jacket against the weather. "Let's hope they tried to come in."

His benign comment made Cora whirl on him and jab her finger into his face. "Don't pretend we're a couple, Matty. You may try to fool the rest of my family, but my sister knows, and she's through with your shit."

He chuckled. "Is that her perfume on ma neck? I doona think she's playing whatever game yer hoping to play."

"Fuck you." She spun and stomped to the paddock.

A small noise fled his lips. "Look. I didna come here to fight with ye; I came to fight *for* ye. I'm sorry."

She tossed her words over her shoulder, not even deigning to face him. "Sorry for what, Matty? Lying to my entire family? Or the reason I hate your guts?"

"Everything. Every bit o' pain I caused ye, ever."

"Oh, so I guess we're fine, then?" She ducked her head into the wind without waiting for a reply. Stinging pellets assaulted her face as she trudged the hundred yards to the barn. Matty kept pace, his kilt knifing between his legs as the wind blasted into him. She glanced from the kilt to his eyes. "That's a stupid thing to wear in a blizzard."

"Aya, it's a wee bit chilly," he agreed.

Most of the horses had gathered by the barn door, their rumps to the wind, their turnout coats flipping up. Cora plowed through the snowdrift and tried sliding open the door to no avail. As she shoved against it, Matty's arms encircled her, and together they managed to roll it open. She shoved him away and grabbed the first horse's halter and pointed to both him and the nearest stall. "This is Penelope. She goes there."

Matty gripped the nylon halter and led the mare to her stall, then returned to the door as Cora loaded the next one. He made his horse wait while Cora loaded hers so she could tell him where this one went. They alternated loading the stalls until the herd outside was safely tucked away for the night.

"Thank God that went fast."

"Aya." But Matty was counting heads. "No. Only nine."

"Are you shitting me?"

"Count 'em yeself, then, lass."

She went down one side of the aisle, double-checking each stall for occupancy and saw Matty stopped in front of an empty stall. "Fuck. Who's missing?"

Matty read the plate on the door. "Nessie."

She raced to the door and raised her hand to deflect the stinging snow to see if she had come in. "Shit. She always gets chased off by the other horses. She could be anywhere." She stepped out into the blizzard and tried calling Nessie's name, but the wind blew her voice right back at her. "This isn't going to work. She'll never hear me."

"She's the bay with the snip on her nose, aya?"

Snip? He really *had* been studying horse terminology. "Aya. I mean, yes," she fumbled.

He grinned at her slip and dropped his hand on her shoulder, making Cora violently yank away. "That one always loved me. She may na hear ye, but she'll for certain hear me." He left her at the barn as he ran back toward the house.

"What the....?" No point trying to figure him out. She bunched her coat at her neck and tugged her cap down lower over her ears as she trudged the fence line. "Nessie! Nessie!"

A few minutes later he returned, his bagpipes cradled under his arm. "Nessie always loved ma retreats. She'd come from the farthest end of the field to listen."

The confession stopped her. "I didn't know you played for them."

"I had to practice somewhere. Ma folks didna want

me rattling the china in the house, so I always came here to play."

The deep frigid breath she took stung her lungs. "Well, let's hope she remembers."

He set the drones on his shoulder and took a deep breath to inflate the bag, but then stopped. "Ye know, I doona play for free anymore. A performance from the star member of Bagpipe Barons is going to cost ye."

"Me?" She glared. "Hit up my mom. They're her horses."

"But yer the one who was asked to fetch them in. I'm charging ye, Cora. Pay up, or ye can spend the evening trying to wrangle her in by yerself."

"That's a dick move."

He only waggled an eyebrow. At least, she thought he did. Hard to see with the snow blasting into her face. She waited for him to recant, but after chattering her teeth for a good ten seconds, he still hadn't changed his mind.

"You are such an asshole. Fine. What the hell is your fee?"

"One kiss."

"No fucking way." A worse fee could not possibly exist. Anywhere. Matty's lips rivaled the cautionary tales that grandparents told their daughters about kissing leading to pregnancy. In Matty's case, his lips encompassed all dangerous elements to Cora's sanity. Like the primal need to breathe when held under water, Cora would desire his next touch, his next kiss. Or how some women shed their clothes when they got drunk, Matty's heated stare substituted for her tequila. Or those dangerous date rape drugs, which left a woman insensate. Being in Matty's embrace always made her weak, malleable. Resistance would be completely futile. Angry as she was with him, she couldn't tempt fate. She emphasized her statement with, "Not on your life."

"On New Year's Eve."

The day of forgiveness and promises of new beginnings. "Fuck you. The answer's no."

"Ye willna get a better price than that, I guarantee it."

Her teeth chattered again, making her snug her coat tighter to her throat. She hadn't been this cold in years. "This, Matty, this is exactly why we don't belong together."

"No, *mo chridhe*, it's exactly why we do belong together. Ye wouldna be fighting it so much if ye didna have such strong feelings for me."

"True. It's called hate."

"Going once."

"No. I don't kiss assholes."

"Going twice." She heard the whine of the bag as he deflated it, folding it down to pack it back up. "Getting mighty cold out here. Going blind, even."

She glared at him, even though she shivered and had to clench her teeth to keep from chattering again and looking weak under his regard. Then she glared some more.

He opened his mouth to say "Gone," but Cora said, "Fine. But only *if* you're able to bring Nessie in. Otherwise, suck off."

"Deal." He unfolded the drones and placed them back on his shoulder. Took another deep breath and inflated the bag, his fingers already in position. He punched air into the drones and marched slowly away from her, up a slight incline, the sad low notes from his tune puncturing the blizzard.

Despite the whistling wind, the biting snow, and the poor visibility, Cora had no difficulty pinpointing Matty as he stood at the fence line, his pipes belting out the sad, low retreat called *Kilworth Hills,* one she'd heard him play a hundred times. Tears sprang to her eyes as the bass drone hummed in the background, the familiar *dum da di, ba da-dum bum* carrying across the desolate pastures. Even as teens, Matty had been able to play tunes that rocked her on a fundamental level, and the years had only lent to his talent. His beautiful Throws on Ds and crisp grace notes, staples of bagpiping, moved her as they always had. And despite the weather, despite her blazing hatred of his past actions, despite her anger at his skillfully maneuvering her into his stupid deal, Cora knew she had never seen a more powerful image than Matty standing in a blizzard, in full regalia, piping and marching in place to help a wayward horse find her way back home.

The pain she felt in her chest felt suspiciously like sorrow. Regret.

No.

Never again.

But as her eyes locked on the surreal image of him, all she could think was *damn.*

Damn followed closely by *fucker.*

Motion caught her eye, and from over a hillock came the wayward mare, her head low as she battled the wind. Cora shuffled her way through the drifts, two thoughts battling in her head: *Thank God she's safe* and *Shit, now I'll have to kiss the bastard.* "Nessie! Come inside!"

It was probably only being so close to shelter that made the mare face her, but Cora waved her near and snatched her halter and dragged her inside, Matty's tune still piping away behind her, like he had no intention of stopping until the horse was safely contained and his reward guaranteed.

Why not add insult to injury?

She led Nessie to her stall and sensed the minute Matty entered behind her, even though he had already deflated his pipes, rendering them silent. One glance proved the instrument was protectively cradled under his arm.

"I'll collect ma payment in four days. Doona forget

now."

She didn't look at him. Made no comment.

Like she ever *could* forget.

She'd have to weasel out on a technicality somehow.

Chapter 7

Thank God she'd brought sweatpants with her, because even sitting in front of the roaring fire with a cup of hot chocolate and a piping-hot reheated meal in front of her, Cora ached to her bones from standing out in the blizzard. The cold permeated every inch of her, from the back of her throat to the insides of her ear canals and even under her arms, which should be the warmest part of her body, seeing as how they had the most layers. But she couldn't get warm. Hadn't been truly warm all year.

Well, technically, fourteen months.

But she wasn't counting.

Nana had shooed everyone away from the fireplace so that her two frostbitten victims could warm themselves, front and center.

So thoughtful of her.

Not.

Beside her, Matty dove into Nana's lasagna, moaning with appreciation after every bite. Could he be more obnoxious in reminding Cora that, despite her numerous attempts over the years, hers paled in comparison? Not that she expected to rival Nana's cooking abilities, but having Matty gush over how *much* he'd missed it and how *perfect* her cooking tasted made Cora want to dump her hot chocolate over his head.

She didn't want to sacrifice her mini-marshmallows to such a senseless death, though—his only saving grace.

With her superhuman hearing, Nana swept in and collected their plates the second she heard the forks scratch across the empty expanse, and then seconds later pushed two more steaming mugs in their hands. "Thank you so much for your help. I can't risk breaking a hip at my age."

"No problem, Grandmamma. They're all safe and

bedded down."

Another horse term he carelessly flung in her face, another way for him to prove he had been studying in his feeble attempt to gain her forgiveness. But then Cora got front-row privileges in watching Nana simper and croon over him. "I heard you playing, Matty. You're even better than I remembered."

He positively beamed, the rotter. "Thank you. I appreciate hearing I did well."

Now Nana's eyes swiveled to her. "Isn't he, Cora? Even better?"

They locked eyes for a prolonged second. Oh, how Cora wanted to chew her out for making her pretend in front of everyone that everything was alright when it wasn't, for practically beating a compliment out of her for her soon-to-be-ex-husband, for standing there expectantly for some kernel of glowing praise until two of her cousins looked over at her, wondering why she wasn't gushing over Matty's skill. She forced a smile and said, "He should be; he's had fourteen straight months to practice without interruption." Take that!

Both of their smiles faltered, and two people listening in frowned, but Cora stirred her cocoa and spooned out her mini marshmallows and fervently prayed Matty's appendages would fall off from frostbite... all of them.

With a little sniff of disdain, Nana left, but not three seconds later her mom came up. "Thank you so much for bringing in my horses while I was on call. I knew I could count on you. You're so good with animals."

"Says the veterinarian. I don't know if I should feel complimented or concerned."

Her mom smiled, too used to Cora's snark. "Matty, move closer to your wife."

As soon as Cora eyed Matty, she noticed her mom draping a heavy wool blanket over them. "You both still look cold. Snuggle up."

But Cora flung off her half of the cover. "I'm fine." She managed to suppress the shiver before anyone noticed.

"No, lass, yer mom's right. Ye've got blue lips." He grabbed the wool and drew it over her shoulders, leaving his arm in place. To her mom he said, "I've got her, Dr. Foote."

"Keep her warm."

"Aya, I will."

He made to inch closer but stopped at her death glare. Instead of being cowed, he lowered his lips to her ear. "If ye've lost feeling in yer lips, I'll consent to let ye pay yer dues now."

She ignored him and pressed her mug to her lips to warm them—something equally hot, but not nearly as dangerous as paying her debt.

He chuckled, clearly expecting no different a reply.

The clock over the mantle chimed; only seven PM. Three more hours before she could even *pretend* to head to bed.

Perhaps he sensed her thoughts, because once more he leaned in. "Roll in to me, wife. Yer family is starting to find ye a wee bit cold to yer husband."

She hissed, "Just because Nana and Mom haven't told anyone doesn't give you *carte blanche* to pretend nothing is wrong between us."

"Aya, everything is wrong. We're but inches apart, yet I canna see over yer walls."

"Walls you put there."

"Aya. Walls I intend to knock down."

"Intend away, but you made your choice. These are the consequences."

"Aya, but a decision made in panic, *mo chridhe,* is no decision at all. I was blind with fear and pain and desperate to prove maself to ye."

Despite his pathetic attempt at a plea, it was his

familiar endearment that made Cora turn to glare at him. "Stop calling me that. I mean it. And panic or no, you had fourteen months to contact me. Which you didn't. Which means we're done."

She couldn't read his expression, but it seemed guarded. "No, lass. We're na done until death. I vowed it."

"You also vowed to honor and cherish. You can't pick and choose."

His eyes swept down, the long lashes fanning against his cheeks, sending shadows along his high cheekbones as the fire undulated before them. "Aya, I've failed ye."

"Yes. You have."

Her declaration made his lips curl. "Ye never mince words, Cora. It's what I've always admired so about ye. Life is black and white to ye. No gray. Ever." He nodded once and got up, tucking the wool around her as he left.

And Cora finally got to sit before the fire in absolute silence to enjoy her cocoa.

Funny, it seemed so much hotter only seconds ago.

By the time 9:30 rolled around, Cora let the day's toll kick in, decrying her long travels and cold weather to finally have gotten the best of her. She bid goodnight to the adults who were around and climbed the stairs, looking over at the cots and sleeping bags filling the bay windows to the right. She heard whispers and shushing and giggling as all the kids tried to knock off for the night.

What a hell of a day.

Some cots were still empty, one definitely for Davey, the newcomer, but she really hoped Nana wasn't packing Sherry into that same corner but rather gave her a room.

Maybe Sherry could share with her!

She slipped back downstairs and found Sherry sipping wine in front of the fireplace. As she approached, she sensed she walked through some kind of invisible barrier, and looked over to see Davey watching her sister. Intently. Cora must have broken his laser vision, because he snapped his eyes to her and then looked down at his drink.

Time to save a fellow Foote-Steppe from the danger and subsequent damage of MacKenzie males. She leaned over. “Stay in my room tonight?”

Apologetic eyes met hers. “Oh, sis, I’m sorry. I told Jemma I’d watch her kids tonight so she and Joe could—” she cut off her words.

They shared a conspiratorial look. “Have some privacy for the Annual Creating of the Next Child Prodigy?”

“At least they’re in the RV this time and not the cellar. Remember when—?”

They both giggled as they recalled how their cousin’s love cries carried through the house that one year.

“So, sorry. I’m winding down early so that I’ll be there if they wake up.”

With a nod of resignation, Cora headed back upstairs, not seeking or seeing her husband. She stepped into her freezing-cold room and shivered. She couldn’t let him stay here. He’d be too tempting, with his radiating heat only inches away from her corpse-cold skin. She knew if he slept here, she’d wake up in his arms, and that couldn’t happen. Ever. She grabbed his duffle bag and instrument case and dropped them outside the door again before closing it. No locks. Damn it, she forgot. So she took a deep breath and got to work.

It took every muscle in her body to shove the bed across the heavy carpet, but even then, she couldn’t wedge it flush against the door. By the time she had barely a foot left to go, Matty opened the door. It banged into the side rail and he frowned. “What’re ye doing?”

“You’re not sleeping here.” She tried to heave the

bed again, but the sheer weight of both it and Matty's resistance stymied her. She threw her weight into the giant footboard, trying to slog it along the carpet, but all she got for her efforts was a Charley horse.

Without preamble, Matty pushed back on the door and slipped inside. He closed the door behind him and hissed, "Look, Cora, I know ye doona want me here—"

"Understatement of the year." She focused on rubbing her stinging hamstring so that she didn't have to meet his eyes.

He growled. "But if ye toss me out now, people are going to start asking ye questions. And I'll be honest with ye, I'm going to tell them I'm trying to win yer heart back."

"Bastard," she hissed. "Anything to make me look bad."

"No, *mo chridhe,* it's the truth."

"*Don't* call me that!" How many times did she have to say it? "If I really were *your heart*, you'd be dead by now. You would have expired the second you walked out on me, leaving *do chridhe* behind."

She watched his shoulders lower at that. "Who says I didna?"

Cora whirled around and sat on the bed, her back to him, ignoring the cramping in her leg in favor of ignoring the bastard at her back. The bed slid back across the carpet, and she gripped onto the comforter as Matty shoved it foot by foot back across the floor. Once he got it situated in its original spot, she felt him sit behind her. "I'm here 'til the holiday, Cora. I'm hired to be here, so I canna leave."

"But I can." She stood up and immediately regretted it, collapsing when her leg spasm gave away under her weight.

Before she even made it to the mattress, Matty was before her, his eyes filled with concern. "Are ye alright, lass?"

Exasperation filled her. "Why do you care? And

what's up with the stupid accent? You haven't had one in fifteen years."

"I just got back from visiting my family in Scotland. And I've always cared."

Now she scoffed and met his eyes. "Scotland. No wonder the courts couldn't find you. Stupid me for not looking there."

"Courts? For what?"

"Divorce, Matt. On abandonment. The fact they couldn't find you kind of proved my point."

He blanched quite nicely. "No, Cora, ye doona want this."

With a whack to his shoulder she yelled, "How the hell would you know what I want and don't want? This is my life now, one which you blatantly demonstrated you wanted no part of, so fuck off, Matt. You don't get to tell me what I want and don't want anymore."

He looked toward the door and pushed down with his palms, indicating others might overhear them, but Cora didn't care if she woke the entire household. "Take your damn bags and sleep elsewhere." She gripped her clothes closer to her neck; the heat must have gone off, because it was even colder now.

"I willna disrespect Grandmamma's decision by moving. She put me here with ma wife, and here I'll stay."

"So, it's okay to disrespect your legal wife, but not her family," she sneered. "Got it."

He rolled his eyes. "Cora...."

"My God, you are one arrogant prick." She winced from the sharp leg spasm as she turned to face him. "If you think for one—"

"Yer hurt."

"Yeah, from trying to keep an asshole from getting into my room."

His eyes softened. "Let me see."

"Fuck off." But he had already grabbed her ankle

and extended her leg, making Cora cry out. "Stop it."

"Where does it hurt?"

She tried to wrench free, but Matty had a sound grip on her ankle and that determined look in his eye that said he'd get his way. She pointed to the back of her leg. "I just pulled it. It'll be fine. Feel free to head out any time now."

"I can help ye."

"Not necessary. It'll go away in a bit."

His brows lowered. "So I should just sit and watch ye suffer 'til it's gone?"

Now Cora thought she had him. "You're right. You're no good at hanging around and watching someone suffer, are you? Again, feel free to leave. I know how much you hate to have to watch your wife in pain."

She could tell her jab struck a nerve. "I'll na leave ye. Never again."

Now she was able to wrench her leg free. "Right. Fine. Whatever. Will you please go?"

"No." He stood and dragged Cora's feet to the middle of the bed, then crawled next to her. "Lay down."

"No." She tugged the elasticized bottom hems of her sweatpants back down around her socks. "Please leave."

He playfully pushed her down and flipped her to her stomach, and when she tried to kick him, Matty sat on her calves. "I'll rub it out for ye."

This was where she usually got into trouble. For all that Cora shoved back, she always respected Matty more when he stood up to her, and he was doing it now. She rallied and said, "I can get somebody else to do it, so get off of me."

"And then they'll wonder why yer not asking yer husband to do it, especially when I'm right here."

She managed one good buck and said, "Because I don't want you touching me!"

That comment seemed to push Matty over the edge,

because he braced his hands right under the swell of her butt cheeks and whispered, "If memory serves, you liked my touches enough to beg for more of them."

"Been there, done that."

"Then this shouldna bother ye, lass."

Shit, he wasn't going to give in, so Cora begrudgingly stopped protesting. One thing about Matty was once he put his mind to something, he never relented until he got his way. Apparently, that included massaging away her Charley horse.

Fuck. It hurt anyway, and he used to be good at working the kinks out, so Cora buried her head under her elbow. "Fine. Whatever. You should know that pinning me to the bed under protest makes you a fucking rat bastard."

"Aya, but I'm yer foking rat bastard."

"Not mine."

"Aya, I am." His voice had softened, but not his hands. He stroked up the backs of her legs and honed in on the twitch, his fingers and palms burrowing into the knot and loosening it.

He must have known that her pain finally abated, but he didn't stop. Matty continued to work the muscles of both legs, starting under her buttocks and working down to the arches of her feet. Then he worked his way back up, his thumbs working the inside of her thighs and rubbing higher, higher...

His touch had always aroused her to no end, and apparently that much had not changed. Maybe it wasn't his touch *per se*, but the fact that nobody else's fingers had gotten that close to her core in over a year that made her female juices slip out.

Right. She wasn't buying her own theory. Matty's touch made her horny.

He rubbed and massaged until her legs liquefied, and as soon as she closed her eyes, he stopped. "Better?"

No. Now the throbbing had simply moved higher.

Internally. Changed from agonizing to taunting. Couldn't tell him that, though. "Yeah. Sure. Fine."

"Yer welcome."

"Whatever."

With a chuckle, he eased off the side of the bed and stood up, then started unbuckling the two side straps of his kilt.

Panic flared inside her. Could he tell he had gotten her wet? "What are you doing?"

"Going to bed." He indicated the clock. "It's after ten, and this place wakes early."

An agonized groan slipped from her lips. "Matty, you can't stay here."

A sexy rogue grin crossed his face, and he unfastened the final buckle holding his kilt to his hips. He held her eyes as he pulled it off, revealing he wore nothing more than the Good Lord gave him.

Cora turned away, but not before she heard him chuckle. "It's nothing ye havena seen before, lass."

The only one she'd ever seen. Touched. Experienced.

And she could tell at a glance that he wasn't unaffected by the massage. So much for wishing all his appendages fell off from frostbite. Not a full cockstand, as he'd call it, but he hung thick and almost ready, like one hot look from her could make him spring to action.

He wasn't going to get that look from her. Ever. She replied, "Obviously, it's super cold in here. Or maybe objects in memory were larger than they appear."

He stopped disrobing, and she knew she'd burned him on an elemental level.

And then she felt like shit. She'd never insulted his manhood before; she'd never had cause. Although Cora had no comparison, she had the experience of her body, the pleasurable memories, and knew Matty had always given her one hundred percent.

The bed dipped as he sat down to peel off his socks and flashes. “It’s not the room temperature I’m worried about, but ma icy roommate that’s a killer.” He cast her a disparaging glance. “Ye going to sleep in yer clothes?”

“Actually, yes.” She climbed in and tugged the blankets to her ear and nestled deep, hating every single second of her life this week.

Chapter 8

Aya, her words cut him deep. Never had Cora assaulted his manhood before, and the fact she did it after he massaged her to bliss truly rankled. He'd aroused her, for certain; he could smell it on her, the heavy musk permeating his verra nose and sending him careening into memories he desperately wanted to relive.

But he wasna worthy, not yet.

He'd messed up in the biggest way a man could, and Cora was right to shirk him, to keep him at bay. This uphill battle wouldna be worthy of her forgiveness if she simply took him into her heart and bed without making him earn back her trust.

He would, too.

No matter how difficult, how much she shoved him away, Matty would regain his wife, his marriage, his *chridhe.*

He stared at the ceiling, the snow light casting soft purple shadows in the room. Herbie nestled in his hay, probably for warmth, and even though the heater in the corner kicked on and off, it couldn't seem to keep the room comfortable.

Cora kept her back to him, her body tucked into a wee ball. She didna sleep though; either she shivered or her teeth clattered. He glanced at the clock. Eleven-thirty. Midnight. One AM and still they remained awake and aware. She hadna moved from her fetal position. They needed more heat than the bloody plug-in could provide.

In all the time Matty had been alone, he hadna slept well. Sleeping well involved Cora wrapped in his arms. Cora, who remained but inches away, across a chasm of his wrongdoing. He tipped his head to look at her. He should tell her to roll into him, despite her refusal earlier today.

How many times had he used that phrase on her? A hundred? A thousand? Ten thousand? Perhaps she'd do it from habit, even if angry and awake. Perhaps, being warm and able to sleep would trump her anger at him.

Perhaps wishes were horses and beggars would ride.

Her teeth chattered again, so Matty turned to face her. He mouthed the words three, four times before his whisper became barely audible. "Roll into me, lass."

"Fuck you."

"Not tonight, lass. You're freezing. Roll into me."

"Not tonight? I think you mean not ever."

Rankled at her second rejection in as many hours, he bit out, "Well then, can ye stop yer bloody chattering and shivering? I havena been able to get a lick of sleep. Yer chattering sounds like castanets, and yer shivering is like a sombrero dance. Yer a goddamned mariachi band banging away in ma ears."

She punched him, hard, but Matty didna care. In fact, he embraced the fact she was so angry with him. It meant he'd rattled her. "If you're so goddamned inconvenienced, then go sleep downstairs. No one's making you stay."

He reached out and grabbed her hand, but she flung off his touch. "Yer freezing, lass."

"Oh, my God, give the man a cigar."

He snatched her around the waist and dragged her across the bed to his side, earning a few elbows to the gut in the process. "I was just getting warm!"

"No, lass, yer still freezing. Come, lay down with me."

Through clenched teeth she said, "I was."

"Not *by* me, *with* me. Come get warm." And he gave her no chance to argue, curling up behind her and pinning her legs between his. He smoothed down her hair and tucked her head under his chin, trusting her not to bash in his throat in the process.

"I hate you. For the record."

"Aya. I know. Now get some sleep." He forced his breathing to stay steady and shallow, his hands rubbing heat back into hers. He could tell she fought it, hated that she cuddled with him, but the blasted room was so cold that Matty had seen his breath.

Eventually he could tell she warmed up, and shortly after that, she slumbered. And shortly after that, Cora turned in his arms, tucking herself right under his chin, her actions so familiar and yet so incongruous with her sharp tongue that Matty wrapped her tightly in his arms.

When she let out a sigh, a lump swelled in Matty's throat. A tear slipped down his cheek. He gathered the cotton of her sweatshirt into his fists and drew her flush against him. It wasna forgiveness, but it was a start.

Baby steps.

And tomorrow, she would hate him even more.

Chapter 9

That fucking bastard. He'd leveraged her hypothermia against her to lure her into his arms. He hadn't taken advantage of her, thank God, but the fact that Cora even fell asleep in his embrace rankled. Like he knew she'd give in or something.

His damned determination, that's what it was. Once Matty set his mind to something, he'd never give it up. She used to admire it, but now she realized she herself was his target, and nothing she could do would deter him.

Part of her growled, but the other part thrilled.

When was the last time she'd been pursued so ardently?

Ah, yes, when Hugh asked her to the Summer Fest dance her sophomore year. Matty had been new to school, but she and Hugh had already been studying together, with her hoping that he'd asked her to be his girlfriend. As soon as Matty found out about the dance, he was at her side every single minute, glaring at Hugh whenever he came near. He fought for her then; it appeared he wanted to fight for her now.

Except Cora no longer wanted the honor of being his wife.

Matty must have had a thousand women tossing themselves at him over the past fourteen months. When he wore that kilt, ten thousand. Matty was seriously hot. Tall, muscular, a musician and now he had an accent. He was driven and unrelenting when he wanted something. A fantastic lover. He was everything a woman could ever want in a man.

Well, other women. Not her. Cora needed more in a man, like trustworthiness. Dependability. Someone who wouldn't run screaming at the first sign of trouble.

The bathroom door opened, and Matty stepped into the bedroom, bare-chested but wearing a pair of jeans that hugged him in all the right places. He scrubbed a towel through his damp hair and shut the door behind him. "It's still warm in there, if ye wish to shower."

"I'll wait 'til you're gone. No locks on the doors."

He rolled his eyes. "I'll na ravage ye, wife, ye have ma word. But if ye shower now, ye'll beat the emptying of the hot water tank."

He made a good point. The collective parents usually tossed three small kids into each tub at night, but most of the adults showered in the morning. At six-thirty, most of the house still slept. Without eyeing his spectacular chest, Cora asked, "Why are you up so early?"

His warm gaze slid down her. "I needed a cold shower. Me and ma wee cock, that is."

She grimaced with shame at how she'd treated him. "Matty, I—"

"Doona fash yerself. I knew ye didna mean it, despite how much I deserved it."

Her face heated as her shame grew. "No, you didn't. I've never talked to anyone like that. I shouldn't have insulted you. I'm sorry."

She could tell he merely stared at her, silently... condemning? Stewing? Loading a scathing retort? Whatever he next said would be deserved. Never in all their years together had Cora insulted Matty's manhood, so she could understand how deeply she insulted him.

"I'm hoping ye havena had cause to gaze upon another man's cock, but if ye have, I've no one to blame but maself. I'm truly sorry for what I did to ye, Cora. As sorry as any man could ever be." His voice lowered. "I'll do whatever it takes to make ye forgive me and win ye back."

The silence grew thick and heavy, as thick as the steam she suspected hung in the master bathroom. She couldn't look at him, couldn't face the hope and sorrow she heard in his voice, the same emotions she knew would reflect in his eyes if she dared peek. The only noise came from Herbie, where he nestled through his hay and dragged his litter box around the crate in one of his "interior-desecrator" moods.

"It felt good and right having ye in ma arms again."

A softly spoken confession. One that both echoed her sentiments and recalled how comfortably they fit together. She cleared her throat and mumbled, "Think I'll jump in that shower." She gathered up her armful of clean clothes and headed between Matty and the wall, but he didn't move over. In fact, he leaned closer. She angled away from him, but Matty stepped toe-to-toe with her and grazed her cheek with a feather-soft finger. "I've missed ye something fierce, Cora. What we have is—"

"Had. What we *had.*"

His swallow told her she either rankled him or irritated him. "Special. Unique. I may na deserve ye yet, *mo chridhe,* but I will win ye back, and I promise I'll never do anything to jeopardize our marriage again."

She nodded, hugged her clothes tighter. "Pretty words from a pretty man." She met his eyes. "I don't do pretty, Matteu. And I'm not a huge fan of forgiveness. Neither was our child."

She meant that attack to the core of her being, and it sent Matty back a step, clearing her path to the bathroom. Tears welled in his eyes. "Ye never told anyone what we lost. Ye never let me tell a soul. I promised ye that, and I kept ma word, but for the love of God, lass, nothing I could have done would have saved our babe."

Truer words were never spoken, but Cora wasn't referring to the miscarriage. She met his eyes and said, "Losing the baby was awful, but that's not what killed me, Matty. It's the fact you disappeared in the aftermath. When I needed you the most. What kind of father would you have turned out to be?"

"The right kind." Fierceness filled his eyes. "I vow it on ma soul. Ma life. It'll never happen again."

She shouldered past him and opened the door to the welcoming steam. "You already vowed that once and bailed. Doesn't matter, because you're not getting a second chance."

Chapter 10

Even way in the back bedroom, farthest away from the kitchen, Cora could smell the bacon. Breakfast! She toweled her hair, tugged on her clothes, and braced for the chill as soon as she stepped out of the bathroom.

God, she'd never warm up in this house. Or, at least, this bedroom.

She let Herbie out of his cage, and he sprinted past her to buck and "binky" and frolic as she shook out his towel and straightened his cage and filled his bowl with pellets and added hay to his box. Since Matty had already headed out, Cora decided to brave frostbite with Herbie rather than see her husband, so she sat on the floor and rolled a toilet paper tube to him. Herbie bolted out from under the bed and bit it and tossed it and nosed it around the room.

She smiled at his antics. The best bunny toys were always the by-products. Paper tubes, single-serving fruit cans, towels draped over chair seats; The Herbinator did not lack for environmental enrichment.

Speaking of riches... Cora glanced up at Herbie's food containers for a mental inventory of his supplies. She hadn't even been able to apply for unemployment before heading here. She'd called the local office, of course, just in case, only to hear a recording that they were closed for the holidays. The sheer audacity of closing the unemployment office at the end of the year, when most people got laid off, left her thunderstruck. Then, *then*, to beat home the point, they had the balls to wish the caller happy holidays!

She'd definitely have to start counting pennies now. Unless she got a job right after New Year's Day, the unemployment checks wouldn't even start for three or four more weeks.

Better load up on the vittles while she could. She lured her bunny back into his cage and headed downstairs, where the tantalizing aroma beckoned. Nana had laid out a spread, with Gramps keeping the coffee pots full and her two uncles running assist at the stove while Dozer barked and attempted counter-surfing until they yelled at her cousin Randy, barely twenty and failing adulthood, was forced to drag him away. One uncle got back to frying the bacon while the other one flipped the pancakes, and Nana mixed a giant bowl of eggs at the island. She looked up and smiled when Cora entered. "Scrambled or scrambled?"

"Hm." Cora pretended to consider her options. "Scrambled. No, wait. Scrambled."

"Egg-sellent choice." She grinned at her own pun, something Cora's boss, Carla, would have found amusing. "Flapjacks? Bacon?"

"Yes. Two each, please."

"Coming right up. Matty's in the sunroom."

So I'll eat in the dining room.

"I made sure the kids saved you a spot at his side."

So courteous. Cora smiled when she really wanted to snarl. "Thank you."

Then her mom came up and grabbed the milk out of the fridge and filled two mugs. She kissed Cora on the forehead with a, "Good morning, Sunshine," and popped the mugs in the microwave to heat. "I'll get your cocoas, Cor. Why don't you head in?"

"*Baa*," Cora said, recognizing a sheep being sent to slaughter when she saw it.

As promised, Matty had a free chair at his side, the small card table being shared with Sherry and Davey. At least her sis was there. As soon as she placed her hand on her chair, Matty stood and pulled it out for her to sit. "Good morning."

"Mm." The best reply she could manage, under the

circumstances.

"We havena met," Davey said, extending a hand over his plate. "Davey MacKenzie, Matty's cousin."

"Hello. I'm Cora." No last name. "Welcome to America."

"Thank ye. I've only been here a wee bit, but everyone's so verra friendly."

"It's only because you have an accent," Cora said. "Women fall all over that shit." She glanced around and saw a couple of her young cousins look up. "Sorry, didn't mean to swear."

They went back to talking about their favorite comics, and Cora simmered in her seat.

"The storm's mostly let up," Matty said. "I thought, maybe ye'd like to snowshoe today?"

Sherry gasped with joy and looked outside, then held Cora's eyes in hope.

Despite the threat of spending hours with Matty, Cora glanced out the window behind her to the serene landscape. The blizzard had stopped, leaving crystalline branches glinting against a cobalt sky. It looked like a postcard outside, a day filled with beauty and promise.

"It's barely ten degrees out," Davey said. "Ye'll have to keep each other warm." He waggled his brows, as if his meaning couldn't be any clearer.

As Cora opened her mouth to decline, Sherry cut her off. "Come on, we haven't done that since we were kids. Do you want to go? I know we always had fun snowshoeing." She smiled and extended an olive branch. "At least it's not skiing."

"Aya, Cora has no talent for that."

"Shut up."

"No, she doesn't," Sherry giggled and added, "I've never seen someone roll down a hill in skis."

"Kiss my can, Sis."

Matty nodded in agreement. "No getting back on

that horse."

"Speaking of rolling," Sherry looked at Matty. "What's that saying you always used?"

Even though Cora leveled him a dark look, he barely glanced at her before answering. "*Roll into me.* It started when I tried to teach her to rollerblade."

"Skateboard," Cora corrected, even though she mumbled.

"Are ye sure?"

She nodded, just barely. She didn't want to rehash the past, especially where it concerned the one phrase that summed up their relationship.

"Aya, I remember now. She wasna any good at it, and I was trying to teach her how to brake. But wee Cora felt she'd crash, so I told her to roll into me and I'd catch her."

"Aww," Sherry crooned, like it was the sweetest story she'd ever heard.

Her contribution made Matty smile. "Then, with the rollerblades. Later, a recumbent bike. Skiing, of course, and even when learning to parallel park."

"Like you'd always be there to catch her when she fell."

Three sets of sparkling eyes turned on her, and Cora had had enough. "Yeah. Right up until he disappeared for a year." She got up and left the table, just as Nana headed in with her plate. "Sorry, Nana, but I've suddenly lost my appetite." Without another word, she headed back to her room.

Chapter 11

Well, Matty could rot in hell if he thought Cora was going to let him lure her out on snowshoes, not after what just happened. Certainly not since the radioman stated another storm was blowing in. Even as she watched, the cobalt blue sky had darkened, and heavy gray storm clouds loomed. Soon enough, the wind picked up, and Cora heard the windowpanes rattle again. She shivered and listened to the kids downstairs get fidgety from being cooped up—a feeling she knew only too well. "Hey, Herbmeister, wanna meet the crew?"

Her rabbit responded by rotating his ears and making a long strand of hay disappear into his mouth.

"Perfect. Let's go."

She gathered him into her arms and headed downstairs. "Whoever wants to meet Herbie, gather into a circle in the living room. I'll let him out to play."

Randy said, "Let me put the gate up. Dozer would love to pounce on him."

"Thanks." Cora smiled. Randy's giant yellow Lab defined *excessive* in every way, from energy to girth to appetite to his giant testicles. She kept telling Randy *neuter is cuter,* but like most men she knew, he couldn't cope with the thought.

Once the gate braced the living room entryway and all the kids had gathered in a circle, Cora set Herbie down. He hopped around the circle, then leapt into the air, kicking out his hind feet in glee. "That, kids, is called a *binky*. Means he's happy." As if to prove Cora correct, Herbie binkied a few times before racing back and forth to nudge each child, looking for treats. Treats! She had lots upstairs. "Stay here, guys, and I'll bring down some toys and treats for him. She stepped over the gate and headed up, only to see Dozer heading back down the hallway....

From her room....

Smacking his lips....

"Dozer!" she screamed, and ran into her room to see he had cleared out Herbie's bowl of pellets. He'd also jumped up and cleared off the top of her dresser. Torn packages of Herbie's Hay & Honey Snackies and even his Fruit Nibblers peppered the floor. But as she got down on hands and knees and looked under the bed, she saw he had eaten Herbie's *raisins*. An entire canister of them. "Fuck!" She raced down the hallway, screaming for Randy and her mom and Nana.

Nana and Randy frantically greeted her at the foot of the stairs, asking what was wrong.

She glanced behind them. "Where's Mom?"

"Colic call."

"Shit!" She'd be gone for hours! Cora pointed at Randy and told Nana, "Dozer ate all my rabbit's raisins!"

Randy rolled his eyes, like that was the stupidest concern he ever heard, but Nana understood immediately. "Oh, no," she groaned and scurried to the cordless phone. "Call your mother."

Cora looked to Nana. "Do you have any hydrogen peroxide?"

"Yes. In the bathroom." Nana pointed as she ran to get it.

At least her mom picked right up away. Without preamble, Cora rattled off, "Dozer ate an entire canister of raisins."

She heard her Mom's groan. "When?"

"Two seconds ago. How much peroxide?"

"How much does he weigh?"

Cora wheeled on Randy. "How much does Dozer weigh?"

Now Randy seemed to realize something was wrong. "What's the big deal?"

"They're fatal," Cora replied as Nana added, "Grapes and raisins cause acute kidney failure," as she handed over the brown bottle.

Cora relayed the weight to her mom, then nodded at the instructions. "I'll keep you posted." She hung up and turned to Randy. "Get your stupid dog," Cora ordered, "and meet us outside."

"Outside?"

"Yes, please." Nana screwed the cap back on the bottle.

"Unless you want to clean up all his vomit," Cora shot back.

Cora couldn't look at Randy, and not because she was mad at him. She was mad at herself for leaving the containers in a tidy pile on top of the dresser instead of in the closet when a giant doofus ran free in the house. She was mad that it was her fault for not closing her door, granting Randy's out-of-control dog access to her pet's only food. She was mad that if anything happened to Dozer, it would rest on her soul. She was mad that she'd have to go out in a storm to buy more food for The Herbinator.

Mostly she was mad that she had no idea when her next steady paycheck would come... if ever. Penny pinching became her norm when Matty had walked out on her and left her in dire straits. She'd downsized to a place she could afford in a skuzzy part of town and lived way below her means. Until today, when thoughts of living out of her car manifested.

Randy tried to find his wayward dog, but Matty was the one who snatched him by the collar at the front door and dragged him over to the stairs. "Back pantry," Nana said. "It's fenced out back, and we can watch him from the window."

Cora shoved her cousin out of the way, since he was useless in training, restraining, or disciplining his own dog, and held Dozer still while Nana administered the appropriate amount of peroxide. "Put him outside and watch him for vomiting," Cora said, then she and Randy waited at the window to monitor the dog. Within seconds, Cora sensed Matty at her back, leaning over her to brace his arm on the sill. She resisted leaning back into the radiating heat, despite the chill in the cold room, forcing herself instead to lean forward, her breath fogging the window as the yellow dork bounded through the snow.

"He's just got too much energy," Randy explained, waiting and watching to see if his pet yakked up his stomach.

"I think ye mean testosterone," Matty said, surprising Cora that he spoke what was on her mind. "Ye'll never calm down a male with raging hormones. Look at ma cousin, Davey."

"He's still a puppy."

"He's three," Cora said. "Two point five years overdue for the big snip."

"He doesn't need it done."

Now Matty's hand landed on her shoulder before she could return a scathing reply. "Aya, what was I thinking? Ye canna argue the benefits of neutering with a wee lad whose verra name means horny."

Now Randy faced Matty, his expression antagonistic. "I'm not a lad."

But Matty only smiled at him. "Maybe na in body, but in here." He tapped his temple. "If he doesna puke, ye'll have to man up and get him to the hospital."

"He'll be fine."

"Or dead," Cora felt compelled to add.

Nana came into the room as Randy paled. "Any puking?" she asked.

"No," they all answered.

Cora glanced at the clock. "Bring him in for another round. If this doesn't work, then you'll have to take him to the emergency center in Syracuse."

His cheeks paled. "Can't we just keep giving him peroxide?" He opened the door and let the dog bound right past him.

"No." Cora snatched the collar and tugged him close for the next treatment. "He'll need apo."

"Can't you give it?"

She looked up as she restrained his dog for dosing. "No, I can't give it. First off, it's a controlled substance, so it's not simply hanging around the house. Secondly, I'm not losing my license because you can't control your dog."

He rolled his eyes. "Does he really need all this?"

Nana laid a gentle hand on his shoulder. "If you want him alive tomorrow, yes."

Cora pressed, "He'll need blood work to determine the extent of his kidney damage."

"Blood work?"

"Yeah. Correct me if I'm wrong, but Nana doesn't have a lab in the house."

Nana sighed at that. "Your mother doesn't even have one at the hospital."

Cora couldn't believe that. "You kidding me?"

"Nope."

Randy begrudgingly leaned against the counter in defeat, and Cora got Dozer's mouth open for his next dose. Nana had to fight to get the correct amount into him, and after ten minutes of wandering outside, he still hadn't produced.

Cora clapped her hands once. "Pack 'em up, move 'em out."

Randy seemed aggravated that he had to drag his dog out when the roads were barely plowed, but Cora knew the dog's life depended on it. Acute kidney failure would be definite with the amount he ingested, and time was of the essence. As Randy tugged on his coat, Matty walked up and clipped the dog's leash to his collar and held him until

Randy found his keys. As Matty handed him the leash, he said, “Ye also owe yer cousin about thirty dollars in damaged goods, which ye’ll need to replace before ye return.”

“Are you kidding me?”

Cora watched in disbelief as Matty stepped threateningly closer. “Man up, lad. He’s yer responsibility. It’s na like Cora packed weeks of supplies when she only planned on being here a few days. Ye owe her, and ye’ll make it right.”

Hard looks passed between them before Randy snatched away the leash and got dragged by his enthusiastic dog down the stairs and into the car.

Nana patted Matty on the back as the car pulled away. “Thank you for standing up for my granddaughter.”

He smiled. “It was the right thing to do, Grandmamma.”

She laughed and swatted him on the arm. “Oh, Matty, you always know just what to say.”

He looked over at Cora, his desire burning into her. As Nana walked away, Matty whispered, “Ma pleasure.”

Cora scoffed and headed back into the living room to collect Herbie.

“Wait!” Nana called. “After you put your rabbit away, I’m going to need your help, since it was Randy’s turn today and now....”

Of course. She playfully chased Herbie around the kid corral, making him leap and buck before she cornered him and scooped him up. “Never ever pick up a rabbit,” she told the kids, “because most of them hate it. Herbie’s the true exception. Got it?”

They nodded, and Matty pulled the tension gate out of the doorway for her so she wouldn’t have to step over it. She nodded thanks to him and headed upstairs, and he followed. Perhaps her bunny sensed her agitation, because once they got close to the bedroom, he squirmed, and Cora barely managed to lower him to the ground before he leapt out of her arms and took off towards his cage.

"Thank God he didn't break a leg," she said. To Matty she added, "We'd have a regular family reunion at the emergency hospital."

He said nothing, but bent to collect the plastic packages off the floor and arranged them on the bed. "Give me yer phone."

"Why?"

He sent her a warning look and put his hand out, waiting.

"Fine." She tugged out her cell and slapped it into his hand, wondering what he was up to.

He took individual pictures of the ruined packages, including the raisins, and said, "Ye have Randy's number, aya?"

She nodded, then took the cell and scrolled for Randy's information. When she handed it back, Matty texted him and sent him the photos. "There. I told him this is what he needs to replace."

She could only look at him.

"What?"

She shook her head and looked away. What could she say? That he was acting like the man she always knew him to be? That this is what she always expected of him? To be her champion? Best friend? But when he failed her, he lost her forever? "Just curious where this man was fourteen months ago."

"Out of his mind with grief. But I'm here now, lass, and here I'll stay."

She stared at the remnants on her bed, so grateful that Matty stepped in and insisted Randy man up. She'd be able to make it home, even if she had to charge her gas, and she had a lot of pantry items for meals, but she never skimped on bunny food. Having all new packages on hand took away a measure of her burden. "Thank you."

He stepped into her personal space and brushed his fingertips along her jaw, forcing her eyes to his. She waited for his fingers to lower, but they didn't. Instead, his eyes skimmed her face like he meant to memorize every detail, and his thumb brushed along the bottom of her lower lip, making her breath quiver in her lungs and her knees wobble. Her heart raced, and heat swept over her, blissful, feverish heat, starting at his thumb and burning its way straight to her belly, her core. She locked her eyes on his, wondering if he was going to lower his head, suck her lips, claim her with a kiss that would blow her mind, make her forget everything.

"Like I said, *mo chridhe,* ma pleasure."

Pleasure. Holy shit! What the hell was she *doing* here? Her lungs sucked in air, pushed it back out. Her heart raced, this time in fear of what she almost allowed. In her haste to escape the hungry look in his eyes, Cora stumbled against the wall. "Nana needs me. Lock Herbie up, will ya?" She turned and raced downstairs, eager to face whatever doom Nana had planned over the seductive look in her husband's eyes and the weakness that surged in her soul.

She found Nana alone in the kitchen and seized both horns on that matchmaking bull's head. "For the record, Nana, thanks for all the help with Dozer, and as much as I love you, I'm fucking pissed—"

"Cora!"

But she continued, "—that you're making me room with a stranger."

Nana composed herself, but her eyes hardened. "Matty is not a stranger."

"Fine. Estranged. Same difference."

"Is not. He's your husband and you two belong together."

"No, Nana. We don't."

"I saw you two united under God, and *united* you

will stay." Her eyes hardened with her none-too-subtle threat. Then she pointed to the room they had all just left, the back pantry. "Now go. I've got it all set up for you."

The abrupt change in topic dragged Cora's focus from the memory of her wedding to whatever waited in the back pantry. "What?"

"The carrots. They need washing for dinner."

Well, at least it was something easy. Trying to blow off Nana's devout belief in *ever after,* she said, "Fine." She headed into the pantry and saw about ten pounds of fresh carrots waiting to be washed, as well as a giant stock pot. So she washed her hands and grabbed the dull knife and the scrub brush and started scrubbing them under the water, taking time to cut off the tips and fluffy green sprouts on top before loading them into the pot. As she glanced at the discards, she realized she might need Herbie food if Randy couldn't make it to a pet store, so she took a handful of both tops and bottoms to set aside for him. Not a minute later Matty came in, ushered in by a not-so-subtle Nana.

"Thought you'd need help." Oh, boy, did Nana look pleased with herself.

"No, I'm almost done."

She looked up, but Nana pointed at the ten pounds of potatoes in a wooden crate in the corner. "Those haven't even been started yet."

Matty nodded and grabbed the crate before Cora could even force out a protest of potatoes not being part of the equation. "We'll get this done for ye, Grandmamma."

"Good. And don't come out till you're good and naked."

"Nana!"

"Excuse me?"

She smiled and pointed. "I was talking to the potatoes. They're covered in dirt."

The potatoes. *Riiiiight.* "Whatever. I'll get it done."

"We will," Matty corrected.

"I knew I could count on you two." Nana smiled and left the pantry.

Matty picked up the potato brush and started washing the spuds in the sink. "I've never heard ye call a dog stupid before."

"I was angry."

"At the dog?"

"Him, Randy, myself." She looked up. "You."

"Me? What did I do?"

Cora faced him. "You really want me to answer that?"

"I tried to help ye."

She nodded and took her own spud to wash. "I know. It's just...."

When she didn't finish, he supplied, "Feel frustrated?"

No word seemed perfect for her feelings and situation. Yes, frustrated, but also angry, betrayed, dejected, hunted/stalked, helpless, corralled... the list went on and on. "Maybe."

They washed in silence for a few minutes. "I've worked hard to be the man ye deserve, Cora. I know ye doona see it, but when ye trust me, I'd like to show ye."

"Stop, Matty. Just... stop."

They each grabbed another potato to clean. "Yer mom says ye've moved into a nice studio apartment."

"It's tiny, and not in a great neighborhood, but it's all I could afford after you ditched me."

He tossed the spud into the pot. "Will ye please stop recounting ma sins? I know I wronged ye, lass. I'm trying ma level best to make it right."

"How? By taking a paying gig from my family to pay your bills?"

"No. I'll take no money from Grandmamma. But I am defending ye. Standing up for what's right."

She shook her head and focused on digging a knot

of dirt from one spud's eye. "It's all just words, Matty. Actions speak louder."

"Like standing in the blizzard to wrangle yer horse?"

God, she'd never get that image out of her brain. "And blackmailing a fee in the process."

"A fee ye once gladly paid, over and over again."

"Once upon a time."

"Aya." He stepped closer. "A fairy tale is what we had, and a fairy tale is what we'll have again. I promise ye."

Now she chucked the spud into the pot, taking some satisfaction in the clanging it produced. "Your promises aren't worth the paper they're written on." She reached for another potato but he stilled her hand.

"Perhaps na the paper ye've seen, but I've another sheet for yer eyes."

"Yeah? What is it?"

"Na yet. Na until ye've forgiven me."

"Don't hold your breath." She shoved past his hand and grabbed another spud.

They scrubbed in silence until the last one was cleaned, then Cora shouldered her way past Matty and plunked the stock pot on the counter. "Here you go, Nana."

She came over and peeked in. "They're not peeled."

"But you said—"

"We've got this," Matty cut in and picked up the pot. He sent her a slightly sanctimonious look as he headed back into the pantry. "You coming?"

"Like I have a choice," she mumbled as she joined him.

After searching through the drawers, Cora only found one peeler and called out, "Do you have another peeler, Nana?"

"Two peelers? Heavens, no."

"We'll take turns," Matty offered, and Cora shook

her head and picked up a carrot to peel. After watching her for a few seconds, Matty said, “I’ve always enjoyed watching ye make the meal.”

“Freeloader.”

“Hardly, since I was the one growing them.”

One tiny nod. She vacillated on adding anything, but then smiled. “Those tomatoes were huge, weren’t they?”

“Aya. Remember how the yams took over ma parents’ garden?”

She smiled and handed him the peeler to use. “Who would’ve thought two tiny slips had such staying power?”

She waited while he dug out the eyes from the spud and sliced off the dark skin until only the white flesh remained. “They were the best we’d ever grown. I used to think it was because ye’d bring the horse manure over to fertilize.”

“I thought it was because you played music for them.”

“But only the tunes ye liked.” A flicker of sadness passed across his face. “I doona remember a time in ma life when ye weren’t in it.” He held her eyes. “I miss ye, Cora. To ma bones.”

She snatched the peeler and took her turn on a carrot. “I can’t, Matty. I just can’t.”

“Na yet, *mo chridhe,* because I doona deserve ye.” His earnest touch stilled her frantic swipes on the vegetable. “But doona push me away because it’s what I deserve; give me a chance because I’m proving I’m worthy of yer love again.”

Fast blinking kept the tears at bay. She never cried, but this week was proving to be her breaking point. “Why should I?” She stopped and faced him. “What guarantee can you possibly give me that you won’t walk out on me again?”

He opened his mouth, but nothing came out.

"Wow, all that?" Cora tossed the peeler in the sink and headed out, but Matty grabbed her arm at the same time Nana blocked her path.

"Are you both done already?"

"No."

"Lass, doona leave."

"I need those ready in about forty minutes. Randy was the fastest peeler we had."

"Fine!" Cora tossed up her hands just to shut them both up. She snatched up the peeler and started on her roots with a vengeance, ignoring Nana's little victory sniff and Matty's long-defeated sigh. She finished and tossed it his way. "Your turn."

He poked out the eyes and started swiping. "Ma guarantee is part of the paper that I willna let ye see until we're together again, as a couple."

"A couple of fools."

"Fools in love."

Softly said, but it made Cora look away. She still loved Matty; she'd love him until the day she died. But love without trust couldn't happen. Their baby had died, and she could have, too. She'd never be able to trust getting pregnant and raising a child with him if history dared repeat itself.

Perhaps Matty sensed he'd crossed a line, because he focused on his spuds for a few minutes, handing the peeler back and forth in silence.

When Cora got down to her last carrot, she said, "I'm done. I'll bring these to Nana."

He only nodded, and his sorrow felt as her own. She hauled the pot back into the kitchen, where Nana said, "I'm making stew. I'll need you to chop these into chunks."

Of course she did. Instead of heading back into the butler's pantry, Cora moved to set the pot on the counter, but Nana's hands flew up. "Oh, not in here, dear. I'm going to start rolling out some dough, so I'll need the counters."

All of the counters, Cora guessed, because that would ensure she went back to Matty's side. So she headed back into her narrow green dungeon and dumped the lot back onto the counter.

"Now what?"

"Stew chunks."

So Matty leaned out and called, "Stew chunks for the potatoes, Grandmamma?"

"Yes, dear."

He whispered, "And let me guess; she only has one knife in here, so we'll have to share that as well."

The fact Matty also saw through Nana's charade made Cora scoff. "I think you're right." She tugged open all the drawers to no avail. "Looks like we're stuck with this one lone semi-dull kitchen knife."

"Ladies first."

She rough cut her carrots into large pieces and then handed the knife to Matty and waited while he worked away, listening to him hum a piping tune. "Which one is that?"

"Hm? Oh, *Flower of Scotland.* It's a march I started playing in Scotland. One of ma new favorites."

In silence Cora listened to his deep soothing hum as his foot tapped in time to the slow march, imagining the sway of his kilt in time to his careful steps. Growing up, he was the only one in high school to play the pipes, with his services frequently requested to lead the parades, start the games, and whatever other school events they concocted to get him front and center. She'd grown up listening to him play, hum, teach her about his music, his passion. Of course she'd tried to play them, was sort of okay on the practice chanter but never wanted to try her hand on the real deal, too afraid of damaging such an expensive instrument.

Didn't stop her from appreciating his talent, though.

He even cut the potatoes in time to the march.

Not entirely sure when the question formed, Cora

heard herself ask, "Why did you choose the Barons over me?"

He stopped his cutting to look at her. "Ye willna believe it, but I went *for* ye, not *instead* of ye."

"You're right. I don't."

When she made no further comment, his shoulders dropped. "I know it looks like I panicked and ran, but once I was at the airport, I knew I couldna go back to the way I was. I wasna any good for ye, lass, any good for either of us, and I knew if I ever hoped at a chance at getting ye back, I'd need to step up ma game."

"So you fled the country."

Instead of arguing with her, or even attempting to defend his actions, he whispered, "Aya, like a cowardly fool. But by the time I got there, I had a plan."

After holding his eyes a second, she asked, "Sharing?"

"Na until ye let me back in, *mo chridhe.*"

An eye roll. "Again with the heart?"

This time, he gave her a sad, meaningful look. "It's the only place ye've ever been, lass. Since the first time I set eyes on ye."

Without meaning to, Cora smiled. "Like when you tried stealing me away from Hugh?"

"Tried? Oh, lass, I fully succeeded. To this day, I still doona know what ye ever saw in him."

For once, Cora felt no need to correct Matty that he'd since lost her. "He idolized me."

"But he never fought for ye, did he?"

"Neither did you."

Matty scooped up the last of the potato pieces and dumped them into the pot. "Lass, I've fought harder for ye in the last fourteen months than I ever thought possible."

His unverified claim made Cora snatch all the green carrot tops off the counter, clenched tight in her fist. "Yeah? Sure doesn't feel like it."

He opened up the cupboard hiding the trash bin, but Cora tugged open a drawer and yanked out a plastic shopping bag to stuff the discards in. Matty waited for her to dump them but she made no move. He closed the cupboard. "I'm sure it will when ye forgive me. It'll all make sense then."

Nothing in Cora's life made sense this week. Nothing. "Nana! We're done!" She squared her shoulders and headed for the doorway, but Matty's arm on hers stopped her. "I've never stopped loving ye, Cora. Na even for a minute."

She shook the bag of carrot pieces at him. "Love is about finding a way to take care of another, even when you have absolutely nothing left to give." She shoved past him and ran up the stairs, the bag held tight in her shaky fist.

Chapter 12

This would be the perfect time to cry. The best time to curl into a little ball and bemoan everything that went wrong this day, this week, this year. But a house full of people and a wayward husband in Cora's bed meant that any moment of an unrestrained pity party would have to wait. Some cans of worms did not need to be opened, especially with spectators.

More hay in Herbie's cage helped keep him warm, and the towel draped overhead did even better to keep him snuggly. Ol' Red's warm air blew into the domed cage, helping to keep him comfortable at her own expense. Like she told Matty, love was about finding a way, she thought as she tickled Herbie's nose with the carrot tops until he yanked one out of her hand and munched away.

She stayed with him for a few minutes, feeding and stroking him as she tried to make sense of her life. For a brief moment last week, Cora had panicked that her license would be compromised, but logically she knew that would not be the case. Her registry was sound, provided she didn't do something stupid, and she had plenty of time before she had to worry about the cost of renewing it. Perhaps she should look into getting a day job, one where she could do dental cleanings again. She missed those, since few dogs coming into emergency needed prophylactic cleaning. One old Poodle had needed it, the poor dog so neglected it broke her heart. That case had resonated with her, left a lasting impression, since her relationship with Matty had just been severed when the dog had come into emergency. Cora had empathized with little Pixel, knowing what it was like to trust somebody only to end up destroyed in the end.

All her life she cared for animals. Her mom had taken her to work as a child and taught her how to take temperatures, check pulses and respirations, even listen to gallops and arrhythmias via stethoscope. While other kids were learning their multiplication tables, Cora learned about milligrams and milliliters and the mg/mL ratio.

A nurse, through and through.

She needed to nurse something.

Faberge. Where was that geriatric Bichon, anyway? She hadn't seen him since yesterday. With an apology and an extra handful of hay, Cora locked Herbie in his crate and headed downstairs, checking the nooks and crannies for the old dog. When she peeked into her grandparents' bedroom, she rounded the bed and found her target cuddled up in his little blankie. She kissed to him and he looked up at the sound. "Hey, boy, how are you?"

Sadness ringed his eyes, and his tail thumped once. Concern made Cora's brows lower. "Fab? What's wrong, boy?" Enough room between the bed and the wall enabled her to squat down, and there Cora sat and stroked him. He smacked his lips, and with a practiced hand Cora tugged on his skin, testing for elasticity and moisture content.

She didn't like what she saw.

Knowing that he had kidney disease worried her. She headed into her grandparents' private bathroom and found the IV bag hanging behind the door, with a medical label stating to give 200 cc at a sitting, but 300cc remained in the liter bag, meaning Nana shorted him—probably from all the commotion, but still. She warmed the bag under hot water until it felt comfortable against her cheek, then went back to Faberge. He seemed really lethargic, so Cora rolled the IV bag down like a tube of toothpaste, put on a fresh needle, and started his sub-Q fluids, electing to finish the bag to rehydrate him.

As she squeezed the bag to increase the flow, her mind raced to her non-existent job. When would she next give sub-Q fluids? Would she get hired again? Where did she want to work? Not a lot of hospitals near where she lived now, so if she found something, she'd either have a long commute—possibly into the City—or she'd have to move. Again. Shit. She'd just unpacked her last box not four months ago.

Fuck. She hated not knowing.

Perhaps Faberge sensed her agitation, or perhaps the fluids relieved him, because he started to get antsy. "Hold your horses, big guy. We're not done."

"There ye are. Thought ye'd be upstairs."

Instead of looking up, Cora stroked Fabby's head. "Did you close the bedroom door?"

"Aya. We doona want yer cousin's dog repeating his sins."

An apt concern, and one Cora hoped Matty applied to his own life these days. She nodded and squeezed the bag, rearranging the dog's skin to allow more fluid to seep in.

Despite ignoring her husband, he settled in at her side. "Always did love watching ye work. Ye've such a soft touch."

A nice compliment, but she shook her head. "You've never seen me work."

"Ye kidding, lass? Do ye na remember how many times yer mom asked us to help her with the horses?"

Oh, yeah, ten years ago, when she'd just started studying towards her license. This time her nod felt more sincere. "You'd hum to them, keep them calm."

"Na, lass. Ye and yer mom kept them calm. I merely held tight to the halters."

"At least you're not calling them collars anymore."

"Told ye I've been studying."

The last of the IV bag drained into Faberge, so she withdrew the needle and put digital pressure on the hole, plugging it. "Tissue?" She pointed at the box on the nightstand.

He stretched over and plucked one to hand to her,

and Cora wadded it up to help stop any seepage.

"Just by watching ye I can see how competent ye are at yer job. I hope yer doing well there and that they appreciate ye."

She didn't answer, but damn it hurt to swallow.

"Yer Grandmamma know yer in here?"

A head shake. "Just went looking for company."

Yeah, that must have smarted, because Matty looked around. "Aya, and ye chose a dog over yer husband." He got up. "I can take a hint."

She didn't refute his comment and had no energy left to placate him or assuage his ego. As soon as he left, Cora forced herself to swallow. Her little fluffy buddy met her eyes, and she didn't know if gratitude or compassion guided his actions, but he got up and curled up in the triangle of her legs. Once he settled, he laid his little head on her knee to gaze up at her.

She didn't know if the wet spot on his fur came from the sub-Q fluids or her eyes.

She dabbed at her nose with the wadded up Kleenex.

Damn the man.

Chapter 13

This time, when Matty couldna find his wife, he checked the coats and discovered hers missing. She was upset then, his Cora. Probably hiding in the loft. In all their years together, he'd only known her to hide there three, na, four times, each after a tragedy, like her friend's car accident right after graduation, or when she thought her parents were divorcing. If he found her there.... He shook his head and took a deep breath.

Determined to make whatever plagued her aright, he searched the house until he located Grandmamma lounging in the sunroom, yesterday's paper folded on her lap. "Do ye have any popcorn to pop?" It was the one thing that always cheered her up.

"Of course. In the pantry. Let me show you." She picked up her newspaper, but Matty stopped her.

"Na, Grandmamma. I can find it, thank ye. Ye doona need to get up for me."

So she settled back in her chair with a deep sigh of gratitude. "There's a ton of leftovers in the fridge," she offered.

He nodded. "Thank ye, Grandmamma. It's na for me, but for Cora." Instead of staying to explain, he searched the pantry, found the box and stuck one bag in the microwave to pop, then donned his coat, boots and gloves. The bag had rounded by the time he retrieved it, and he plucked it up and headed outside.

Jesu, the wind bit. At least he wasna in his kilt today. His boots crunched across the driveway, the wind blasting him as it picked up over the empty pastures. The red barn loomed dead ahead, and on the other side of the paddock he could make out the white house where Cora grew up with her family. She had explained that people of her grandparents' generation sometimes did that, built smaller homes on the same property so their children could raise their own families while still maintaining the larger family farm.

Twenty more excruciating feet. Ten. He gripped the barn door handle and slid it open, grateful for the warmth inside. He tugged the door closed and went looking for his wife. Stall by stall he searched, then headed upstairs, into the loft, where he found her in the corner, stroking the ginger barn cat with one hand and holding a tool with the other. Na good, being here. After inhaling a breath of courage, he joined her on the hay bale, the cat startling enough to get up, but not enough to actually run away. He bit off his gloves and dropped them on his lap, then tugged the corners of the popcorn open and tipped it to her.

She didna even look up at him but asked, "How did you find me?"

He blinked, surprised at both her question and that she held a pair of tin snips. "Yer kidding, right?" He shook the bag and listened to the kernels settle to the bottom as he tipped it her way. "Still hot."

Nothing. So he tried again. "I know ye havena had anything to eat today. Ye must be hungry. Eat some, lass."

Even though her stomach rumbled loudly at the tantalizing scent of his butter-flavored offering, she didna move. A mischievous grin found him. "I've seen ye force feed yer mom's horse once. Do I have to plug yer nose and slip some of this piping hot food past yer lips?"

She glared at him, but he saw a hint of a smile fighting to curl the edges of her mouth. She raised the tool like a weapon to ward him off. "Do it and die."

"Ach, lass." He made a playful pinching motion with his fingers. "I'm going to plug ye."

She swatted him away. "Stop."

"Mm," he said, jokingly reaching for her nose and chin to get her to open up. "We'll strap this on like a feed bag." Popcorn spilled on the bale and rolled to the floorboards, where the cat jumped down to crunch on it.

She caught a noise that may have been a laugh and turned away. "Matty."

"Look, even the cat has more sense than ye. Dig in." He snatched the bag before more tumbled out and handed it to her again.

"Fine." She took a handful but only stared at it, the motion so incongruous with the Cora he knew that he braced with alarm.

Without realizing it, his hand reached for her cheek. "Jesu, yer ice cold."

Again, no response, unless opening her hand to feed the barn cat counted.

He cupped her cheek, then slid his fingers to her nape. Cold through and through. "Let's get you before the fire. Any longer out here and I think ye willna be able to move."

"I don't want to go inside."

He couldna let her sit out here in the cold, na when no blood flowed through her veins. "Ye need warmth, lass. Ye of all people should know about hypothermia. Even the cat's warmer than ye are."

"I want to stay out here."

He stood and unzipped his jacket. "Then roll into me."

"Matty." She heaved a sigh. "Just leave me alone."

"Na an option. Come here." He pulled her to her feet and unzipped her jacket, then picked her up by the buttocks and sat down with her on his lap, chest to chest, the way they used to cuddle on the couch before bed. The tool thunked as it landed on the bale. "Put yer hands on ma back, love."

He heard and felt her deep resigned sigh, but then she bit off both her gloves and slid them around his ribs, nestled between his sweater and coat. Immediate chill seeped through from the contact. It wasna safe for her to be this cold. He yanked up his sweater and did the same for her despite her feeble protests, drawing their bare skin together. He didna know which was worse: her body temperature or the fact she barely resisted. "Now put yer hands on ma back."

"I hate you."

Better. "Aya, I know. Get warm, lass."

Ach, her fingers touching his skin made him brace, shiver, instinctively flinch away from granting the warmth she desperately needed. "Ye've dumped ice down my back warmer than those fingers."

"Only when you deserved it."

"Deserved or no, I've never felt ye so cold, lass. Move yer fingers."

Lord Almighty, he'd never get warm again with such spears chilling his body, but he wouldna leave his stubborn wife to freeze. Having her in his arms, even begrudgingly, made every emotion he ever felt for her surge to life. He loved how she molded to his body, how she smelled, breathed, draped against him. Loved how she argued with him, infuriated him, made him feel things he'd never felt with anyone else.

"What's up with the pliers?"

"Tin snips," she corrected.

"And why do ye need tin snips?"

"They're not for me."

"Who, then?"

A sigh. "Does it matter?"

"Is everything aright, lass?"

"Yeah. Fine. Sherry needs them to get laid, okay?"

"Tin snips?"

She shook her head, and he felt a wave of sorrow pour from her. Right now, equal measures of worry and love filled him. They worsened when she gave a little hiccup. Something definitely was verra wrong. "What plagues ye, lass?"

"Nothing."

He stroked her back, his fingers leaving warm spots along her skin, a stark contrast to the icy trails hers left on his. "It's na nothing, Cora. Ye canna lie to me; I know ye too well."

Instead of answering, Cora curled her fingers under his arms, the icy tops of her bones sending an electrical current straight through his chest, strong enough to make his heart stutter. He tightened his hold on her, giving her time to reply.

After what seemed like ten minutes of freezing torture, she mumbled, "I'm worried about Faberge."

Grandmamma's dog? Of course she would be, but despite her natural inclination to help animals, the dog's condition didna seem dire enough to warrant a self-imposed exile to the barn in a storm. "Aya, he's been yer most constant companion whenever ye came here. He was happy to see ye."

Again, no reply.

Heat suffused her limbs, and by now Matty had no more cold spots along his back, only blissful heat from their skin-to-skin contact. He dared ease away to try to meet her eyes, knowing she hid the truth from his ears. "What's really bothering ye, lass?"

He didna mistake the glisten of tears as she turned away, but though she tried to shove off, Matty anticipated her and clenched her tight. Whatever it was, he would be the first to hear of it. No secrets ever lived between them, and he didna want to break that pattern now. "Yer safe, lass," he crooned as he rocked her in his arms. "Whatever it is, we'll get through it."

She squirmed in his arms. "There is no 'we,' Matty."

This again? So he nestled her cheek against his. "We are always a 'we,' lass. There'll never be another one in ma heart." He could tell she heard him, listened. "What's wrong?"

Now he heard the barely-contained sob. Felt the tear run down his collarbone. He rocked her tighter, crooned to her, told her everything would be aright. His Cora never cried, never showed weakness, except to him, and even then, only on the rarest of occasions.

She exploded out of his arms, scaring the cat as she railed, "*We're* what's wrong, Matty. Don't you get it?" She tugged down her sweater and dashed away the tear trail as she glared. "We don't belong together. I can't trust you. I don't trust you. Stop trying to make things *aright.*" She shoved her cap tighter on her head and snatched up her gloves. She didna even try to zip her coat, only clenched the edges closed, snatched up the tin snips, and raced down the stairs.

He'd rarely seen such fire in her and knew something awful had happened, but to whom? Despite her protests, Matty knew Cora, knew only a dire circumstance drew her to reflect in solitude.

The cat peeked out from behind a stack of hay bales, watching him. No sense freezing to death out here. He stood and zipped his coat, tugged on his gloves. He dumped the rest of the popcorn and told the cat, "One of us might as well enjoy life. Dig in."

Chapter 14

She should just go home. Pack up her bunny and get the fuck out of Dodge. God, she'd come so close to telling him, so close to sharing how scared she was, how uncertain her future looked from her myopic viewpoint. She'd never been unemployed before. She'd shadowed her mom as a child, learning firsthand about veterinary medicine. When she started working kennels at a vet hospital at 16, she already had decent medical knowledge. So they started asking her to assist with surgery prep, then cleanup, even anesthesia. All *before* she became licensed. She would have stayed with that hospital indefinitely, but Matty's gigs were mostly evenings and on weekends, so working overnights meant they could see more of each other, so she took the position at the Long Island Emergency Center and never looked back.

Now, she didn't know how to look forward.

It certainly did *not* involve a Scotsman, though.

She kicked off her boots and yanked off her coat, her instinct to run upstairs and snuggle her bunny and start packing.

But her body felt cold again on the inside, the type of cold that settled into joints and marrow and had no intention of leaving before July. Going upstairs meant leaving the warmth of the banked fire, the smell of grilled cheese sandwiches, the comfort of a sister who could keep an errant husband at bay. She looked around at the gathered masses and located the blondest head in the room, then squeezed beside Sherry, even lifting her wool blanket to steal her warmth.

"Whoa, I'm not that kind of girl," she joked.

So Cora tossed her arms around her sister's waist and snuggled close, joking back, "You won't know until you try."

"Geez, you're freezing."

"I found tin snips," she whispered, making Sherry nod and relax. Then, louder, said, "I just took care of the horses." Sort of.

But her mom heard and looked up from her crossword puzzle. "You did? Oh, thank you, Cora." Then she glanced out the window and frowned. "You went out in the storm?"

She looked up from her sister's shoulder to clarify. "I didn't muck the stalls, but I followed the whiteboard and gave them all their grain and pellets. By the way, how was the colic call?"

Relief poured from her mom's shoulders. "So far, so good. I think she'll pull through." A grateful smile. "God, I've missed having you around. I never had to worry about getting to their grain whenever you came to visit."

"I nominate Peter to muck. He likes getting dirty," Cora jabbed, daring a glance at her mechanic brother in the corner, engrossed in his cell phone. He gave her a snide face until their mom looked away, then he itched his ear with his middle finger, surreptitiously flicking her off.

She smiled and snuggled against her sister's side as the front door opened. No point looking; she knew Matty had returned. She released Sherry and drew the wool blanket up to her eyes as she slouched deep into the couch, below the top cushion, hoping he wouldn't see her. Whether he did or didn't, he came and stood before the fire, blocking her heat as he warmed his hands.

With his coat off and his back to her, Cora couldn't help but admire the view. From any angle, Matty looked magnificent. His jeans hung just right on him, the dark denim a perfect counterpoint to his raven-wing hair. The sweater he wore was one of her favorites, blue with enough green to augment the intense jade of his eyes. Even without a kilt, Matty was one hot Scot.

He must have sensed her looking, because he turned around and locked concerned eyes on her. "Are ye warm enough, lass?"

She barely nodded, wishing she had acted a millisecond faster and closed her eyes to feign sleep. Now she couldn't tear herself away, locked in that impasse where one of them was expected to speak, and the other would shoot them down.

She placed money on herself.

She could tell he wanted to offer her to roll in, but must have sensed she had no intention of leaving the warm couch and blanket, let alone her sister's solidarity.

He came over and stopped before her. She watched his lips descend as he kissed her forehead. "Ach, lass, yer barely two degrees shy of the grave. I'll be right back with some hot chocolate." He addressed Sherry. "Any for ye?"

Cora liked that Sherry looked to her for permission, like she was going to tell him to fuck off on her behalf, but then Sherry ruined their moment of commonality when she replied, "Actually, that would be nice. Thank you."

When he rounded the couch, Cora jabbed her sister in the ribs. 'Really?"

"Ow. What'd you expect? You froze me. I'd like something warm."

"Traitor."

"It's hot chocolate, not a renewal of vows."

"Great," she muttered. "Now I have *that* to worry about."

So Sherry lowered her head and locked eyes. "The man is falling over his own two feet trying to win you back."

She hissed, "I don't want him back. What's so hard to understand about that?"

She shrugged one shoulder and settled back into the couch. "Then you should stop undressing him with your eyes." She dropped her voice and whispered, "Maybe *you're* the one needing this belt." She tapped her chain link and raised a teasing brow.

"Kiss my ass."

"Again, not that kind of girl."

Stewing in her anger actually helped Cora warm up, as did the hot chocolate that Matty soon pressed into her hands. She had barely mumbled her thanks when the doorbell rang. Since Matty was up, he said, "I'll get it."

Two dogs beat him to the door, and Cora was happy to see both the giant yellow doofus was back from the emergency vet and that the fluids had roused Faberge from his funk. Everyone in the room had spun in their seats to see who had arrived, and the dogs had not quieted down. With a firm grip on Dozer's collar, Matty stepped aside to welcome in the newcomer.

"Matty?

"Darlene?"

"Oh, my God!"

Somehow Cora knew her sister's eyes were on her, waiting to see her reaction to their neighbor Darlene, the evil band leader from high school, at the door. She watched as Matty accepted a one-armed hug from the back-stabber before glancing down at the lump in her arms.

The bitch gushed, "It's so good to see you! When did you get back?"

His eyes darted from the bundle she carried to Cora. "Just this week."

Now Darlene's eyes scanned the room, resting barely a second on hers before returning to Matty, shifting the bundle in her arms like it was heavy. "We're having a party at my house on New Year's Eve, right across the street. Everyone from school will be there. You have to come."

He took a step back, his expression unreadable. "That's verra kind of ye, but I was hired to play ma pipes here."

"Well, afterwards then."

Cora seethed as she watched the reprobate fawn all over her husband. He did a credible job of acknowledging Cora before asking Darlene, "What brings ye here?" He looked again at the bundle in her arms, which Cora thought was now squirming.

"Oh. I need to see Dr. Foote; is she available?" She scanned the room as she asked and flashed a smile when she located Cora's mom.

Cora watched her mom get up and step near. "Hi, Darlene. What happened?"

She shifted the bundle in her arms once again, hefting it to her shoulder. "Roscoe got trapped under a trash can, was out all night. Can you help him?"

"What is Roscoe?" her mom asked.

"A pygmy goat."

Her mom's gray eyes locked on hers, and Cora hopped to her feet before her mom even waved her near. A pointed glance from Matty to Dozer had her husband dragging away the straining yellow Lab, the dog so intent on seeing what was in Darlene's arms that Randy had to come and lift him to his back feet to haul him away. With the barking and whining commotion gone, Cora stepped near and played nice. "Hey."

"Hi."

Instead of starting an awkward conversation centering on Matty, Cora looked at the pygmy goat in Darlene's arms as her mom slipped her hand under the towel. "Wow, he's cold. Bring him before the fire."

Cora turned on the additional lights for her mom as Darlene brought the goat to the middle of the room. Her mom got down to business, making the goat stand to assess cognitive function, checking his eyes for pupillary response, getting a complete history of how poor little Roscoe got stuck in a garbage can. Cora hoped her mom would ask why Darlene was more concerned with inviting

Matty to a party than helping her goat, but apparently her mom didn't feel the need to resort to snark.

Bummer.

Her Nana appeared with a rectal thermometer, which Cora put to immediate use. After a minute she held it up for her mom to see the readout. "He's moderately hypothermic. Cora"—she pointed to the door—"can you run home and get my bag from my office? I don't want to move him until he's a bit warmer, so I'll need my stethoscope; also, can you grab some blood tubes and syringes? Oh, and the Bair Hugger."

"Want dextrose and fluids?" Cora asked.

Her mom considered as she watched the goat collapse back into his towel. "Yeah. Why don't you. I'm going to start CPR."

The statement made Darlene frown and cock her head. "But he's breathing."

Her mom opened her mouth to tout the litany of merits for using CPR, but Cora beat her to it. "Warm air in, cold air out. Be right back."

"I'll come with you," Matty offered, and Cora was actually going to accept his help when her mom butted in with, "Actually, Matty, can you fill some hot water bottles for me?"

She and Matty locked eyes for a second, then Cora snapped away to don her coat. She could carry everything. The Bair Hugger wasn't that big, just bulky, but the perfect item to wrap around a chilled patient to warm them up. She tugged down her hat and braced as the wind blasted her in the face, yanking the door shut behind her and chattering her teeth as she trudged her way to her old home.

Once inside, she stomped off the snow and salt and headed into what used to be her downstairs bedroom, now converted to a makeshift office. The black doctor bag came first, and Cora located the stethoscope already inside. Next she added a handful of syringes and a few butterfly needles in case the veins were too small. Blood tubes. She opened a metal drawer and grabbed a few tiger tops and red tubes. An upper cupboard held the bottle of dextrose. Lower cupboard held the IV bags. She added a couple IV lines and needles for the fluids. Tape in case they inserted a catheter. Ditto for the bandage material. What else? She mentally ticked off each item on her mom's list as she looked into the doctor's bag, happy to put her skills to good use.

The final item she needed was the Bair Hugger to help warm up the goat. She managed to gather the small air mattress under one arm, but the shop-vac sized canister to pump the hot air into it was a little more difficult to carry, and the electrical cord kept falling out of the grip of her gloves. "Damn it." She wrapped the long, thick connecting hose around her neck to keep from tripping over it and bunched the cord until she thought it wouldn't tumble out.

Then she banged her knee into the canister as she tried to walk, making her growl. Where the hell was Matty when she needed him? The black bag slipped out of her gloves and thumped on the ground. "Fuck!" Her fingers were too cold to hold on well; she bit off the glove and opened the bag, relieved that nothing broke.

She snatched everything back into her arms and headed for the door, ready to help save the life of a sweet pet owned by a stuffy rich bitch. One thought rattled around and around Cora's brain as she counted the steps back to Nana's house: *that little bitch better have kept her goddamned hands to herself.*

Chapter 15

Watching Dr. Foote work away on her tiny patient sent Matty back in time, back to when he and Cora would help deliver foals, nurse newborn kittens, even help with C-section puppies. He missed this, even though he did little but provide a few hot water bottles and stand nearby, ready to help. He watched Dr. Foote cup her hands around the goat's mouth and puff air in, administering CPR for a few minutes until the little buddy's eyes cleared up.

Where was Cora? He kept looking towards the door, thinking she'd been gone maybe five minutes.

She should have been back by now.

Darlene maneuvered close to his side, even though he'd already put space between them twice. With Sherry on one side and Darlene on the other, Matty feared Cora would go plumb barmy when she walked in the door. But it didna stop Darlene from whispering, "You and Cora on the outs?"

He looked over at her, tearing his gaze away from the goat. "What?" Her eyes scanned him like she appreciated what she saw. The action irked him; why Darlene and not the woman he married?

But Sherry came to his rescue. "Don't be a ninny. In fact—" she faced Matty "—why don't you check on Cora? Hm? I'll help Mom."

She was no ally, but she wasna his enemy in this battle, either. He gave her a grateful smile and nodded once to Dr. Foote before heading to the door. He heard an unladylike cuss on the other side of the door and yanked it open, not surprised to see Cora unduly burdened. He stepped onto the porch and unwound the flexible pipe from her neck, then took the canister from her hands. He looked at the black doctor's bag. "You got that?"

She nodded, not seemingly grateful for his help, but then again, she looked too bone weary to muster more than a yawn. His concern grew. He hastened the items to Dr. Foote, then stood before Cora, helping her out of her coat. Jesu, she still was cold. He lowered his voice. “Lass, yer too cold to be out in this weather. Come stand by the fire.”

No argument, only a nod. He wrapped his arm around her shoulders and guided her to the flames with zero resistance on her part. Not good. While Dr. Foote fussed with the goat, Matty devoted his attention to warming his wife. While she offered no resistance, he took advantage of the chance to wrap his arms around her belly from behind, draw her shoulder under his chin and press his cheek to hers. He laced his fingers with hers and wrapped them tight about her stomach as he watched the firelight dance upon their joined hands.

This, this was what he remembered, missed. The long touches, the comfort. Taking care of her when she’d lost the ability to take care of herself. He maneuvered his chin to her other shoulder, warming her other cheek. Then he squeezed her, drawing her tighter into his embrace. The words formed before he could stop them. “I’ve missed ye. This. Snuggling.”

Her hands twitched on his; not quite a squeeze, but definite recognition of his words. He’d take it, take any crumb of affection she tossed his way. She wasna herself, and he didna like it. Something plagued her, and he wouldna let it rest until she spilled her tale.

Behind them, he heard Dr. Foote wrap up. “I’ve done all I can, Darlene. The rest is up to him. I’ll keep him with me overnight. Cora can watch him while I set up a pen at home.”

In his arms, Cora turned to meet her mom’s eyes. “Sure. No problem.”

Aya, his wife loved tending to those wee beasties in need. A tender heart thumped away under a salty crust, but

Matty knew Cora took her patient care as seriously as Dr. Foote did.

Instead of acting grateful, Darlene seemed to brush it all off, especially when she came near and said, "I'll see you at the party." Then she met Cora's eyes. "It's a bunch of musicians; doubt you'd have any fun." She spun away. "Thanks, Dr. Foote. Bye."

One... two... three... four.... Cora shrugged off Matty's embrace as soon as the door closed, just as he knew she would, the accommodating wife act played solely for Darlene's benefit. She knelt on the carpet and stroked the goat, talking softly to him. Matty crouched across from her, watching her tender motions of compassion. It's what he loved most about her; he saw who she was inside, and not the person she portrayed to everyone else.

She liked keeping people away, but na Matty. Never Matty. He was the one she always let in.

Until now.

She studiously avoided his gaze to the point he found it comical. She couldna ignore him forever, na when she sat but three feet from him. He heard Grandmamma call Dr. Foote into the kitchen, granting him a moment with his wife, but still she said nothing. So he stood and brought over the Bair Hugger. That's when his wee wife looked up. "I'll get that."

"Na, wife, ye stay by the fire. I'll hook it up for ye."

He couldna tell if relief or exhaustion lingered the most in her eyes, but either way he would help. He attached the long white hose to the canister and plugged it in, then fastened the hose's other end to the air mattress. He turned on the unit and watched the small mattress inflate and heat. With gentle hands, Cora lifted the goat, smoothed out the towel, and set the wee beastie back down on the plastic before covering him. He thought he heard a sigh but couldna tell which shivering creature produced it. He touched Cora's shoulder. "Why don' ye lie down, curl around him?"

Aya, she wished to argue his logic merely because it came from his mouth, but her need to warm herself must have won out, for she scooted her back to the fire and wrapped her arms around the warm Hugger. He couldna stop his own hands from covering her icy ones, trapping them between his own heat and that of the mattress. She didna move, but after a few minutes, he could tell she'd fallen asleep.

Aya, she hated him fiercely, for truth, but perhaps the way to warm his wife to the idea of having him back in her life lay in the warming of her body.

A notion he would put to good use tonight.

Chapter 16

Stew. Of course it would be stew. Hadn't she suffered through half of the creation process this morning? So how could she forget today's meal item? But despite how little she enjoyed recycled Christmas beef and the veggie battle experience from this morning, the meal was hot and thick and helped raise her body temperature until the goose bumps settled down.

True to form, Matty stabbed most of the beef chunks out of her bowl, replacing them with equal-sized carrots, and then he got up and returned with two slices of buttered bread for her to help battle the upcoming indigestion the beef broth would soon cause.

Damn him for remembering.

She couldn't believe she'd fallen asleep on the living room floor with him. While taking care of a patient. Never in all her years of working overnight— even in the beginning, when her body still adjusted— had Cora fallen asleep during patient care. But the warmth of the fire, of the Bair Hugger, of Matty's hands, the soft sounds of conversation and the homey clattering of pans in the kitchen undid her. She zonked out for a good hour, waking only because Matty's hand squeezing her shoulder roused her as her mom's car pulled in the driveway.

"How was our patient while I was gone?" Mom asked as she handed the basket of dinner rolls to Matty.

Had she missed anything? Her eyes darted to Matty's, and he gave a tiny nod. "Fine," she replied. "I didn't take his temp again, but he didn't feel cold anymore, and was trying to stand right before you got back."

"Good. Thanks for sitting with him. Can you believe I had to make another house call?"

She smiled but couldn't meet her Mom's eyes,

electing instead to shove a thick chunk of carrot into her mouth. If anything had gone wrong, Matty would have awakened her. She chewed and swallowed. Even after all this time, she still trusted him with the important things, like patient care. Like helping her truthfully answer her Mom's question. Like falling asleep in his presence.

The only thing she couldn't trust him with was her heart.

She chugged a glassful of milk to help the lump go down. Snatched a roll from the basket and bit into it before passing the wicker down the table. The warm food helped stave off the chill, but it seemed like only Matty had the heat she desperately sought. Even now, the right side of her body warmed as his elbow occasionally brushed hers.

She had to get out of here, away from him. She excused herself and went all the way upstairs, closing herself in their frigid bedroom. She shut herself in the bathroom and turned on the water, then dialed Carla to see if there was any news about getting her job back.

No answer.

Shit.

She left a message and double-checked her reflection for changes. Did she look single? Married? Estranged? Confused? She placed her hand over the elbow that Matty kept brushing, finding it warmer than the rest of her body. A shiver worked through her. Damn it. She didn't want to rely on him, but as another shiver worked through her, she had no choice but to go back downstairs.

She'd find out her future soon enough. Then she could finish this week of hell with a definite goal in mind, be it returning to work or heading to the unemployment office on January 2nd.

Fuck.

She headed back downstairs and headed towards her chair. The second Matty saw her, he frowned and stood, pulling out and then tucking in her chair like a true gentleman. But his frown never left his face.

"Yer lips are blue, lass. Where were ye?"

She glanced at him and then flashed a smile at her nearest cousins. "Powder room."

"Ach, must have used ours. I'll warm ye." He braced her shoulders and started scrubbing his hands up and down her arms, the friction causing delicious heat to ignite her skin.

Across from them, her cousin Jemma smiled with approval. "You two ever think about having kids?"

The innocent question made Cora brace as pain jolted through her, but Matty laughed, obviously running interference as he stopped scrubbing and picked up his roll. "Well, coz, if ye think we're going to announce our attempts like ye two did that last time...."

Half of the table burst out laughing. Fighting her gut reaction, Cora looked up and noticed the two bright spots on her cousin's cheeks. Jemma sputtered and added, "I'm just saying, you two would totally make great parents."

Now Matty set down his roll and held her eyes as he chewed and swallowed, his expression earnest and honest. "That is a right fine compliment coming from ye. Thank ye."

His comment seemed to startle Jemma, because her eyes darted between them. So Cora added, "It's true. Matty and I mentioned it a few times. You don't overreact when the kids fall or injure themselves, you make them accountable for their actions, you let them play and have fun but then insist they behave when the situation requires it. You're both exceptional parents."

Yeah, those were tears of gratitude in her eyes, but Cora didn't need them. What she needed was a faithful husband who would stand by her side and not run screaming into the night at the first sign of trouble. So, lest Matty think they were sharing a moment, she added, "Of course, you have the perfect partner in Jonah. It takes the right kind of man to be a father, and most of the ones I know aren't up for parenthood. You're lucky you two have each other." Damn, that was hard to say, especially with Matty's eyes drilling a hole into her temple.

Apparently her honest conversation was too much for Jemma, because she wadded up her napkin and dabbed at her eyes. After a long mooning glance with Jonah, Jemma looked back to Cora. "We've said the same about you two. That's why we think you should totally start a family. We can let our kids play together. It'll be totally cool."

Ugh, the stew threatened to repeat at that moment. She leaned back and eased the bowl away from her. "Like I said, most men I know aren't up for the challenge."

At the alarm in Jemma's eyes, Matty wrapped his arm around Cora's shoulder, the move both proprietary and silencing. "Most men you knew *werena* up for the challenge. This man would be right happy to have a few MacKenzie bairns rolling around at his feet."

With a giggle, Jemma leaned over the table, her eyes bright with mischief. "You can totally borrow the RV tonight."

"No thanks," Cora started to say, but Matty said, "Yer on."

His eagerness made Cora glare at him. "We're not taking over their RV."

He leaned into her ear and said, "It might be warmer for ye there than in our room. I'll crank the heat for ye, lass." Then he faced Jemma. "Do ye mind a wee rabbit in yer room?"

"I'll take your room for the night," Sherry said, and Cora felt her mouth drop open. Had her whole family gone bonkers today?

"Well," her Nana harrumphed, "this is hardly a dining room conversation," and Cora glanced up at her in relief.

The comment seemed to easily steer Matty onto a different course, because he looked over at Peter and asked, "How's the garage business going for ye?"

He swallowed his mouthful and replied, "Busy. Some days I don't get out until nine."

Then her Mom jumped in. "I keep telling him to knock down that wall and take on an employee, but he's too stubborn."

"It's a load-bearing wall."

"A good architect can work around that. You need staff. You're too busy."

This was all news to Cora. "What wall?"

Now Peter focused on her. "It used to be a three-bay car wash, with a separate room for the manager's office. Now that I converted the bays into work zones, I can't use that space."

"He already made a front desk inside one of the bays," her Mom said to her.

"Ah." Cora nodded, then asked her brother, "You try renting it?"

Peter got as far as opening his mouth.

"Of course he has," her Mom answered. "I've been telling every one of my clients about the available space, too, when I make house calls. No one wants to work next to those air drills zipping off all day."

Poor Peter, Cora thought. No wonder the man never spoke; no one ever gave him a chance to answer.

Perhaps Matty sensed her Mom's need to be the star of all conversations, because he turned to her. "Where's your husband been all week?"

The question shocked Cora, because Matty and her father really didn't get along... well, they had been fine until her dad caught them when they were seventeen. But now, ever since Matty walked out on her, Cora's dad kind of had it in for Matty.

"Oh, he's been getting the hay barn ready for the

party."

"Na willing to have a hundred people tramping through the house this year?"

"Nope. We added a floor and rented six generators. It's going to be the warmest barn in the history of barns."

Matty had been suggesting that for years, and Cora was glad her grandparents finally capitulated to good sense. She turned to her Mom. "Did you ever install the indoor plumbing like you wanted?"

A head shake. "Not really. We added sinks, but we rented Port-O-Potties. Oh, and your father partitioned off two rooms for them, so we actually have men's and women's bathrooms."

Matty grinned and asked, "Still focusing on horses and livestock?"

She smiled at him. "Oh, yes. Anything to get me out of the office. That man...." she trailed off.

"What man?" Matty asked, but Cora knew this story.

"My boss," her Mom replied. "He's insufferable. He should have retired fifteen years ago, but he didn't want to. Now he's deaf and so miserable that he's trying to sell the hospital, but he's lost so many disgruntled clients that no one will buy a place with zero clientele."

"You could buy it," Cora pointed out.

She shook her head. "I'm a horse vet by nature. Yes, I could, but I really love working on the farms, being outside."

Cora thought back to Dozer and the raisins and pointed her thumb at Randy. "You really don't have a blood machine at work?"

"Oh, we do." Her mom shook her head. "It's brand new, still sitting there, three years later, waiting to be used." She leaned forward. "He didn't understand how to run it, mostly because he can't hear the instructions, so it's never been used."

The statement made Cora frown. "The techs usually run all the blood work. All he'd have to do is let the sales reps train the techs."

"Preaching to the choir, doll. We also have a therapeutic laser sitting under a tarp. And he said he was buying a digital x-ray, but, if it even got delivered, it's in the barn where no one's seen or touched it." She shook her head. "Such a waste of a hospital." She met Cora's eyes. "I wouldn't mind being a full partner, but even if everything was working to potential, I still don't want to be stuck behind an exam table all day." She shrugged, then narrowed her eyes. "You don't know any vets looking, do you?"

"In Skaneateles? No, sorry." No one she worked with had ever given any indication of wanting to run a startup, and even then, they'd have to move here.

"Can you ask? Next time you're at work?"

She met her mother's eyes, felt a giant fist crush her heart. "Sure."

"You okay?"

"Fine."

But her mom must have latched onto Cora's nuances, because she didn't let up. "When do you go back, anyway? You've never managed to get Christmas week off before."

"That's true," Matty added as he looked at her. "Ye always liked getting double-time."

She certainly wasn't going to announce her run of horrible luck at a full dinner table, so she said, "Carla begged and pleaded with all the doctors to have this week off. They love her to pieces, so she's not due back until midnight on the second. I'm her assigned tech, lucky me." She smiled and shrugged, letting them assume what they would.

Now Matty's arm draped her shoulders, and he gave her a squeeze. "They're lucky to have both of ye working there, but I'm glad we get ye this week for a change."

No words came to her, but she shared a brief smile. "Thanks."

"What about you?" Randy fired off to Matty. "You ever *man up* and get a real job?"

Oh, a challenge. Cora couldn't help but ping-pong her glance between her cousin and husband, curious to know how Matty was doing without daring to ask.

She watched the hooded expression lower Matty's brows, but then he smiled. "Ye mean beyond being the highest paid musician off Broadway? I get to play ma pipes for a living, something I've always loved to do, which makes ma work a pleasure. So, aya, lad, I have, but I live ma days with passion. But if yer na familiar with the pipes, ye probably wouldna know the joy of striking in the drones, marching to the beat of the most beautiful music in the world." His gaze drifted off, wistful. Then he focused on Randy again. "In ma free time, I've also been writing tunes."

Her cousin scoffed.

But Matty grinned. "Mock me all ye want, but I made a month's income off a tune that took me forty minutes to write. The next three took less than that. And no, it doesna include the royalties, residuals, or book sales." He laced his fingers and leaned forward. "That's beyond ma *real* job. What about ye, *lad?"*

Man, Randy's face turned beet red. "I'm working for the water plant. You know, septic, sewer, water mains. It's good money."

She watched Matty back down at Randy's defensive tone. "Aya, a good honest job. I'm sure yer a right fine worker."

He blinked. "I am."

Cora tipped up her glass, draining the last of the milk, and Matty plucked it from her hands and stood. "I'll get ye a refill."

Because he knew the milk would settle her stomach from all the beef. Was there nothing this man forgot?

Except her hatred of him?

Bedtime, and not a moment too soon, but then Cora remembered she was supposed to be staying in the RV tonight. With Matty. Alone. Even though she slowly found herself getting readjusted to spending time with the man, the idea of bundling up and heading outside to walk fifty feet in a blizzard for a warm place to stay seemed counterproductive. Couldn't she just sleep before the fire? On the floor with everyone else? Where it was warm?

Like his radar detected her movement, Matty stepped to her side, placed a warm hand on the small of her back. "Ready to call it a night?"

Too tired to answer, Cora attempted a nod, then aimed for the door to collect her winter gear, sending a yearning glance to the fireplace and the five small sleeping bags filled with giggling children that surrounded it. Why hadn't she claimed her own spot by the fire?

"Too bad they didna park at the foot of the steps. I bet we could have made a run for it."

"I'd trip and fall and break my neck."

"Then we simply walk," he said, his smile the warmest thing in her vicinity.

They turned and waved goodnight to everyone, then Matty held the door for her and helped her down the stairs, across the uneven driveway, through the drifts to the RV's door.

It was locked. And rocking.

Breath pillowed before her as Cora gasped, "Are you fucking kidding me?"

"Shh, listen," Matty said.

Seconds later, Cora heard the unmistakable sounds of her cousin screaming Jonah's name, interspersed with,

"Ride me, cowboy!" and "Be my stallion, be my stallion!"

They locked eyes, and Cora tried her damndest not to laugh at what she heard, let alone visualize. She assumed Matty wanted to be doing the same thing once they got situated in the camper, but all Cora really wanted was to get warm. Now. She spun away from the door, pissed that her cousin forgot she offered use of the RV tonight. "Fuckin' A."

"That's exactly what they're doing," he laughed as she stomped ahead of him. Two steps later, Matty caught up, supporting her elbow. "Guess she forgot. Heat of the moment, and all."

"Not funny."

He chuckled and quieted for a few steps. "Maybe we should get them a branding iron for Christmas next year."

The comment made her laugh. Loud. God, when was the last time she had laughed?

Matty raced ahead and opened the front door for her, ushering her in and helping her off with her coat and scarf. When Sherry looked up and frowned, Cora answered the unspoken question. "Owner occupied."

"I thought—"

"Yeah, us too." She kicked off her boots and trudged up the stairs, not surprised to hear Matty two steps behind. They entered their frigid bedroom and Cora stopped when she saw the plastic shopping bag on the bed. While Matty went into the bathroom to brush his teeth and get ready for bed, Cora peered into the bag.

Rabbit pellets, the good kind. Yogurt treats. Honey Snackers. Some dried fruit nips. A bag of treats that had a little too much sugar in it, but came from a reputable company. Randy must have asked the sales clerk what to buy, because she knew the store her cousin went to carried both good and questionable brands and only a few of the types she normally purchased at the store nearest her.

Matty did this for her.

She should tell him. Thank him. Tell him that standing up for her was more than defending his wife, that he literally kept food on the table while she survived the limbo and uncertainty of the next few weeks. The intent was fully on her lips when she entered the bathroom, but seeing Matty in only his skivvies made the thought flee her mind. She picked up her toothbrush and went through the motions, the familiar comfort of having a sexy Scot at her side a little unsettling.

He finished brushing and squeezed her shoulder as he passed, and Cora stripped off her clothes and tugged her nightshirt over her head, the moment for full disclosure gone. Heat from the hot water had steamed the mirror to the point that she couldn't see her reflection to comb out her hair, all the better that she didn't have to look herself in the eyes right now. Colder than mere minutes prior, she darted around the bed and leapt under the comforter and balled up to stop her teeth from chattering. The light snapped off, and a minute later Matty slid in beside her. She heard him take a deep breath, low, like he readied for a battle. "Roll into me, lass. I willna take no—"

She rolled in before he could complete his threat, the heat of his skin tantalizing her after the toll the blizzard— hell, the week— had taken on her body. She heard his breath catch in shock, and she contained her smile that she surprised him. He relaxed, wrapped his arms around her, even though she detected him bracing with the icy chill of her skin.

"Jesu, lass, just when I thought ye couldna get any colder, ye proved me wrong."

She wanted to say it was fun proving him wrong, but she tucked her nose into the crook of his neck, inhaling the lingering scent of his cologne, and found both her mind and tongue had numbed from exhaustion. Her shivering, though, remained.

After a minute or two, Matty gave a little growl of frustration. He leaned back to look at her, the tiny motion allowing icy air to seep in between their bodies. The barest touch of his fingertips grazed her jaw, and ambient light from the window glinted in his jade eyes. "I'm going to give you CPR."

Determined to protest, Cora drew in a breath, but the cold room air made her lungs stutter.

He must have sensed her upcoming refute, because he quoted her with, "Warm air in, cold air out."

Warmth. From Matty. All she could do was hold his eyes and wait. Wonder. Pray. Hope. Was it too much to want to be warm inside and out? Too much to wonder what the press of her husband's lips on hers would feel like after a year apart?

Too much to hope to be happy ever again?

She dared not pray. Nothing she ever prayed for ever came to pass.

When no refute came to her lips, Matty eased closer. His hips maneuvered closer to hers, and the fingers on her jaw firmed up. His thumb ran along her lower lip, slowly, slower, and she found her lips parting as she looked up at him. The expression in his eyes intensified, blazed as his eyes roved over her face.

The hand on her jaw slid under her nape and tugged up, exposing her throat to him. His other hand brushed hair off her forehead, smoothing it down and away from her eyes, making her heart race as he smiled down at her. He pressed down on her forehead while simultaneously pulling up her nape, opening her windpipe like they learned in school all those years ago. Eyes locked on his, Cora remained transfixed as Matty's mouth descended lower and lower, and she closed her eyes as he plugged her nose and sealed his lips to hers.

He breathed deliciously hot air into her lungs, filling her with his minty essence. Her chest rose and expanded with the bliss he provided, and when he released her, a measure of cold air vacated her. More. She wanted more. More heat. More lips. More gentle touch. More, more, *more.* Her eyes locked to his, and he sealed his mouth to hers yet again, filling her with what she craved. Her essential organs perked to life, her brain and heart and lungs feeling vital and alive as they hadn't all week. Sensation filtered down to her fingers and toes, and she noticed she curled them all as Matty withdrew and locked his eyes on hers.

In the stillness of the moment, Cora found her lungs taking in tiny gasps of air in contrast to the long pillows of warmth Matty had provided. Her heart beat faster than it had in days, and a measure of heat suffused her body. She felt alive.

Captured.

Ignited.

He hadn't pulled away, hadn't released her forehead or nape. Didn't blink. "More?"

She nodded.

But he didn't bend to breathe for her this time; he slowly mounted her, covering her body with his own. His hands spanned her cheeks, his eyes caressing her as if he'd never seen anything so precious in his life. One hand slid down to tug the end of her nightshirt up over her breasts, and she felt his naked stomach quail against her chilly bare flesh. "Yer getting a wee bit warmer, lass."

"Aya," she whispered, and using his own word made him smile.

His hands trailed down her arms until they laced with her own fingers, then Matty pulled them over her head and slid them under the pillows. Aroused by the slow seduction in his eyes, Cora found her body writhing underneath his in anticipation of his lovemaking. She hadn't forgiven him, but damn, Matty always knew how to make her body respond to his touch.

Like he sensed her thoughts, she watched his lips descend to hers, his intent clearly not to breathe for her but rather to take her breath away. His tongue traced the sensitive inside of her upper lip before pressing his firmly to hers.

Fresh heat exploded in her mouth as Matty kissed her. They breathed as one, drawing in and expelling air back and forth between them, like both halves of them had been split asunder and now sutured back together again. His tongue explored the corners of her mouth, arousing her with his ability to take control. When she tipped her head back, Matty thrust his clothed hips against hers, overpowering her with his body as his tongue thrust powerfully into her mouth.

God, he was huge against her stomach.

He dry-humped her, teasing her as he mastered her mouth, making her squirm with need beneath him. His hands released hers to slide down her body, cupping her buttocks and parting her thighs. He ground his length along her seam, her body now so wet and hot that she felt moisture seeping into her panties. She wrapped one arm around his neck and drew him close to whisper, "Be my stallion."

He sniffed out a laugh and stopped to study her. In the hazy purplish light of the room, his eyes glittered like a wolf's, hungry with intent. He propped himself up on an elbow and stroked her cheek with a fingertip. "Do ye forgive me?"

She blinked. "What?"

"Do ye forgive me, lass?" At her silence, he persisted, "Are we back together again? Moving back in together? Picking up the pieces?"

No words came to her. How could they? What could she possibly say to him that would not be an out-and-out lie?

His deep breath pushed his chest against her breasts,

making her nipples thrust into his chest hair and tease her with what she may never have again. His finger stroked a tendril from her forehead, and he stared at it as he wrapped it around his finger. "I willna make love to ye today, wife. If ye want me in yer bed, I've first got to be back in yer heart." He pressed a scorching kiss to her brow. "I think yer hot enough now to keep *me* warm overnight."

She watched him roll off and lay on his back. Watched him stare at the ceiling. The comforter jutted up from his lap with proof of his desire. She wanted to reach out, stroke him. Feel him thrusting inside her, bringing her long-denied pleasure. Her fingers slid across the sheets toward him. If she straddled him, she'd be able to orgasm. Just once. Just one more time.

But he caught her wayward fingers and pressed her hand to the mattress. "Goodnight, *mo chridhe.*"

He rolled over, his back to her, and all Cora could do was stare in disbelief. Fever prickled her skin, her nerve endings electrified with desire and unfulfilled need. Cora was no longer cold; she was hot, burning hot. An out-of-control flame desperate to be quenched.

As her eyes bored a hole into Matty's back, one thought plagued her: What the hell was the difference between love and lust?

She knew only her heart could answer that question.

Chapter 17

After an interminable night split between lust-filled dreams of Matty and hours of tossing and turning, Cora couldn't take it anymore; she needed relief. Or release. Something that involved orgasmic waves cascading through her torso and down her legs and crumbling and tumbling her walls until all her cares melted away.

But she was married.

To *him.*

The bastard taking over half her bed merely to tease and then torment her.

She'd never attempt to reach out again, not after he rejected her last night; she had her pride. He'd left her. Deserted her. Now he'd upgraded to spurning her. He didn't deserve a second chance at working anything out, not after revving her up and then turning away while her motor ran hot. She'd never have a child with him; she could never risk her heart or her child's mental health on a man who'd already walked out on her. He'd shown his true colors twice now and they were bleak.

Didn't mean she had to suffer, though. He'd made it clear he wasn't going to loan himself out to stud; not this week, at least. Although the bedroom remained frigid, sweat had dried on her skin, a result of both Matty's torment and the troubling hours that followed. She needed a shower. It was far too early to be out of bed, not even six, and the *ping* of snow on the windows would ensure that most of her family would sleep deeper into the upcoming storm.

She slipped out of bed and grabbed fresh clothes, noting Matty remained deep in slumber.

The jerk.

She closed the bathroom door and cranked on the

hot water. Once a measure of steam filled the room, she turned off the lights over the sink, leaving only the fan light on near the tub. She looked back at the door to make sure it was closed tight. She hung her nightgown on the hook by the door and stepped into the blissful heat. As the hot water sluiced down her body, Cora looked up at the shower head. On a long hose. With adjustable pulsations.

No. She shouldn't.

Should she?

Who would know?

Her body tingled from the inside out, her needs having crested unfulfilled over the last few hours. She reached up and slipped the nozzle from the holder and let the stream beat against her thigh. She turned the setting to a soft rain and allowed herself to remember....

The gentleness of Matty's hand sliding up inside her knee.

The brush of his lips against her nipple.

The swipe and flick of his thumb as he whipped her into a sexual frenzy.

With her forehead resting on the shower wall, Cora allowed herself to drift into memory, into sensation, back when Matty had been her world, and she his. When they would spend hours abed, searching, exploring, learning about each other.

Back when the only thing between them was love.

She wouldn't think about that now. Only recall his touch. The pleasure he once brought her. The fulfillment she knew at the end.

As she envisioned moments of her past, she adjusted the settings, amplifying each memory with pulsing or gentle sensation. She felt hot, hotter, like she burned away on a beach under a summer sun as she felt her body ebb and crest with the experience. She had loved how Matty would brush his chin stubble along her clit, waiting until her body was so sensitive that the sheerest caress would cause her to erupt.

She was so close, the memories paradoxically so far away. Tears welled in her eyes, but the shower kept them at bay. This was not a time for regret, but for release. Alone in here with only the blissful heat of the water, Cora could find a moment of peace. No other lover, no damage to her vows, just a body on the brink of reprieve and hopefully exhaustion.

She perched one foot on the tub edge and whimpered, desperately wanting what her body experienced to be a direct cause of Matty's tongue and not some creation of super-soaker technology, but her pleasure sensors didn't seem to care. She mouthed words she hadn't uttered in fourteen months: "Matty, take me there, take me there." She raised her chin and tipped her hips into the spray, feeling her womanly lips swell until her body bucked and exploded with the climax she had so desperately sought.

She had let out a cry, but no matter. Leaning against the cool tiles helped soothe the inferno within, taking the flush of her pleasure down to a post-coital euphoria.

All without allowing the jerk back into her bed.

Smiling and feeling drowsy, Cora slipped the shower head back into its holder and remained propped against the tiles, gyrating in place until the orgasmic swelling had gone down and the pleasurable waves had ebbed. A long moan of overdue relief passed her lips, and she heard herself say, "Oh, Matty," in a sad tone.

True, she missed him, deeply and painfully. Having him at her side this week had been both heaven and hell. It felt so natural to lean on him, talk to him, at one time, trust him, but then the reality of how that had backfired made her snap back.

Her life had become a tragedy.

She lathered up and rinsed off, and a few minutes later, the water pressure dropped. A blast of chilly water sprayed her skin as someone turned on a shower elsewhere in the house.

Perfect time to get out.

She flicked off the water and fumbled for the towel outside the tub, electing to stay in her little steamy cocoon to dry off, her eyes closed as she enjoyed the last orgasm she'd have for a long time at the rate things were going.

She tucked the towel end between her breasts and fumbled for the hair towel and dragged that inside the tub as well. She scrubbed her hair and knotted the mess at her nape and found her legs sliding together, her mind automatically recalling how one orgasm was never enough for Matty. If he saw her like this, he would want to add one more. Maybe two.

He had always been a fantastic lover.

Some girl would be happy to have him.

The thought made her angry. He'd probably fuck up her life, too. Maybe Matty should just avoid women. All women.

But her legs slid up and down a few more times, the ingrained memory of her flesh more enduring than her intent to keep him at bay.

When the clearing steam allowed a blast of chilled air to sneak around the opaque shower curtain, Cora realized she'd taken far too long in the shower. Matty would certainly be awake by now and wondering if she'd broken her neck in here. Resigned but relaxed, Cora tugged open the shower curtain and saw Matty standing there. The opaque shape she had assumed was her nightshirt had been her husband.

He was naked.

He was fully aroused.

And his eyes brooked no argument as to what he intended to accomplish.

Never in all their years together did he know his wife to explore the limits of her own body, and the fact Matty got to see it firsthand made his cock strain at his verra skin. He'd stood with his back to the wall, at first in disbelief of what he witnessed, but then turned on as he'd never been.

Aya, his wife was a looker, as Davey would call her, but right now Matty thought her more fey, like the Selkies who inhabited the shores of Scotland, beautiful women who would shed their seal skins to slip into a man's home and steal his heart and seed, only to slip back into the oceans to raise their new babes alone, leaving the man lovelorn and missing his family.

Aya, his Cora for certain could be one of those fair creatures, so natural and ethereal did she look as she gyrated under the water spray. She had slipped into his life and bed and secured his ring to her finger. She'd even stolen both his heart and seed. But there the resemblance to the myths ended; *he* had left, not Cora.

Men were not Selkies.

Men were the hunters, the keepers.

He wanted to track her, win her, keep her.

He needed his wife back, in a powerful way.

As he crossed the chill tiles, his eyes locked on Cora's, he watched the heated flush in her cheeks pale before turning crimson. Still she didna look away. Ach, the pain of wanting her tripled in his skin, made his cockstand yearn to nestle between her thighs.

He came close, closer, until her chest heaved and the knotted towel at her breasts bumped into his stomach. He couldna help but look down at the flushed skin above the soft terry, the rounded swell of her bosom straining for freedom, the fear and arousal portrayed in her eyes. The smile that curled his lips welled from deep within, and his voice rumbled as he asked, "Miss me, lass?"

Fire shot out of her as she snapped, "No."

He liked that flames now filled her instead of ice, but that didna mean he was buying her lies. He dipped his head to her shoulder, his lips nary a scant inch from her ear as he whispered, "I watched ye, ye know."

Anger flared in her eyes, and when she went to spin away, he caught her arm but didna move, only pulled her closer. "Was it ma tongue ye thought ye had thrusting into ye? Ma fingers?" He drew her marginally closer and tipped his hips toward her, his cock nestling into the thick terry of her towel. "Something far larger?" This wasna no wee cockstand he had working, nay, perhaps the largest he'd ever been, and he felt a measure of pride in letting his wife feel the solid length of him against her flesh.

She trembled, and he didna imagine the longing in her eyes.

She may desire his cock, but Matty desired his wife back. All of her. Body, heart and soul, no half measures. His pride may have been injured, but na his body. He released her arm and lowered his hand to the knotted towel. Holding her eyes, he tugged it free, letting it pool at their feet.

She didna move to cover herself. A good sign.

His gaze lowered, his thumb traveling everywhere his eyes went. He grazed her nipple and watched her chest heave as her skin pebbled, her pink bud thrusting into his palm. He fought down a moan and instead raised his hand to brush her jaw. "Yer more beautiful every time I see ye."

Both anger and appreciation shone in her eyes, and Matty thought he may have tipped his wife into the realm of forgiveness. Somehow his throat clogged, so he cleared it and rumbled, "I never spent enough time bringing ye pleasure, did I?"

Something registered in her eyes, but he didna want to take the time to analyze it or have her backslide, so he pressed on. "I should have worshipped every inch of yer body. If I'd have done that, perhaps ye wouldna have resorted to such a saucy display in there." He flicked his eyes to the shower.

"That wasn't for you to see."

"But I did, lass. I did." Now his hands skimmed over her ribs, down her hips. Lightly, gently. Waiting for her to repel his touch even though the flush of her skin betrayed her desire for him to continue doing so.

So he did.

With painful slowness he lowered his head to her breast, nipping her peak with his teeth before drawing her entire aureole into his mouth. Her wee hands landed on his shoulders. Emboldened, he claimed her breast once more, sucking hard and then letting her slip back out until he sucked her deep into his mouth again and again and again.

She gripped his head with both hands and cried, "Matty!"

Pride filled him, pride and love. Aya, he lusted his wife, but even better was knowing he knew her weak spots, her favorite ways to be touched. He licked her other nipple, then flicked the tip repeatedly with his tongue, enjoying the way she tightened with his touch. He returned to her first breast and sucked her hard. She rewarded him with yet another wee whimper.

One hand slipped around to the curve of her buttocks as the other delved into the damp curls at her thighs. He said, "I got to watch a Selkie dancing in the rain, tempting me as I've never been tempted. Making me ache for ye, lass." He slipped his fingers into her slit and moaned as her lubrication allowed him fast entry. "Ach, Lord o' mercy, Cora, I've missed ye as much as ye've missed me."

"Just horny," she breathed, but the way her head tipped back and her mouth parted open told him otherwise.

Nay, he couldna. Not like this. Lord above, he craved her like air. Needed her. Desired her more fiercely now than ever he had. But he wouldna have sex with her. No matter his straining cockstand and forthcoming blue balls, he wanted his wife to forgive him, to want *him* and not simply the pleasure he knew they could both find.

She'd want a hard tupping, but Matty wanted his wife back.

"Tell me ye forgive me, and I'll take ye back to bed to finish what we started."

A firm head shake. "What if we just hook up for sex?"

Now he shook his head, but he stroked her G-spot as he did it. "Na, lass." He stepped close and suckled her ear. "Let me love ye like man and wife."

She panted now. "How about man and woman?"

"Man and wife," he repeated, pumping his finger into her to augment his meaning.

"Friends with bennies?"

He dropped to his knees and nestled his nose into the top of her slit, causing Cora to cry out and almost collapse back against the wall. Her hands clenched into his hair as his own fingers clawed into her buttocks, holding her close.

Her scent. Lord, he'd missed her scent. He inhaled it deep into his lungs before flicking out a tongue to nudge her clit.

"Whiskers, Matty."

Aya, he knew what she wanted, but he wasna going to give it to her until they both got what they wanted. "Tell me what I want to hear."

He waited, knowing she wouldna lie to him. As the seconds ticked by, Matty blew across her clit, causing her to buck in pleasure. "Tell me."

"Later."

"Now."

He looked up, watching and waiting. But Cora's head remained tipped back, her eyes closed in pleasure. She wasna about to forgive him.

Perhaps ever.

With Herculean resolve, Matty stood and stepped away, the lack of spousal attention making his wife's eyes open and find his. Questions filled her gaze, but he knew she'd find all she needed to know in his own expression: *forgiveness before fucking.*

"Come on, Matty, stop torturing me."

"All ye have to do is take me back." Aya, he didna mistake the tears in her eyes as she whisked her gaze from his, but when she looked back a moment later, only hardness filled them.

"No."

He nodded once in dismissal. Turned his back to her and cranked on the water. Yanked on the shower. Dunked under the heat and blasted the temperature down forty degrees until his cockstand shriveled.

Lord above, this was going to be a hell of a long day.

Chapter 18

Dear God, she'd been so close. So close to saying his stupid words and getting trapped into the same situation she had so narrowly escaped last year. Bills barely getting paid. Landlord waiting outside the door for rent. Charging groceries and gas and praying Matty would get a few gigs that might give them the tiniest breathing room for a week or two.

She couldn't.

She didn't even know where her next paycheck was coming from, or when.

She already had a fur-baby to take care of, someone who truly needed her. Even if Matty *was* the highest paid musician off Broadway, she had no intention of ditching her life and wandering the world at his whim. Herbie had already been abandoned at college when his former owner moved back home; he deserved better than another part-time mom.

So, thanks, Matty, but no thanks.

With her husband scouring himself under the frigid spray of water, Cora took her cue and dashed from the bathroom. She scrubbed herself dry and tugged on the heaviest clothes she had. Between her wet hair and the stark contrast between Matty's attention and scorn, she expected icicles to chime from her hair ends.

Damn the man.

She recalled the conversation between Matty and Randy and wondered how much of it was true. Was Matty really the highest paid musician off Broadway? What did that mean? Not enough to rival a rock star, right?

He was probably just trying to make himself sound more accomplished than he really was.

Didn't really sound like something he'd do or say,

though.

Didn't matter. Cora didn't need to entangle her life with his. Been there, done that.

Thank God her Nana had come through during those rough months. She knew her grandparents had a healthy retirement they lived off of, and although Cora never asked, after she had had to move to the studio to live, every month she received a life-saving money order from Nana. At the time, she had been *this close* to having to rehome her bunny—a fear that ruined her sleep for six straight days. She'd been living off groceries from the dollar store for almost two weeks by that time, washing her dishes with only hot water because the extra dollar went to soup instead of soap, or a box of hamster seed because she couldn't afford his premium bunny food.

Soon afterwards, the money orders swelled in size. No longer enough to simply cover groceries or gas, but enough to cover rent. Then car repairs. New tires. And after Cora finally had some financial breathing room, she tried paying Nana back. Ripped check after ripped check came back to her, though, with a beautifully penned letter from Nana wishing her well, sharing little joys of her day, family news, and prayers for better times ahead.

It almost became a game. They penned handwritten notes back and forth month after month. She treasured them now as keepsakes. In the age of instant messaging and emails, those handwritten notes became her lifeline to her family.

Barely four months ago, she'd gotten completely out of debt, the bulk of each check having gone straight to bills, and lately into savings.

Matty would plunge her straight back into debt, probably bigger this time, since he most likely had developed some expensive tastes over the last fourteen months.

Didn't matter. She couldn't risk it.

But damn, her body vibrated with need.

She should hate him; it would be so much easier.

She toweled her hair as she attended to Herbie, making sure his food bowl and water bottle were full before adding hay and some more carrot tops. She left both males behind the closed bedroom door and hastened downstairs, into the heavy aroma of bacon and the greasy smell of pancakes on the griddle.

Her sister was already awake, mooning away at Matty's cousin, Davey. Since Sherry had apparently reserved two spaces at the card table, Cora had no choice but to join her. She managed a smile for Davey, who today looked so annoyingly like his cousin that Cora thought she may have flashed fangs instead.

"My, my," Sherry said, raising her brows.

"What?"

Her sister scanned her and with a sanctimonious smile said, "Someone's got some color to her cheeks today."

Noting children in the vicinity, Cora managed a sweet smile and said, "Like the sheep say, *flock ewe*."

No comment, but her sister raised a querulous brow, daring her to comment further.

"Aye, are ye thinkin' ma cousin buggered her, Sherry?"

Mouth open with his bald statement, Cora blinked at him. "What my sister thinks is none of your concern."

"No, lass," Davey leaned forward. "It is."

That comment made Sherry's face turn Christmas red.

Now Cora raised a brow at her sister. "Anyone else wish to discuss *flocking?"*

"No," Sherry fired off, her tone stating she'd say no more on the topic.

"Huh," Cora said, grabbing a paper napkin and pouring herself a glass of orange juice. She couldn't decide if stress eating or sulk/starvation was the better choice after having Matty's tongue and hands on her, so all she did was tilt her glass back and forth and watch the liquid slosh to and fro, to and fro, completely at her whim.

Davey and Sherry got into an animated discussion over something they had obviously been discussing already, but Cora barely tuned into it, still bothered over her morning.

As she debate before her raged on, Nana rounded the corner, interrupting her sulk. "There you are."

Fuck. Cora looked up. "Me?"

"Yes. I need your help."

Although she smiled, Cora sensed another setup. "With what?"

"Griddle." She waved a spatula at her. "You're being promoted to short-order chef."

"Demoted, more like it," she mumbled, but to Nana said, "Why not sous chef?"

"Because you can't cook, dear. You told me so yourself."

With a glance to Sherry, Cora stood and said, "Actually, I said Sherry can't cook. At all."

Her sister's mouth fell open on cue, but Cora dodged away from any retort, back into the kitchen. She spun the spatula in her hand as she headed toward the stove.

Shit.

Of course.

Time Out with Matty.

Courtesy of Fairy Grandmamma.

"I'm in charge of the bacon." Matty smiled as he used thongs to peel the long strips from the package and set them to sizzling. His damp hair flopped roguishly over one eye, tempting her to comb her fingers through it and back into place.

The thought made her growl at her own stupidity.

"Here's the batter and the spray oil." Nana pointed to each of them. "Brace for the next wave. The adults will want to eat now that the kids are fed."

"Starvation is undervalued," she mumbled.

"What's that?" Nana asked.

Cora stirred the batter and smiled at her. "I'm ready."

Nana said, "Perfect. Then, I'd like two strips and two cakes, please." She smiled and added, "I'll be seated at table nine."

With an eye roll, Cora hefted the silver bowl and tried pouring a dollop onto the griddle, but it spread so quickly that it reached the edges. She dropped the bowl to the counter and lifted the griddle, intending to pour it back into the bowl.

"Ye canna do that, lass. It's already frying."

"Can too."

"No, ye canna. Let me show ye."

Like a dutiful wife, Cora stepped back, watching Matty quarter the massive pancake for her. "Count the bubbles, lass. Twelve bubbles, time to flip, like this." She watched him shimmy each quarter from the blob, then flip and drop them apart to finish cooking. "Once they're golden brown, table nine awaits ye." He winked.

She waited a minute, then flipped the cakes over. "I never knew you knew how to make pancakes. Or, anything involving a heat source."

"Ma uncle taught me. He'd had to learn to feed Davey on his own after ma aunt died. Vacuums suck down less than Davey, I trow."

She eyed him, not sure she wanted to ask, but then had to know. After all, she thought she knew everything about this man, and this was new. "When was this?"

"I had six weeks off at a stretch, so I stayed with them. We always ended in Edinburgh, so it made sense for me to stay there."

The sharp reminder of how grand his life was without her had Cora turning away. She nodded once and placed two pancakes on a plate, then accepted two strips of bacon from Matty, which she delivered to Nana. She waited until a few more of her cousins showed up, and soon she and Matty found themselves elbows deep in grease and flour and oil for the next hour. By the time the teenagers dragged themselves downstairs, Cora and Matty dubbed Sherry and Davey as the new short-order chefs and took their own plates to the empty dining room.

As Cora drowned her pancakes in syrup, Matty studied her. “Ye did good, lass.”

“Whatever.”

“I forgot how well we worked together.”

She knew where this was going, so retorted, “Not surprising, since you’ve had plenty of time to forget.”

His gaze swept to his plate. And although Cora knew she was being an ass, the angst of how he left her unfulfilled twice in as many days rankled. Was this the female version of blue balls? Rancor and acidity?

She heard him exhale, then he sawed into his food and chewed in contemplative silence. After an awkward minute, he said, “I really want to share something with ye before the New Year rolls in, but I doona want to say it when ye hate me so.” Now his eyes met hers. “It’s hard to share when ye know the person doesna trust ye.”

“It’s hard trusting someone who already shattered you.”

Were those tears? No... maybe. Transfixed, Cora studied Matty, waiting for him to say more. She really wanted him to fight for her, to be there for her, but she couldn’t tell him. Didn’t even know how to allude to it. So she jabbed and jabbed, pushing him back and watching him move further away, proving her point that he couldn’t be trusted.

Yeah, she knew it was a self-fulfilling prophesy, but

her heart couldn't handle any more pain, any more rejection. She'd lost too much this last year. Her baby. Her husband. Her home. Her job. What the fuck more did she have left?

If anything happened to Herbie, she'd cash in her chips, quit the game. Done-zo.

Job. Her thoughts turned to her boss, Carla. Had she heard anything from HR? Was this week of torture about to come to an end? And what about that hot guy Carla said she met on the plane? She really wanted to grill Carla on whether or not she creamed the guy's Twinkie.

Filled with self-loathing and self-doubt, Cora chewed her soggy pancakes and crunched on the perfect bacon, taking no joy in the meal she and Matty had created together.

Sure. The one thing they had done well together all year, and she couldn't even enjoy it.

She would have enjoyed the sex.

Not the complications, of course, but the sex? Oh, it would have been mind-blowing.

Another reason to hate him right now.

Matty shoved his plate away and leaned back, startling her enough that she looked up. His eyes locked on hers. "I've done so much for ye, Cora."

She snorted. "Yeah? Like what?"

His eyes glittered, his expression hard. "I willna tell ye until ye've given me the barest benefit of doubt. I doona know what else I can do, so please, tell me. How can I make it right?"

Now the tears truly appeared in her eyes. "You can't."

"No. I doona believe that, and I doona think ye do, either." He leaned forward, his voice urgent. "Give me three honest-to-God ways to make everything right between us."

Three? Super challenges? Impossible feats of

manliness?

As if he sensed her thoughts, Matty said, "Three things that I can do to make you forgive me. Guaranteed."

The question should have been easy. Get a normal job. Pay back all the debt he'd left her to pay off. Never walk away again. But those words stuck in her throat, strangling her until she felt more tears threaten from forcing them so hard to stay down. So she tweaked those words to make his quest more difficult, something to buy her lots of time. "Write me a viable check for eighteen thousand dollars to cover all the debt you left me to pay off."

He grimaced at the reminder.

"Hypnotize me into forgetting how forgettable I was to you."

Oh, she could tell he didn't like that one. "You were never forgotten."

"Oh, no?"

His jaw twitched. "How about a real request?"

"Oh, it's real. I don't see how else I'll ever be able to forgive you for breaking practically every single marriage vow we exchanged."

"I never cheated on ye."

"Well, you didn't exactly stick to love, honor and cherish, either."

He leaned back, crossed his arms and glared. "Fine. And the third?"

The one impossible task, something he'd never be able to accomplish. "It doesn't matter."

"Of course it matters."

"It doesn't matter because *I* don't matter. To you. The third and final request is to choose me, *us,* over your music."

Now his arms loosened, and his expression turned incredulous. "Do ye have any idea what I've accomplished, lass? I canna go anywhere in public without people recognizing me. Some go plum barmy and beg for autographs. But I did this for *ye.* For us. You'll never have to live below your heart's desire again, *mo chridhe.* I worked far too hard this past year so that I'd have something to offer ye, us, when I returned."

But Cora had heard this line of BS too often to fall for it. It sounded good right up until the venue fell through, or the people didn't budget enough to pay him until next month, or the bagpipe needed a new reed or seasoning or plaid and suddenly, whoops, which card had enough room on it to buy peanut butter this month? "I'm not changing my mind on this. It's me or your music, once and for all."

"That's not fair."

"Neither is what you did to me." It physically hurt to breathe, but Cora managed to shove away from the card table. She stood and picked up her plate and glass, felt her shoulders catch as she choked down the lump in her throat. Before any tears grew large enough to drip off her lashes, Cora deposited her dishes in the sink, then bolted upstairs.

She shut herself into her room and opened the crate for Herbie. He hopped out and shook out his long ears, then ambled around before getting frisky and binkying around the floor. His happiness was the only thing that mattered to her right now, and she couldn't even enjoy it. She lay on the comforter and dragged half of it over herself for warmth as she wallowed.

She was getting too close to him again. Every minute in his presence weakened her will, crushed her spirit. She'd never loved anyone like she loved Matty, but love without trust held no value. She knew this. Bone-deep knew this.

Herbie stretched up towards her, his whiskers almost brushing her cheek. She reached down and hoisted him onto the bed, where he flopped down beside her, keeping her side warm. As Cora buried her fingers into his soft fur to keep them warm, she heard a knock.

Well, Matty wouldn't knock, so she asked, "Who is it?"

"Me," Nana replied. "May I come in?"

"It's your house," Cora said.

She heard the groan through the door before Nana opened it, and Faberge shuffled into the room right ahead of her and headed for the bed. Nana shivered and crossed her arms. "Oh, my goodness, why is it so cold in here?"

Cora tried to shrug, but the effort seemed beyond her. "Don't know." But she did manage to reach down and assist Fabby so that he could curl up beside her, too.

Nana dropped a stack of bills on top of the dresser by the door, then tried pulling the piece of furniture away from the wall. "You should have told me."

Cora took the cue and came to her aid, tugging the heavy dresser away from the mopboards. "You had enough on your plate, hosting a bazillion Foote-Steppes."

"Still, I don't freeze my guests."

"Um, why am I moving furniture?"

"The thermostat is behind here."

Heat? That motivated Cora like nothing else had all week. She practically craned her foot on the wall to haul the piece out enough to reach behind it. "Why is it behind the dresser?"

"It wasn't," Nana said as she reached into the space and flicked the switch. "We moved the dresser to make room for your rabbit. It must have gotten bumped."

The scent of burning dust from the electric register smelled like salvation. "Oh, thank God. I don't think I could have taken another night of freezing."

Her Nana honed in on that comment. "Still... *estranged*, are we?"

Wow, maybe this was where Cora got her bluntness. "Yup."

"Hm." Nana picked up the stack of paperwork and sat on the edge of the bed and looked at Cora until she took the cue and joined her. "I came to tell you that Randy and Matty are in charge of plowing the driveway, and Randy put that beastly dog of his in the plow truck with him. Anyway, it'll take them a good hour, so if you want to keep your door open to warm it up in here, feel free."

An open door without endangering a lunatic Lab's life? Perfect! "Thanks. I will."

"Secondly," Nana fiddled with the envelopes in her hand. "I can sense you're conflicted about... things. About Matty."

Did Cora's groan carry? Or was it silent? "So?"

"So." She flipped through the stack. "I thought you'd like to know about these." She met her eyes. "I'll make sure you have at least an hour before he gets back."

Though her eyes asked the question, Nana made no reply. She set the envelopes on the bed and left, leaving the door open. Herbie must have thought they looked delicious, because he hopped over and stretched to pick one up right as Cora snatched them away from his hungry lips. "Stop being naughty," she scolded him, then glanced at the handwriting.

Handwriting she'd known almost half of her life.

Unlike most of the guys at school, Matty had great penmanship, a side-effect of the Scottish Catholic school system. He wrote as nicely as her grandparents, a trait she'd always admired. But these were all addressed to Nana. She checked the postal stamps and frowned.

The first one was sent only two weeks after he left her.

Trepidation filled her, but curiosity won out. She flipped open the envelope and pulled out the letter.

Dear Grandmamma,

I've made a terrible mistake. I'm sure you know by now the level of my guilt and shame, an act for which I fear I can never redeem myself nor expect apology. My soul is plagued by the deaths I've caused and I do not know how to forgive myself. If I cannot forgive myself, how can I ever expect my wife to do the same?

I spent eleven hours at the airport, needing to run but scared to leave and hating myself more with every passing minute. My soul aches for the wrong I've caused and the trail of hurt and betrayal I've left behind.

I don't know what to do or how to come home. I don't know how to look my wife in the eyes and beg for her forgiveness.

I can't even look at my own reflection without feeling a sound measure of disgust.

I cannot write to Cora; I've tried, but the letters get returned unopened, the checks untouched. She never tried to reach me at the airport, so I fear she is truly lost to me.

Cora lowered the letter in thought. She remembered Matty *had* written to her, twice, and she wanted to tear them into bits and set each piece on fire, but then she knew he would have assumed he'd made contact, so, since she'd already begun looking for cheaper apartments, Cora elected to write *NOT HERE RETURN TO SENDER* on each one.

Damn. He'd been trying to send her money.

Or purchase her forgiveness, an angry thought voiced in her mind. But what did he mean about trying to reach him at the airport? How the fuck would she have known to look for him there, when she'd been frantically calling home? With a head shake, Cora continued reading.

Now when I try to write her, my mouth dries and my pen refuses to touch paper. I've hurt her on so many levels that I no longer qualify as a man, let alone her husband. She deserves every kindness the world has to offer, and I have given her nothing but pain and betrayal.

I need to become the man she deserves. I need to find a way to overcome the depths of the harm I have caused her. I don't know how to go about it, but I'm hopeful my idea will pan out.

By the time you receive this letter, I will be back home in Scotland.

I'm enclosing a money order for $150. It's not much, but it's what I earned this past weekend playing my pipes at a wedding. Will you please see that Cora gets it? Don't tell her it's from me; she needs it more than I do, and I want, no, ***need*** *to provide for my wife.*

I love her, Grandmamma. I've loved her since the day I first saw her, long before we ever spoke. My time away from her will be torturous, but I will return when I am able to right my wrongs.

All my love,
Matty

Somehow, Cora tore her eyes away from the letter, watching the words blur as she lowered it to the comforter. She'd never thought of how difficult that day had been for him, but really, she'd been hospitalized, so her immediate concerns were on surviving and mourning her miscarriage. But Matty? For the first time, she tried to envision what pain he must have felt— to kill a deer, which killed an innocent cyclist and also aborted his firstborn child. Without meaning to, she reread the letter. *My soul is plagued by the deaths I've caused.* She reflected on the agony of her own job— at least, her former job— when an animal's pain became too great and ultimately the owner would choose euthanasia. It never became easier. Never. But how did she feel that first time, witnessing it?

Like shit.

Like she was a horrible human being.

Like she had let both the animal and the owner down, even if the pet was suffering.

Logically, she could separate an animal's death from that of a human being. But Matty? He never saw death before that day. Never went to a funeral, never saw a car crash on their quaint little back roads before that day.

The sight probably fucked him up.

It *did* fuck him up.

To the point he ran away to try to deal.

She let that thought settle for a moment, then picked up the next letter.

Dear Grandmamma,

Thank you so much for writing back to me. I'm glad you were able to sneak the money into Cora's purse and laundry pockets. She always wads her money up, so she'll think she simply forgot about it.

And to answer your question, no, I don't mind that your daughter knows I'm writing to you. I'm glad Dr. Foote's alright with it and I hope she's doing well.

I'm renting a furnished room in this rundown house on the edge of Edinburgh while I wait for my turn to audition for the Bagpipe Barons. I think the walls are alive with a level of insects and rodents that would keep Cora researching their genus and species for weeks. I'm renting month to month and am counting the days until I can move.

I've been in contact with a Pipe Major back in Toronto, and he's agreed to take me on as his corresponding apprentice. I'll only do it if I don't get in with the Barons. The position is unpaid, but he is willing to help me work on my music-writing skills. In the meantime, I found a seasonal cleanup company who took me on, so I'll be raking leaves this autumn and learning to snow plow next month. The pay is great, but the hours are horrible, and of course I'd have to quit if I can get a job with the Barons. Cora would be so proud of me getting such a boring job! As soon as I get my first check, I will send you another money order for her. Will you please see that she gets it again?

That's about all for now.

Miss you, Grandmamma.
Yours truly,
Matty

Cora remembered that wad of money that showed up in her purse and jeans pockets. She even called Nana and asked if she put it there, but she only laughed it off, proclaiming she wished money would magically appear in her own laundry. So Cora shrugged it off as a stress-induced memory lapse, but she always wondered.

And Matty got a job? Doing something he hated to pay the bills? Noteworthy. She picked up the next letter.

Dear Grandmamma,

I got the callback! I'm officially a member of the Bagpipe Barons! I'm on rotation and will only work backup, but I'm on the payroll, doing what I love.

In the meantime, I'm staying in this God-forsaken room for another month just so I have more money to send you for Cora. My entire paycheck is enclosed. Since I don't have a computer, and no time to go to the library between raking and band practice, would you mind picking up something special for her for Christmas? Call her boss, Carla, who can give you the specifics, but there's a new stethoscope that she's been wanting for months. It has an additional feature, something special to listen to small animals' heartbeats, like bunnies and lizards. They're not cheap, so please don't have a heart attack when you hear the price. (But if you do, Cora would have the right tool to listen ha ha!) She wants the green one. Would you mind ordering that for her, please?

Cora lowered the letter. Although Nana made no bones afterwards about calling Carla for gift ideas, Cora had never considered that Matty had paved that path.

The triple-head green stethoscope had never left her

neck at work. It was her single most expensive and prized instrument.

Because of Matty.

Damn him.

She resumed reading. *I know she'll be so happy to toss the cheap one she had to buy when someone stole her last one.*

As far as the Pipe Master in Toronto, I'm learning how to write bagpipe tunes now, corresponding by mail. I'm actually paying him student fees, can you believe? Ian says I have a natural ear for it, which is nice to hear. (Like that pun?) I've written three retreats, which are slow, sad tunes, and he wants to include them in a music book to sell. Imagine that for a moment. My name will be under a score! And I'll have rights to every sale. He has two other students trying to compose, but mine are the only ones he's forwarded to other musicians to rate.

So far, my music is the only thing not suffering.

We don't celebrate it here, so Happy Thanksgiving to you, Grandmamma.

All my love,

Matty

She stuffed that one back into its sleeve, fast blinking to keep the world from smearing.

Why did he have to be so thoughtful? Generous? Even funny?

Why could she not find it in her heart to forgive him?

Why? Why? Why?

She yanked the next one out of its envelope to read, then the fourth, fifth, sixth. All sweet, all funny, poignant. Filled with burning drive, lament, humor— everything she believed to have boiled beneath his stubborn and lazy surface.

Last week, Cora had advised her boss not to date Phil, some guy from work, because he was a POLR, a term Cora dubbed for people who took the Path of Least Resistance. She resented Phil for not having drive. For just coasting through life. For not having passion or drive or giving a fuck.

Cora knew firsthand what that was like. She'd lived with it, fought with it, begged it to try, to care, to put some muscle into their marriage. And when that man walked out on her and proved her theory, Cora knew with certainty she couldn't bear to let the same thing happen to her friend. Carla needed someone to fight for her. To care. To give a fuck.

The seventh letter was from France. The ninth from Germany. The eleventh from Venice. In the twelfth one, Matty had returned to his homeland, where he took hiatus with his uncle and cousin before resuming his world tour. There, he continued learning how to build bagpipes, an exacting art, according to his growing résumé, something he had learned to do as a child. He now qualified as Pipe Master, song-writer, and budding Bagpipe Maker.

As Cora folded the thirteenth letter back into its sleeve, she wondered if she'd gotten Matty wrong all this time. He *did* give a fuck.

Just not about her.

Chapter 19

Bitter wind slipped underneath Matty's coat, making his skin brace despite the fact the chill air eased the sweat of his labors. While Randy and his barmy dog enjoyed the comfort of his enclosed Bobcat as he plowed his way around the U-shaped drive, Matty hacked his shovel into the ice, chipping away giant chunks of it until he reached both steps and concrete.

He'd never win Cora back.

Chopping down towards the sidewalk helped him chop through his options. Aya, he could for certain write her a viable check, but to Cora, that would merely be an admission of his measure of guilt. She'd take the money as his due penance and wouldna look back.

Na an option. He'd paid off that debt already, although most likely she didna know it. Besides, the next time he wrote a check that large, it would be as a down payment on a house for them, ideally here in Skaneateles, the land so like his lochs back home that he wouldna want to leave ever again.

He *didna* want to leave ever again, but how could he convince his wife of such?

Aya, Option Three. Give up his music. Truly? How could he ever give up that which filled his soul? His music got him this far in life; he'd never have been able to provide her what he wanted to if he hadna followed his heart.

Well, technically, not his heart, but his passion.

Aya, she had him there.

She believed he chose his passion over her. He didna, but he *did* choose one passion over staying at home with his wife.

Truly, he was a buggered rat bastard; she had the

right of it.

But then a wee voice at the back of his skull challenged the familiar retort—that he'd never asked Cora to give up teching, her own heart's passion. But then their battle would start anew, with her stating technicians didna work per diem, and her degree was too valuable to her to let fall to waste.

She fully believed Matty could work days and take gigs on weekends, something he had no interest in doing.

Well, that only left hypnosis. Aya, it would be a fine idea, wiping the slate clean and starting over, but no magic wand to his knowledge existed. Even if he found someone willing to wipe her brain clean of his wrongdoing, he wouldna do something so cruel. He deserved her scorn, but he also deserved her forgiveness. He couldna have the second without overcoming the first.

Skipping that felt akin to cheating, and Matty didna cheat.

The larger part of the problem, as far as he could see, was that Cora never told anyone anything about that night in the hospital. Not only that he'd walked out on her as a husband, but also that he'd failed her as a father to their child.

If she'd never told their families, how could she have grieved?

Regardless, she'd forbidden him to do as much.

Fourteen months for certain he'd held his tongue, doing her bidding as requested, the least he could do since he'd walked away. But seeing her again, having her family surrounding them, surfaced all his buried pain.

He knew not how they could ever move forward until they addressed the past. She might na need to, but he did. He wasna as strong as Cora, couldna put aside that which broke him.

He feared he'd fully shatter before the broken pieces could ever fit again.

He just didn't want to take Cora down with him when that happened.

He thought to the small box hidden inside his duffle, his gift to Cora should she grant him a measure of trust. A voucher for her to join him on his next tour. The next leg was the Romance Tour, hitting Amsterdam, Venice, Paris, Florence, Budapest and Prague. Although the Pipers would be playing jigs and reels, most of the tunes would be ballads and retreats. They had upgraded the show this year, adding actors to play silent roles in romantic plots, letting the music speak for them. It was akin to the old black and white movies, something Matty himself had concocted and which the director had agreed to cast.

He thought for certain Cora would love to join him. She could quit her job and travel Europe with him, see the world, cheer him from the front row. Nothing he would like better than to look down from center stage and see the glowing smile of his wee wife. A gust of wind pelted him in the face, making him think something Divine punished him for his thoughts. Aya, Cora for certain wouldna want to leave her job, and his tours would take half the year.

Buggered rat bastard yet again. Why had he na thought this through?

Aya, because once again, he chose his music over his wife.

The rumble of the Bobcat had Matty turning around to see Randy push a mound of snow at the foot of the sidewalk, blocking the path he'd just cleared. He shook a fist at him, but Randy, safe inside his warm cocoon, laughed and wheeled away.

Another rat bastard.

As Randy took one final turn about the driveway, Matty scooped the fresh pile off the sidewalk end, then sprinkled ice melt down the stairs and path. By the time Randy and his wayward Lab parked the Bobcat and crunched back, the entryway had melted clear down.

He had no solutions to any of Cora's requirements.

And now, realizing he'd made the wrong choice of gifts, he was even more buggered than before.

The bright red spots on Matty's cheeks told Cora just how cold he was after shoveling, and he sat before the fire chattering his teeth, although, knowing Matty like she did, Cora knew he tried not to let on.

Stubborn bastard.

She thought to tease him and said, "Did you scrape off my car?"

"Doona know what yer driving these days, lass, so no."

"Jerk. It's the same car, parked in the same spot as usual."

He nodded. "Maybe when ma hands warm up, I'll go back out for ye, then."

A measure of compassion filled her at seeing the shiver rip down his back. She only today felt heat return to her body, courtesy of Matty's scorching kiss and a working room heater, and a surge of empathy filled her. She didn't think he had seen her as she came down the stairs, the stack of his penned letters to be returned to Nana's bedside, so now she headed through the kitchen and into the back pantry in search of bouillon cubes. She shook one small square out of the container and dropped it into a small pan and added water. Low heat and five minutes later produced two steaming mugs of broth, one of which she wrapped in a potholder and delivered to one hypothermic man.

She tapped his thigh with her toe. "Use the potholder. It's hot."

He looked up to her, then to the mug in her hands. "Broth?"

"Chicken. Don't burn yourself. You look frozen."

He grinned. "Can I put ma hands on yer neck for a professional diagnosis?"

A familiar taunt, and a ghost of a smile warmed her chest. "Over my dead body." Now she grinned. "Are you going to drink this, or should I dump it over your head?"

He chuckled and slipped his hand into the mitt, then scooped the mug under his nose, breathing deeply of the steam. "Thank ye, *mo chridhe.* Yer the best."

Deep inside, she growled. "Shut up." She spun away, intending to clean up her pan in the kitchen, but stopped when she passed the ottoman with the wool blanket folded on top of it.

Damn it all.

She shook out the heavy material and draped it over Matty's shoulders, and he made a noise of appreciation and tugged it closer to his chin.

A scoff made her look up, and Sherry shared a haughty little smile.

Cora flicked her off and stalked into the kitchen to drink her cup of broth.

Alone.

When she returned to her bedroom about an hour later, she heard Matty playing his chanter before she made it halfway down the hallway. She stopped and closed her eyes to listen. She had always loved hearing him play. This time, though, the fumbling of his fingers told her he was in the throes of creating and not simply playing, and using the recorder-sized plastic chanter instead of the behemoth pipes made sense.

She turned the handle and peeked in. "Okay if I come in?"

"Of course." Matty moved his sheets of paper and his pencil off her side of the bed and shook the pink eraser shards peppering them onto the floor. He'd always loved when Cora would sit with him while he worked, and the fact she showed up while he struggled with a riff was fine by him.

Matty frowned as he tried a few different endings to the tune, finding his fingers playing *dum da di, ba da-dum bum*— the repeating riff from *Kilworth Hills*— instead of creating something new. He pursed his lips in concentration and looked at his sheet music again, humming the last few bars leading up to the place he kept faltering.

Damn. He needed something with an equally entrancing pattern, something lively and memorable, but his brain kept filling in the same pilfered riff.

"Something wrong?"

He looked up at Cora and back down to his sheet. "I'm trying to write a new ballad, but I find my fingers playing notes of their own free will."

"*Kilworth Hills?*"

"Aya. Recognized it, then?"

"Aya." She flashed him a tentative grin. "What are you trying to do?"

"I need to finish this tune, but I'm having a wee bit of trouble with it. I'd love yer help. Here, let me hum it for ye." And he did, right up to where he faltered. "Here's where I need to wrap it up."

"Okay, so instead of *dum da di, ba da-dum bum,* what if you went with, *di dum, ba rum ba, bum.*"

He tried it but lowered his recorder. "Not quite. It needs another beat." He played it again for her, and then said, "How about, *di dum, ba ba rum, ba bum.*"

She actually wrinkled her nose. "No. Play it again, the one before."

So he piped *di dum, ba rum ba, bum.*

"Try this. *Di da dum, ba rum, ba bum.*"

He played it, knowing she had nailed it. "That's it."

"No, do it once more."

He played it again, and she pointed at the *ba rum ba*

part. "Instead of that one, can you do the crazy one?"

He smiled at her familiar description. "A Toarluah?"

"Yeah. Try that."

So he replaced the Double C with a Toarluah, the sound much richer with the more complex arrangement.

"I like it." She leaned back. "You?"

That was it. She'd solved his week-long problem in two minutes. All he could say was, "Perfect, lass." On so many, many levels. He wanted to smile, but the fact she helped him overcome this one particular quandary told him how invaluable she was to his life, how perfectly they belonged together. He grabbed her nape and ached to press a long kiss to her lips, but at the last moment angled instead for her forehead, keeping his lips there for as long as she let him linger. At her first sign of unease, he released her. "Thank ye."

Pink spots blossomed on her cheeks. "Yeah. Whatever. You're welcome."

He looked down to pen in the notes before they disappeared to time, but he had a feeling he'd hear this particular tune in every dream, in every waking moment.

Death Himself could not steal this from him.

"Mind if I let Herbie out while you practice?"

"Not at all."

She opened the crate and let Herbie out to stretch while Matty sat on the bed, playing and watching her and feeling so content with life he ached with what might never be.

Chapter 20

Fresh assorted submarines and tubs of condiments from Wegmans grocery store in nearby Auburn were arranged along the counters on pretty trays for lunch, and as Cora and Matty stepped into the kitchen, she wasted no time plucking a turkey sub for her plate, as well as a pouch of nacho chips.

"Grab me a ham piece, will ye?"

She blinked and remembered submarines were called "pieces" in Scotland, but then said, "You've got two hands."

He was pouring two glasses of root beer for them and looked up at her words, and the fact he was providing for her made Cora relax and force a smile. "Kidding. Want mayo?"

"Aya, please."

So she slathered mayo on them and picked up another bag of chips as Matty collected their glasses, and two minutes later they joined Sherry and Davey at what was becoming their usual dining card table. Barely a bite into her meal, however, Nana came up.

"The crews are here already with the stage and chairs. Can you show them where everything's supposed to go?"

Her stomach rumbled its complaint at the interruption, but she knew the drill. Today would be their busiest day. "Sure."

But Matty clamped a hand on her shoulder and gave her a warning glance before turning to face Nana. "With all due respect, the men are going to have to wait until ma wife's done with her meal."

"But they're here now."

She watched him continue, "Three squares a day

served in this house in the last three days, and ma wife hasna had two hot meals under her belt. In a house of thirty people, Cora's been the one to wrangle the horses, prep the stew, tend a neighbor's wee goat, deal with Randy's dog, and then she trudged back into the storm to tend the horses again. She's na leaving this table until her belly's full." To augment his point, he opened both of the single-serving pouches of nacho chips and dumped one onto each of their plates.

"But..."

Those fingers returned and flexed on her shoulders, reminding Cora of a cat flexing its claws. "No buts, Grandmamma. Tell them they can start to unload, and we'll be out shortly."

Her sister swatted Davey on the arm and stood up. "We got this, Nana."

"But Cora—"

"Is eating," Sherry finished. "Really, Nana, we got this."

Throughout the exchange, Cora hadn't budged, only her eyes moved as they flitted back and forth between speakers. As Sherry and Davey left the table, Cora waited for some kind of backlash, but all she received from Nana was an appreciative gleam.

Wait. Was that what Nana had hoped for? That Matty would jump in to defend her? Or was she merely happy with the results?

Mouth open, Cora turned to face Matty, who mowed into his chips.

"Yer gonna catch flies with yer yap hanging open."

She smiled at him and bit into her sub, only to discover it lacked cheese. Perhaps he could tell by her expression, because Matty picked up her plate and headed into the kitchen, returning a minute later with a remedied sandwich.

"Thank you."

He kissed her forehead. "No thanks are needed, *mo chridhe.* I've let ye down in the past, but ne'er again. If I'm man enough to right ma wrongs, I'm man enough to make sure it doesna happen again."

She watched him chomp into his own sandwich and chew away, oblivious to the fact that somewhere deep inside her, a tiny seed of forgiveness had sprouted.

Aya, she tried to race flat out through her meal, but Matty wouldna let her, insisting she take her time. "Yer father's out there, and Sherry. And Davey. The men get paid to load and unload. Enjoy yer piece and stop worrying."

"I was born worrying."

"Aya." He grinned. "I'm sure ye were. But this isna yer job, with innocent lives on the line. It's about folding chairs and snap-together flooring."

"It's the single biggest event of Nana's year."

"It'll be fine. Drink yer pop."

It felt good and right watching over her, tending to his wife. Felt even better she let him. Aya, her job must place ungodly demands on her if she accepted them so readily at home with nary a complaint, but he wouldna stand by for it.

Na today. Na on his watch.

He smiled as she sipped her root beer, obviously savoring it, and asked her, "Are ye enjoying this time off from work?"

Steely-gray eyes snapped to his. "What do you mean?"

Odd. He clarified, "Not working on Christmas or New Year's for a change. Ye must be enjoying it. Spending time with yer family instead of punching a clock."

"Mm." She wiped her mouth with her napkin and stood. "Now that I'm finally warm, let's tackle the movers."

He joined her and wrapped a possessive hand on her waist to tug her close. "Tackle *me,"* he whispered in her ear, then swatted her bum. "Tonight."

She elbowed him, making him laugh, but a few seconds later he caught her eyeing him, a look of consideration on her face.

He tried na to feel too hopeful.

They donned their heavy coats and trudged down the U-shaped driveway, where Randy had plowed the private road between her parents' and grandparents' houses that led to the hay barn. Old it was— one of the oldest barns in town should the stories be believed— but once they drew nearer, the sounds of gasoline generators and sparkling glow of electric lights brought it squarely into the twenty-first century. As they entered the door, a wave of heat greeted them.

He'd always loved this long, narrow barn. The beams were wrought a full eight-inches squared, with some of them composed of entire tree trunks, complete with bark. Yellow string lights were being wrapped up each of the twenty columns from floor to ceiling. Blue-white icicle lighting already dangled from the crossbeams and ended at each column. Fresh white tarps overhead spanned wall to wall, lowering the ceiling, most likely for warmth. Four giant paper lanterns dangled in equal measures beneath the tarps, their light surprisingly bright. And at the narrowed ends, two old wooden wagons lined one wall, while a loft filled the other.

To the right of the entrance, rows of rolling silver garment stands with hundreds of empty coat hangers awaited guests, and Matty hung Cora's coat and then his. The movers' cube van had already been backed into the barn, the rolling overhead door closed to keep the warm air from the multiple generators inside. All the folded chairs and tables leaned against the back wall, near a small trailer proclaiming itself to be a mobile bar. Storage lockers to the side of it likely held replacement vats of spirits. Thirty feet away, Davey and Sherry ran orange extension cords along the wall, supervised by Cora's father.

Matty looked away, then down at the floor. "I like the new floor."

"Me, too. Customized rubber mats. Six months ago. And the generators have been running long enough that even the ground's warm."

"Aya. Ye'll want to cool it off some before the guests arrive."

She considered his words for a second. "You're right. We'll turn off half of the generators tomorrow."

"A fine idea." He helped the lads lift the snap-together squares for the dance floor off the truck and set them aside. Because his back was turned, he didna see Mr. Steppe until the man had pounced.

"Not here. Your grandmother wants the floor over there." He pointed to the wagons.

"And the bar goes here?"

Her father nodded once, like he needed to answer but preferred na speaking to Matty.

From all his experience on stage, the proposed arrangement made no sense. He looked from the mobile bar to the wooden dance squares and knew they'd also have to make space for the caterer and band, since they hired those every year. "The dance floor should be front and center. People will be hot, and the door opening will cool them off. Also, the bar and the caterer should be on opposite ends. Ye'll get people moving around that way."

"I didn't ask you."

Aya, he didn't expect Mr. Steppe to agree to a word he said, but he expected even less for his estranged wife to champion him.

"No, that makes sense," Cora looked between him and her father. "Otherwise, people will just grab food and wine and never leave the tables."

"So?"

"So!" Cora glanced at him for support and wheeled on her father, "Have you ever heard Nana rate the quality of her parties afterwards? If people don't dance, she considers it a failure."

A car horn blared, and Cora peeked out the door and motioned the driver. "The rental company is here to set up the band's equipment. I signaled them we need five minutes to get this van unloaded."

Now Matty scanned the barn for solutions. "Where's the band going?"

Her father pointed to the loft. "Up there."

"With all those hay bales up there? And three-hundred pound speakers? How are they getting them up there? Where will they fit?"

"Not my problem."

"It will be if Nana complains."

Now Cora's father rounded on him, his eyes as cold as the outside sky. "I assume you have a stellar idea?"

The question had Matty evaluating the acoustics of the barn. Then he pointed to the long wall directly across from the main door. "Keep the music centered on the dance floor. That's where people want to feel the beat, and those that doona can move to the ends, where it'll be quieter."

Her father for certain understood his logic, but his hardness told Matty he wouldna agree to a single thing coming out of Matty's mouth. Should lava rain from the sky, Mr. Steppe would have to have the flesh seared from his bones before he'd believe it.

"No. My mother-in-law told me how she wanted the barn set up, and that's how we're going to do it." He leaned menacingly closer. "That's how a man in this family honors a woman."

Aya, the blow for certain took a measure of wind from his sails, but Cora once more championed him.

"Nana's never set up the barn before, Dad. Matty does this shit for a living."

"Are you going to go against your grandmother's wishes?"

Matty found himself holding his breath. He loved the fact Cora came to his aid, but he didna want her to create a rift in her family. She looked between the both of them. "I think what Matty's suggested makes the most sense."

"Me, too," said one of the moving lads. "It's how we set up most of these events."

"Aya," Davey chimed in, hiking a thumb Matty's way. "The Barons always rely on this bugger to set up the stage right."

Pure anger seethed in Mr. Steppe's eyes, and he sent a withering glace Matty's way, but Cora championed him yet again. She patted her father on the arm. "I'll tell Nana we're going to make this the best New Year's Eve party ever. Don't you fret."

"Fret is not the word I'm thinking of," her father said as he zipped up his jacket and headed into the wind. Sherry followed him to the door, trying to calm him down, and Davey spared an apologetic shrug before returning to his orange electric cords.

Matty couldna help but smile down at his wife when she returned. "Thank ye."

She shrugged off his words. "I did it for Nana," she muttered as she turned away.

But he grabbed her arms and held her still. "I think I may have a wee bit of hero worship floating around in ma gut for ye."

She smiled and tried to tug away again, to blow it off like she did all his compliments, but Matty wouldna let her go. Instead he leaned down to whisper, "Ye've made me happier than I've been in a long time, wife. If ye like, I'll return the favor. Tonight."

She looked up at him, and he couldna help but share a saucy grin as he imagined all he'd like to do to her. He leaned close again and whispered, "Whiskers."

Interest and exasperation both crossed her features, and she did manage to break free of his hold and move away. But he grabbed her elbows from behind and leaned into her ear once more. "Think on it. Tonight will be all about ye. Yer wants. Yer pleasure. Just keep showing yer family that we're a united front, and I'll do anything ye ask of me." He turned her to face him, holding her eyes. "Anything."

Chapter 21

Fuck, she hated that he suggested something sexual, because now Cora couldn't get the thought of sex out of her mind. Sex with Matty. Matty's hands. Matty's tongue. Matty's thrusts. Matty making her orgasm. Matty making her orgasm again. And again.

Oh, he would. She knew it.

And he knew she knew it.

The bastard.

As she labored side by side with Matty, carrying two chairs while he and Davey carried the long folding tables, she noticed how hot the barn had become. Sweat worked across her brow and dripped into her cleavage. She set down the chairs and wiped off her forehead. "Is it hot in here?"

"Aya," Matty replied as he looked over his shoulder to her. "I'll shut off some of the generators." And then he gave her this little victory smile, his *See? I was right* look. "And this is with only a dozen of us. Imagine another ninety folk wedged into here."

"Yeah, yeah. I already agreed with you, so shut up."

He chuckled, fully expecting her usual retort.

Comforting, actually. Of all the people she knew, only Matty, her sister, and her boss Carla, understood her *salt,* as Nana called it. Everyone else thought she pushed people away, and she did, but not out of anger or vanity or self-righteousness. Only out of self-preservation. In her line of work, nothing was long-term. Her patients never stayed for more than a few days. Sometimes longer than some of the staff. Life was precarious, vulnerable. Too easily ended by a fall, an animal attack, or a deer slamming into the hood.

Damn, were those tears? She looked back at the

remaining chairs and tried counting them, a diversion intended to dry her eyes. She calculated probably thirty more trips to finish setup. Maybe forty.

"Ye alright, lass?" Matty frowned at her as he turned off the nearest generator.

Damn. It. All. Since her eyes had dried, she looked to Matty. "Why are we the only ones working here? There are fifteen other people inside the house who are fully capable of helping."

"Yer right." He reached around her and started groping her ass.

With a swat, Cora tried to back away. "What are you doing?"

He plucked her phone out of her back pocket and held it up, his expression one of pure innocence, although the gleam in his eyes betrayed his enjoyment. "Why, calling yer useless cousin, of course." She watched him dial and hold her eyes. "Randy, get yer useless arse into the barn to help us set up. Ye and everyone else with a good back and two working hands."

"Don't bring the dog," Cora said. Dozer and a few thousand dollars' worth of liquor? The thought made shivers prance down her spine.

"No dog," Matty added. "Unless ye wish to mop the entire floor before nightfall."

He held the phone away from his ear as Randy ranted, but then he said, "If I come in there, I'll be dragging ye out by yer ear, lad, in front of yer whole family." He paused for effect, then added, "Doona make me come in there."

He grinned as Cora heard Randy yell, "Fine!" Then he handed her cell back.

Championing her again. Defending her again. Protecting her again.

She snatched up her cell and stuffed it back into her pocket, then picked up her chairs again. Damn. She could still feel the heat of his fingers sizzling where he touched her butt.

Matty had set up a few tables, some parallel to the barn walls, some perpendicular, and she watched him and Davey count and discuss their options.

He was taking this far more seriously than she was.

After a few more minutes, Matty and Davey swung them perfectly parallel with the long sides of the barn, leaving an obvious space for the caterer's tables. As she walked up with more chairs, he said, "I'd prefer perpendicular, but there willna be room at the ends to move around them, so this way will have to do."

"I like them this way."

But Matty shook his head. "Too institutional. Makes me think of a school lunchroom."

He had a point.

"But this way," he continued, "it willna crowd the dance floor, or make people trip in the aisles."

Yup. Way too seriously. "Whatever."

"Yer welcome."

His sarcastic comment made her grin. She held his eyes. "Thank you."

Fifteen of her cousins and second cousins trudged inside and shucked their layers. While the rental company set up the band's light and sound system, the guys divvied up the tables to either end, and the youngest moved the chairs. That's when she noticed Matty staring up into the loft, a line of concentration furrowing his brow.

"Uh oh. It's thinking," she teased.

He smiled at her comment and turned bright eyes on her. "What if we drop a few of those bales to the ground? Stacked, they'd make good bar tables." He pointed to the mobile bar. "A few tables over here, interspersed with the bales, would get people mingling."

"I like it," Davey chimed in.

Cora did too. "Have at it, but you're both going to

have to put them back up there."

"Aya," he agreed, shoving out a breath as he obviously weighed the merits of this plan. To Davey he said, "Let's go."

They headed up the stairs and shoved and maneuvered the first stack of bales to the edge. Then Matty called out, "Hey, Randy!"

When her cousin looked over, Matty flagged his attention and said, "We're going to drop these. Stand below and catch them, will ye?"

Cora caught her laugh. Randy's face reddened with biting back his retort.

The guys burst out laughing and shoved four bales to the floor, where Cora and Randy collected them and moved them aside so more could rain down. They stacked a handful of bales three high, then Matty and Davey came back down and arranged them, even pulling the mobile bar into the desired position. Then they shoved the liquor lockers near it and headed back to the other side of the barn. While the movers finished up and backed out, Cora watched the sound guys test their speakers and stage lighting. The younger kids swept up the scattered hay while the slightly older ones finished moving the remaining chairs. Then Matty and Davey completed setting up the tables, leaning forward in scrutiny to make sure they were completely straight.

All Cora could do was stare.

Did he always put this much effort into his work? This critical eye for detail?

Why couldn't he do this for her? For them?

A tiny voice in the back of her head warned her he was doing just that. Better not to scrutinize what she wasn't ready to admit was already happening.

She waited another minute for him to finish, and he came to her side, draping a heavy arm around her shoulders. "Yer Grandmamma will have no complaints this year, *mo chridhe.* I'll make sure this will be a party to remember."

Yeah, she was sure he would, that was the problem.

Cora wanted this to be a party she could easily forget, which wasn't going to happen if her hot Scot hubby kept trying to undo all the damage he wrought so long ago.

The question, of course, was how permanently he undid it.

They decided they'd done all they could do for the day, so Cora and Matty bundled up, then Cora veered from the path and went into the horse barn to check on the horses. Since she was already sweaty and gross, she took a half hour to muck their stalls and run the hose to fill their water buckets, with Matty hauling and dumping the wheelbarrow onto the trailer, where her dad would later dump it in the field for composting.

She pulled out her cell and glanced at the clock. "Should we feed them while we're here? They're not usually given grain this early in the day."

"No," he said, his voice stern. "Ye've done enough. I'm sick of watching ye work yer fingers to the bone for yer family. I love them too, Cora, but enough already. Let yer mother come tend her beasts at their regular feeding time."

She rolled up the hose as she considered his words. "You know she's going to ask."

"Then I'll tell her no on yer behalf. We did the party setup; that's enough for today. Ye need yer rest. Yer a guest here. Besides, yer supposed to be on vacation."

Perhaps permanently. Cora found her arm rolling up the hose slower than normal. She should tell him. Now. While they were alone. Damn. She'd never kept secrets from Matty, ever. She'd always told him everything, and this silence was killing her. But she didn't want to see the sadness in his eyes, the compassion, or worse, the hope that she could now just drop everything and be his groupie. She'd read those letters, and she knew Matty well enough to know he'd come back to try to win her back with intent of having her tour the world with him.

But veterinary technicians did not have "traveling nurse" employment benefits. If she got hired as a tech, she'd be expected to stay there. People didn't hire *per diem* LVTs, not like human medicine.

She'd be stuck in hotel rooms for the remainder of his career, letting her degree fall uselessly to the wayside.

Now that she'd talked herself out of it, Cora looked at him and attempted a smile. "Fine. You can tell my mom that. Right now, I'm ready for a shower."

"Aya. I can smell ye from here."

"Ha, ha." She squeezed the hose nozzle, letting the remaining water drip out to alleviate pressure, but then she felt a retaliatory desire crest in her, one borne of years of familiarity. She reached for the spigot and aimed the nozzle in his direction. "Care to say that again?"

His eyes crinkled as he laughed, and damn it, he was the most gorgeous man she'd ever met.

"Na, lass. I'm sure I'm a wee bit more ripe than ye are. Let's head back. I'll let ye shower first."

She grinned and released the nozzle, then zippered up and braced for the chill air. Once they deposited their coats and boots at the door, they headed up to their room. She showered and turned over the bathroom to Matty, then sat on the floor to let Herbie out to play before dinner. Soon enough they were called down to a nice meal of spaghetti, with fresh artisan bread from the local bakery in town, the toned-down fare telling Cora that Nana was rather through with entertaining.

While Matty and Randy went back outside to shovel and plow, Cora headed back upstairs to play with Herbie again. She looked at her cell phone and checked for incoming calls.

None.

Damn it all.

She couldn't handle waiting any longer. Hated the agony of limbo. So she called Carla and couldn't believe she actually, *finally* picked up. She could sense the stall when Carla asked if she was still in Skaneateles.

"Yeah. How's the dream vacation?" She really wanted to know about Carla's hot dude.

"Right now, fantastic. Two days ago, sheer hell. How's your family doing?"

Sheer hell? What the fuck happened? She was about to ask that when she heard a few of the younger children running outside her door, so she focused on answering instead. "Great. Everything's going... well, as good as can be expected."

"Not the highest endorsement."

Should she tell her? Of course she should. Carla would expect the whole truth, because Cora never held back. "Nana invited Matty."

A gasp. "Matty, as in, *Matty*? The one you never wanted to talk to ever again?"

"The one and only."

"The one you told me to surgically remove your tongue if you ever spoke to him again?"

Damn. She did tell her that. "Yeah. That one."

"Why would she do that? Are you okay?"

The heater kicked on, sending a waft of Matty's cologne and soap to her nose. She thought about their hot CPR kiss, how well they worked together in the barn, how badly she wanted to get naked with him again. Was she okay? Would she ever be? "Yeah, whatever. Look, you know I'd never bother you on vacation, but I kinda gotta know what's going on."

A sigh carried to her, followed by what sounded like bedsprings creaking as Carla likely sat on her hotel bed. "I only just heard back from Mary today." An awful pause filled the line, but Cora didn't interrupt, electing instead to hold her breath. "She didn't sound very optimistic about taking you back. And now I'm under the microscope about, well, you know."

Fear and panic crashed into Cora's chest like a tidal wave, making it hard to breathe. Damn it, but she really wanted to go back to working with Carla, and now, it seemed that holding out, hoping, praying, had all been a useless waste of time. She was officially unemployed, floating about at sea, snatching at leads with the intention of finding a job, any job, to keep Herbie living the life he deserved. But, better to have a definitive answer than five more days of this fucking limbo, and once she wrapped her head around that fact, she realized what *else* Carla was saying.

Under the microscope about... Phil? That useless statue her boss had started dating before meeting the hot dude? Ire crept into Cora's spine and tone. "Well, I sure as hell didn't say anything about him. To anyone."

"I'm not blaming you. News travels fast at work."

Time for a lateral subject change. "What about the guy you met?"

Another pause. "As far as....?"

Damn! Carla was holding out! "Come on! Don't leave a gal hanging. You hook up or what?"

"Karrolin's here."

Well, that sounded like a classic tactical aversion technique, but Cora frowned and asked, "What's she doing there?"

"She's from the sheer hell part of my vacation that I'll tell you all about when I see you next."

"Hmph." Definitely a classical tactical aversion technique. But Cora felt her world tilting and teetering this week and really needed help sorting out her brain."Well, since you're under the microscope for fraternizing, and you won't tell me about the hot new guy, want to come to the New Year's Eve party? You know it's a standing invitation, and I kind of need a familiar face. Yours."

Another pause, this one considering. "Can I bring a date? And a child?"

Would Nana mind? Nah. "Absolutely. The hotter he is, the better. For you, at least. Anyway, there'll be, like, a hundred people coming. What's two more?"

Carla must have covered the mouthpiece on the phone, but Cora still heard her ask someone if he'd want to come to her party. The new guy was there! And then he said the sweetest thing ever: "I'd go anywhere with you."

Cora would normally puke with the sugar rush of that comment if it didn't smack so strongly of why Matty was so tragically wrong for her. He'd never stay here with her. He was officially a wandering minstrel, taking his music on the road for all to hear.

Fuck. She couldn't resent Carla for having such a sweet and stable guy in her life.

It just sucked that Cora didn't.

Someone knocked on her door, and Cora said, "Great! I'll tell Nana you're finally coming. See you soon." They hung up before Cora realized she never even gave Carla directions. Oops. She'd text them to her in a minute. "Who is it?"

"Your incredibly awesome sister."

She smirked but remained on the bed. "*Who*?"

"Not funny. Can I come in?"

Even though she should be moping or ranting that she didn't have a job, the fact she was going to see Carla tomorrow made her spirits lighter. "Yeah."

The door opened, and Sherry peeked in, then stepped inside and closed the door behind her. "Matty's outside, right?"

A nod, and then Cora opened her mouth in understanding. "You want that thing off."

"Oh, God, please."

So Cora slipped off the bed and rummaged through her shucked jeans in the closet for the tin snips. "I put it in one of my pockets... here it is." She pulled it out and snipped the air.

"Bathroom?"

"Yeah." They went into the private bath and closed the door.

"I'm glad I bought this, but holy shit, I'm ready to have it off."

A thought blasted its way into Cora's head, and once it lodged there, it made its presence fully known, pressing until it spilled out her mouth. "Need to get hot and heavy with a Scot?"

"No." But her tone sounded defensive... or lacking conviction. "I'm chaffing. It hurts." She unzipped her jeans and peeled down the material on one hip.

The raw skin made Cora grimace. "Ouch. You wore this willingly?"

"Yeah. But try not to ruin it. I might go back, and these things aren't cheap."

No challenge there. Cora slid two fingers under the chainmail hip strap and snipped her way down in a straight line. It only took a couple of minutes for the garment to clatter apart.

"Thank God." Sherry wiggled the one leg still bearing the chastity belt and shoved the chainmail down until it rattled around her ankle.

"That needs a bandage, Sher."

"Nah. I'll be fine."

"Shut up, Doctor. You have pus."

"I do?"

"Yeah." Slipping into tech mode came so naturally to her. She ran the hot water and grabbed a clean washcloth, then washed and dried the infected area. Next, Cora rummaged through the medicine cabinet and found some antibiotic cream, as well as non-stick gauze. She applied the medicine with a cotton swab and pressed the gauze to Sherry's hip, then taped it in place with white tape. "How's your other hip?"

"Fine."

"Yeah. Right. Turn around."

With a loud grumble, Sherry did, and Cora inspected the flesh. "Just chaffing." She got up and returned with a tub of Nana's cocoa butter cream. "Put this on. It'll help."

"Yes, Doctor." The tease was strong in Sherry's voice as she slathered on the proffered cream. "I think I put on a few pounds stateside. Nana's cooking and all."

"Well, if I had to eat your cooking every day, I'd starve, too."

"You're such an ass."

The comment made Cora grin as she stood up. "Feel better?"

"Yeah." Sherry gathered up her chastity belt and balled it into her palm. "The question is, who do I now ask to fix it?"

"Peter?"

They looked at each other and laughed.

With the kids all asleep, and the older adults cozy in the living room watching *It's a Wonderful Life*, Cora found herself getting antsy. She didn't want to call it a night, not with a horny husband waiting to repay her kindness to him. No, not at all. But she didn't want to play a board game, didn't want to head into the basement for the tiny TV and start another movie. Certainly didn't want to think of what Sherry might be doing, now that her chastity belt was gone.

No. Cora wanted to relax, maybe burn off some steam, but not alone. She leaned on the banister and watched everyone conversing in the living room, not sure where to go, what to do.

Davey came up and leaned low, waving her in with his intent on sharing a secret, and Cora cocked her head for him, curious but guarded where her sister might be concerned.

"Me and Matty found a locker open. We've got a bottle of rum ready to share."

She recalled the storage lockers stacked by the mobile bar. "You're stealing it?" she hissed.

He looked around and put up one hand to calm her down. "Matty checked with your grandmother. All the spirits are paid for already. We're just... sampling for quality." He wore a shit-eating grin, which made her relax.

Well, she could use a good beer, so why not? She followed him to the front door and put on her coat. "Matty's out there?"

"And your sister, and yer cousins with the RV."

Jemma and Jonah. A night "out" without getting onto the icy roads. "Perfect."

When they made it to the hay barn, she noted only the holiday string lights were lit, the effect both serene and magical. To the left, Jonah stood in front of the mobile bar, an attached computer screen lit and working. "Check this out!" He pointed to the monitor. "You type in your drink, and the machine makes it for you. What'll you have?"

Waving off the thought of strong alcohol, she said, "Just a beer."

"Long Island Iced Tea it is," he said with a grin, and she looked and saw they all had glasses with the same drink.

"Never had one," she admitted.

Matty raised his glass to her in a toast. "Ye'll like it, lass. Sweet and goes down smooth."

"I like anything that goes down," Jemma said, then giggled.

"I know," Jonah said, sending her a look hot enough to make her red.

"Ew," Cora said. "Really, guys, aren't you sick of each other yet?"

"Not remotely," Jemma quipped.

Matty left to fiddle with the stage equipment, and a few minutes later soft jazz music from his Smartphone filled the barn, the volume low. Her sister and Davey had claimed a nearby table, so she sat across from Sherry, and soon the rest joined them.

Dang, Matty was right; the first tea went down smooth.

The second was hot on its tail.

By the time she reached the bottom of her second tea, someone— she thought Jonah— suggested tequila shots.

"Great idea!" Cora had never had a tequila shot before, but how bad could it be?

"Lass," Matty cautioned, "I doona think yer in a position to handle much more alcohol." To Jonah he said, "She doesna drink, so doona load her up anymore."

"Psh," she waved him off. "You don't know me."

"Aya, wife, I do. No shots for her. She's a wee slip of a thing, canna handle her booze."

"No," Cora flagged Jonah, or, at least, where she thought he should be. How did he get to the bar so fast? "Don' listen t' him. He doesn' know... thing... 'bout me no more."

Yeah, she could tell Matty didn't like that.

"Aya, I do. No shots for Cora. She's already drunk."

Now she whined. "But I feel good right now. Really good. And Mr. Matty... Meaniehead," she waggled her finger at him, "isn't gonna take it 'way."

She held his eyes, no easy feat, since he seemed blurry. "Fine. One shot, Jonah. That's it. Any more, and ye'll answer to me."

"Yeah, yeah," he said, then told Cora, "You're gonna love this."

She watched as Jonah doled out lime wedges for

each of them, then brought out the salt shaker. He poured shots for each of them, then said, “Lick your wrist.”

She did as instructed, then licked off the salt he sprinkled on it. She downed her drink and fought the tears stinging her eyes, then sucked on the lime wedge. “Holy shit.”

The rest of the table reacted about the same.

Damn, she felt good. Spinning and woozy, but good. Alive. Warm inside and out.

Jemma gasped and said, “We should totally play Truth or Dare. Who’s in?”

“Oh, I’m in.” The hot look Jonah sent Jemma made Cora woozy.

Matty placed a proprietary hand on Cora’s shoulder.

Everyone seemed to find it a grand idea. Somewhere in the darkest recesses of Cora’s mind, she thought she should object, but she couldn’t remember why. “Sure.” She waved to Jonah. “Bartender, one more tea.”

“That’s the last one, lass.”

“Whatever.” She waved Jonah to hurry, and he went to make her one.

“I totally want to start.” Jemma smiled at Cora, then looked to Matty. “Truth or Dare?”

A grumble. “Truth,” he said.

But Jemma added, “We can only tell five truths. The rest are totally dares. Okay?”

“Sure,” they all agreed.

“So, Matty.” She leaned back and stirred her straw in her drink. “When was the first time you knew you were in love with Cora?”

For a long moment, Matty held Cora’s eyes, but then he turned his focus to Jemma. “That’s easy. The very first time I saw her.”

“He... he wanted to ask me to the dance, but Hugh and I were shtudying.”

“No,” Matty said. “That’s the first time we spoke.

Na the first time I saw ye."

What was she missing? Cora frowned at him, but Matty smiled. Then he addressed Jemma. "It was the beginning of eighth grade, and Da had gotten hired, but he wanted me to check out the schools, see which one I liked before we moved." He smiled at Cora before continuing. "She was in a biology class, and I watched the teacher pick up a snake and ask for volunteers. Some boys raised their hands, but Cora simply walked to the front, eager to demonstrate how to hold it for the class." Now he addressed Cora. "Ye were the most fearless, confident thing I'd ever seen. I told ma Da right then and there, that was the school I wanted to be in. So we secured an apartment that day, and I've never regretted a moment of it."

"Oh, that's so sweet!" Jemma sipped her tea and looked between the two of them. "Your turn."

But Matty only looked at her. "Ye, or me?"

She considered. "I'll go." She lingered on Matty's words for a moment. "I 'member that snake. Red-tail b-boa. Sweet. Her name was... was... Repticia." She narrowed her eyes at Matty. "And I *thought* someone was creeping 'round... behind that door."

"Not creeping. Watching and choosing."

"Creeping." Cora focused on her attack for a moment, stalling long enough for her third tea to arrive.

"Sorry." Jonah placed the glass into both of her hands. "Had to change out the container."

"Already?"

"Aya." Davey patted his chest. "We MacKenzies are a thirsty lot."

"Thanks, pal," Cora told Jonah, then looked between him and her cousin. "So. Jemma. Truth or Dare?"

"Oh, truth."

"Good. Where'sh the last place you two've done it?" She chased her straw around the glass with her tongue until she captured it and sucked away. She thought she heard Matty groan but couldn't be sure.

Jemma and Jonah exchanged looks, then Jemma pointed to the hay bales not five feet away. "Right there, maybe two hours ago."

"Ew!"

Matty stood up. "Now I gotta flip it over. I don't want your jackoff in someone's drink."

"It's biodegradable," Cora said, then giggled when he glared at her as he flipped the bale over.

"I'm next." Jemma fused her gaze on Davey. "Truth or Dare?"

"Dare."

She looked around and focused her gaze on the bandstand. "I dare you to sing a song to Sherry. On the stage."

"What song?"

"Anything."

"Aya, what about *Oh, Sherry?*"

"Never shaw that coming," Cora quipped, then giggled as she pointed at Jemma. "Coming! Ha!"

With a wry grin, Davey stumbled over to the mike and tugged it out of its stand. After a minute, he got the speakers turned on, then performed a terrible rendition of Steve Perry's song. Terrible because he didn't know half of the words, but his voice, truthfully, was rich. Soothing.

The whole time he sang, Cora thought how nice it would be if someone would ever serenade her. Someone strong and devilishly handsome, perhaps with a career in music. She tapped Matty on the arm and whispered, "If you shang to me like that, I'd forgive you. For everything."

He pulled his attention away from Davey. "I doona sing, lass. I play. I've a terrible voice. Ye knew that."

She shoved away. "Ne'er mind. F'rget it."

"I'm working on your challenges," he hissed back. "Doona give me more."

Not more, she shook her head, but the motion made

the room swim. *Instead of.* But Matty didn't respond, and she didn't want to yell it. Wait, did she say it or think it? "Did you hear me?"

"Aya. I heard ye."

"You seem kinda pissy 'bout it."

When Davey finished and jammed the mike back into the holder, he said, "Alright. My turn." He returned to his seat and considered everyone for a moment, then he faced Matty and gave a cocky grin.

But then looked to Cora. "Truth or Dare?"

"Dare."

He grinned. "Take a close-up picture of your twat and send it to me."

Knowing that would piss Matty off, she opened her mouth to agree, but got cut off.

"Over ma dead body," Matty growled as he leaned over the table.

"No," the others shouted. "It's got to be something we can all see."

"Fine," Davey settled back into his chair in thought. "Straddle yer husband and give us a show."

"Okay," Cora said, seeing nothing wrong with the request. "He *is* the shexiest man in th'room, idn't he?" She reached behind herself and managed to unclasp her bra, then straddled Matty's lap. Still standing and facing him, she lifted her shirt, then tugged it down over his head, making everyone laugh.

Matty's hands gripped her back and tugged her close, and his chin rasped across her chest, down one boob, nudging the material aside to brush her nipple.

While everyone cheered, all Cora could focus on was Matty's whiskers.

Then his lips.

Then his teeth.

Zinging pleasure shot straight through her, right down to her slick core. Before her orgasm ripped out of her, she pulled away and backed off, then tugged down her shirt. When she turned around, they all cheered.

She found her seat, feeling a rush she hadn't felt in over a year. Her skin felt branding-iron hot, and all she wanted was Matty thrusting inside her now. But she couldn't, for so many reasons, the most immediate of which was the game wasn't over. She grabbed her boobs to settle the burn, making the guys moan. "Me next." Cora pointed to Sherry. "Truth or Dare?"

A sigh. "Truth."

Now Cora pointed between her and Davey. "You two a couple? Like... fucking?"

Davey leaned back in his chair as Sherry turned bright red. "We're just friends."

"The whole truth," Cora insisted, even raising a finger at them. "Friends with bennies?"

A head shake from both of them. "Just friends," Sherry insisted. "You know I'm not ready to date."

Maybe she didn't want Davey seeing her fresh hip wound, but Cora didn't share that thought. "Boring. You should bang him. MacKenzies are fucking hot in bed."

Sherry spared a nervous glance to a grinning Davey, who cocked a thumb at Matty. "Can't speak for him, but I am, ye ken."

Matty chuckled and looked to Cora. "Never did hear a complaint, what with all the screaming and writhing."

"My turn." A bright-red Sherry faced Jemma. "Truth or Dare?"

"Dare."

She thought for a moment, then giggled. "Fondle your husband for three minutes without making him hard."

"Impossible," Jonah said.

"Try." She pulled out her cell and set the timer.

They watched Jemma slide her hand into Jonah's pants, and they all laughed as Jonah crunched his eyes and gripped the chair and started singing the alphabet, then the birthday song. Then he started reciting baseball stats. When the timer went off, he launched out of the chair and turned his back to them, but Sherry called out, "Nuh uh! Turn around!"

Jemma cheered and pointed at the missing jumbo bulge in his jeans. "We did it!" Now she whirled on Jonah. "Truth or Dare?"

"Dare. Definitely."

She grinned. "You have five minutes to—" she leaned in and whispered in his ear.

"Absolutely." He gripped her hand and together they bumbled their way into a dark corner of the barn, hitting only three tables as they went.

"Five minutes to what?" Sherry yelled as she set her timer, but they got no reply.

Sherry shrugged and fumbled her cell to the table.

"Drunk, lass?" Davey asked.

The question made Sherry face him and nod once. "Feeling it."

Soon they all heard the grunts of two people getting down and dirty behind one of the heavy barn beams. The sounds were making Cora fucking horny. She'd never been a voyeur before, and knowing two people were getting it on made her acutely aware of Matty at her side.

His hand maneuvered to her thigh.

Then it inched higher.

He squeezed.

She parted her thighs for him, and he moved in.

"More shots?" Davey asked, and Cora wasn't sure, but she thought he looked pretty aroused, too, listening to Jemma's love cries. He uprighted all their glasses and tipped more tequila into it. Cora licked her wrist and sucked off the salt, then downed another shot before Matty could stop her.

Jemma's cries became faster, more fevered.

Then she screamed.

The timer went off.

They all exchanged cautious glances. Cora found her lip curling when she whispered, "Who wants to see Jemma naked?"

With a shrug and a less-than-graceful stand, Sherry found her feet. "I guess, since I'm a doctor, it'll have to be me."

But Davey touched her wrist. "We doona even know what she dared him to do."

But Cora found herself giggling and holding Sherry's eyes. "Don't we?"

"He did it!" Jemma called out. "I came. Hard."

Davey waggled his dark brows at Sherry. "I think the doctor should determine the truth of that." And he angled his head towards the dark corner, indicting she should go.

"Ew! I don't want to see my cousin naked, thanks." But Sherry looked into the dark shadows for answers.

Jonah adjusted his pants as he led Jemma back into the lit area of the barn, then chuckled as he addressed his wife. "Oh, I needed that. Now, my turn." He sent a devilish look to Sherry. "Truth or Dare? And you're running out of truths."

"Fine. Dare."

He pointed to Davey. "Give him a hickey."

Cora watched her sister consider the dare. "Okay."

"On the inside of his thigh. In three minutes."

Oh, dear. Cora figured Sherry knew how to give a hickey, but outside of her work, she wasn't sure her sister had ever seen a naked man.

But her sister said, "Okay."

"You have to pull off his pants for him."

Cora leaned back in her chair. "Da... Davey, you mi...might be the first man my sister's ever shtripped."

"Shut up." Sherry tugged Davey upright, and with

semi-economical movements undid his zipper and tugged down his pants. Then she guided him back to the chair and knelt at his feet.

"Two-keela gives my sister some balls," Cora announced, but then she turned away when Sherry's head nestled into Davey's lap.

But no one else did.

What if Sherry was the one to get laid tonight? What if taking off her belt gave her free rein? What if Matty got sick of his wife's refusals and finally took Sherry up on her offers?

Matty seized the moment of distraction to nestle his fingers between her thighs, stroking along her swollen sex until she squirmed. Then he probed her folds through her jeans until liquid seeped from her. His motions both calmed her fears and aroused her, bringing her back to the present, to Sherry's head in Davey's lap.

"Suck! Suck! Suck!" Jemma and Jonah chanted.

When the timer went off, Sherry popped up and sat in her chair, beaming. She waited while an aroused Davey tried tugging his pants back up, with the girls eyeing his stiffy with interest while the guys jeered.

"See it? It's right there." Sherry pointed. "My first hickey," she told Davey, then faced the table. "Now it's my turn." Sherry scanned everyone, then landed on Cora again. "T or D?"

"Um... D."

"No more dares," Matty said. "Ma cock hasna shrunk from her last one."

Cora looked down and appreciated his heaving bulge. "Fine. Truth."

So Sherry leaned over the table and locked eyes with Cora. "You two together again?"

"Wait," Jemma interjected. "What do you mean?"

"He left her." Sherry pointed an unsteady finger at Matty. "This is the first they've seen each other in over a year." Though Jemma gasped, Sherry faced Cora again. "So, are you?"

"Um," was all Cora could say.

"That's not an answer."

"Na yet," Matty added. "I havena earned back her trust."

"What do you mean, he *left* her?" Jemma asked. "He's right here."

"He's back, but he left her." She turned from Jemma to Cora and said, "Cora has yet to answer." She leaned closer when no reply fell from Cora's lips. "If you won't answer that one, answer this. I watched Matty fondling you. Are you going to do it with him tonight?"

"Atta boy," Jonah and Davey both cheered.

"No," Matty said at the same time Cora said, "Maybe."

They looked at each other.

"My turn." Cora turned to face Matty.

"Wait!" Sherry said. "You can't leave it like that!"

"But I don' know the answer." She faced Matty again. "Truth or Dare?"

Despite his last protest, Matty's lips settled into a thin line. "Dare."

Oh, she wanted to feel him. Now. She leaned close and placed her hand on his glorious chest. She knew what she wanted to say, but the words wouldn't form on her tongue. When they did, she had a hard time pronouncing them. "Lemme sit on yer naked lap for the resht of the night."

His eyes rolled back, kind of like he was in pain. "Better be a short night."

"I knew he was short," Davey chimed in.

"If ye want to compare cockstands, *wee little* Davey, I'll be happy to show ye the error of yer assumptions."

Now all Cora could think about was Matty's

cockstand. She stood and stared at his bulging lap. "Drop 'em."

While seated, he shimmied off his jeans and spun Cora around and sat on his lap. His huge erection throbbed along her backside, and he guided her forward so he could tuck himself underneath her, where she squirmed atop him.

"I need another shot," Matty said, and Jonah poured them all another round.

God, Cora hadn't felt this good in a long time. Certainly not this horny. Definitely not this reckless. Some part of her thought she might regret this in the morning, but right now, all she could focus on was Matty's erection bumping into her swollen sex. She smiled at Sherry and asked, "Ishn't he the hottest man alive?"

Sherry grinned and glanced at Davey for a second, like she meant to argue the question.

Now Jemma looked between them and said, "I never understood why you two hadn't started a family yet."

She tensed at the comment, but forced herself to tuck it away like usual.

"Family," Matty scoffed as he slammed his glass to the table. "Ma turn." He locked onto Sherry. "Pick Truth."

"Okay. Truth."

With Matty's hand between her thighs and his erection shoved into her cleft, he asked, "Did Cora ever tell ye the truth of that night? The night of the accident?"

"Well, yeah," she hedged. "That woman died."

"Three deaths," Matty clarified.

Cora felt her face pale. She glanced at him over her shoulder, but he only met her eyes for a second. "Don't," she whispered.

"I'm sick of the lies, lass."

"They're no' lies. They're... *shecrets*. And shecrets aren' meanta be shared."

"But grieving is. Either ye tell them or I will."

Her heartbeat tripled. "No."

"Two deaths," Sherry corrected, her brows lowered in concentration through the fog of alcohol. "The deer died when you hit it, and its body crossed the median and killed the motorist."

Now Cora felt the tears gather and burn the backs of her eyes as that moment came back with crystal clarity despite the alcohol burning through her. She swung her knees to one side of his lap and twisted her torso to face Matty. "Don't. Please."

He adjusted his erection and leaned toward Jemma. "Ye asked when we're gonna have kids. We have to have sex for that, don' we, *mo chridhe?* And we havena had sex because of the lives I ended. All of them."

His fingers gripped her inner thigh, and all she could focus on was sensory, but his words pushed past that, made her focus on pain and not pleasure. He released his grip and tipped her chin up to face him. "I'm na strong like ye, Cora. I've done as ye pleased, but I canna take it anymore."

The burning ache inside her now leaked from her eyes. "No."

"I miss him, Cora. For fourteen months I grieved, but ye didn't."

"Who's he talking about?" Sherry asked. "The report only mentioned a female motorist."

"Matty," Cora whispered. "I can't. I can't. I can't." She dashed away the hot trails on her cheeks as she implored him to silence with her eyes.

"Ye have to," he said. As she looked at him, tears welled in his eyes. "I canna be with yer family and na speak the truth. I need them to know. To know why I left ye. Why they think I broke yer heart when ye're the one who really broke mine."

A sob worked out of Cora, and she covered her mouth as she shook her head.

"I've died a thousand deaths since that day, *mo*

chridhe, and ye never told anyone."

"Told us what?" Sherry demanded.

"The baby!" Cora yelled, then covered her mouth again. "He's gone."

Chapter 22

It was awful. Awful. Sherry and Jemma rounded the table and pulled her up to hug her, and all Cora could do was cry.

"How come you never told me?" Sherry's hand covered her mouth in sympathy.

"Too late, too late," was all she could say. Behind her, Matty stood and zipped up his pants.

Cora looked down as Jemma's hand rubbed her arm. "We lost one, too, and never told anyone." Now she stroked Cora's hair and tucked it behind one ear, and the maternal act only made Cora cry harder. "How far along were you?" Jemma asked.

Might as well share it. "Eleven weeks," she whispered.

Sherry dug fingers into her eyelids, like drunk thinking taxed her. "That's medically too early to tell."

"I knew. With all of mine, I totally knew." Jemma wrapped her arms around Cora's neck and cried. "Ours was a girl. I totally knew it right away. We lost her at ten weeks. I'm so sorry."

Now Cora found herself consoling Jemma, the comforting words she spoke hundreds of times at her job seeming inadequate when it came to someone she knew. "I'm so sorry."

"It's why we always have tons of sex at Christmastime. That's when we lost her. And we either have lots of sex to help me forget, or I turn into a crying mess." The last two words disappeared to her tears, and Jonah gathered her close.

After years of witnessing euthanasias, Cora realized people coped with loss in different ways. Some left their pets alone with strangers, some cried for hours over the body, some sang to them or read books to them or brought their pets cheeseburgers, fries and ice cream as a final treat. Since Cora hadn't even acknowledged her loss—to anyone—she was not the person to judge.

Now Matty's tears were evident, and Jonah's, as the family tragedy spread. The only one not crying was Davey, but Cora wasn't surprised. He hadn't lost a baby.

Matty waved to Cora and said, "Roll into me, lass." He pulled Cora to his chest and wrapped her tightly in his arms, then tighter still, as if holding her would keep the pieces from falling apart. She felt the hitch in his lungs, the rumble of his chest. "We were going to name him Logan. Logan Sean MacKenzie." Matty drew her off to his side and faced everyone. "If ye doona mind, I think we're done for the night."

They nodded, and Davey and Jonah agreed to clean up while the rest headed inside. Matty's arm never left her shoulder, and when they made it into their bedroom, Matty left her side and went into the bathroom, then came out a moment later with a glass of water. "Drink this."

She gulped it down, and he refilled it. "One more."

She complied.

When he returned the glass to the bathroom, Cora said, "I needta roll in," before she walked back into his arms again.

God, she'd missed him. Missed holding him, kissing him, loving him. He was the one she always came to with her problems, her secrets, her joys.

He was the one who always held her the few times she ever cried.

She gripped him tighter. "I'm so sorry, Matty. I never realized how much my... silence hurt you."

"Shh."

"No." She leaned back and held his burning green eyes. Her words slogged out of her, each one more painful than the last. "I was s...so caught up in m-my own pain that

I never thought of yours. God, I'm such an ass."

"I'm the ass who left," he said as he tucked her back under his chin.

Another sob ripped out of her. "I sh-should have told my family. M-maybe they would have understood."

"Or yer Da would have lopped off ma head for leaving ye after such a loss."

"No. He wouldn't have. Because if I told... if I'd've told... it'd all be alright. But I didn't. I shut it all in. It's my fault. All my fault. I'm so sorry, Matty." She kissed his neck, the highest she could reach. "So sorry."

He drew her closer, and Cora kissed his throat. God, he smelled so good. The memory of his cologne brought back a rush of happier times, and she found her lips parting and sucking on a delectable bit of his throat. Then she slid her hand up to his nape and speared her fingers into his soft hair. She tugged his head closer.

"Lass, what are ye doing?"

What was she doing? Hugging him, holding him, kissing him. Everything she always knew, everything she ever relied on, was in her arms this very moment. "Kissing you."

His voice seemed strained to her ears. "Yer drunk, lass, and grieving. Ye shouldna be kissing me like that."

"Like this, then?" She tugged his head down and stretched up on her toes to lock her lips against his.

God, it was great. All that she remembered. More, even. And when Matty gripped her in his arms and bent her backwards, overtaking her mouth with his tongue, Cora knew she'd made the right decision to kiss him. He tasted faintly of salt and lime wedges, the rest distinctly him. Between his flavor and fervor, Cora found her resistance gone. "Take me there, Matty."

He pulled away. "Na, lass. Na like this. Whatever we do tonight, ye'll likely hate me for in the morning."

Tears—this time of frustration—fell. "I was wrong

to shut you out, Matty. Wrong to force you to silence. I hurt you far worse than you hurt me."

"Lass...."

"No. I see it in your eyes. I heard it in your voice. You should hate me for what I did to you."

"I could never hate you."

"But I hurt you."

He made no comment.

She let the silence linger on for a moment. "We would lessen our pain together."

She let his eyes search hers while he decided. When he seemed on the verge of deciding against it, Cora whispered, "Roll into me."

Pain filled his eyes, pain and desire, and his breaths came hard and fast.

So Cora pushed him, stepping into his space to press her point. "I need you, Matty, and you need me. Take me there."

He growled and braced her hips, holding hers away from his own. "I've na been with anyone, lass. No one since ye. And if I get ye under me, I'll na be giving ye up for hours yet. Ye know that."

She could tell he spoke the truth, and the fact he remained true to her blossomed the kernel of hope she tended. "So let me be on top."

He held her still, studying her.

"Lemme be on top, Matty. That way, I'll have no one to blame but myself."

He didn't budge. At all. "Ye'll hate me for going along with ye."

Panic flared at the chance he might back away, and she was so close, so close. "I'll hate you more if you turn me away again. Please, Matty, we don't have to feel this pain alone anymore."

Her words struck him hard, she could tell, even with the fuzz of alcohol blurring her world. So before he could refuse her again, she reached up and tugged his head down once more, and this time, Matty joined in.

Hard.

She was way more blitzed than he was, because he stripped out of his jeans and sweater while Cora still struggled with her only button. So he popped that open and tugged off her pants, flung off her shirt and her already-unfastened bra and lay on the bed on his back.

Cora took a moment to scan him: the hard, flat plane of his stomach, the dark hair swirling around his pectorals, his long, hard length jutting straight up. “God, you’re beautiful.”

He got up and tugged off the covers before reclining again. “Yer gonna catch a chill standing there all alone.”

She smiled and turned off the light as she headed to the bed. Holy shit, was she really doing this? Seducing her husband?

Forgiving him?

Most likely, yes. She knelt on the bed and then reclined beside him, trailing her fingers down his side as he pulled the covers up around them. Down her fingers went, and down, until she gripped his rigid length in her hands.

“God Almighty,” Matty breathed.

She smiled and bent to capture his nipple in her lips, making him moan. She smiled broader and licked her way across his chest, reveling in the scent of his deodorant and cologne until she felt dizzy. She sat up and straddled him.

“Are ye sure, lass?”

She nodded. “Just don’t come in me.” But she wanted more, first. Curling her lips with her thoughts, Cora shifted higher on his chest, then higher. “You said you’d do anything.”

“If we’re together, aya.”

“Anything, Matty.” She pointed to her damp curls. “I want your tongue in me.”

He moaned or growled, she wasn’t sure, but then

his hands locked around her hips. "Aya, I'll take ye there, *mo chridhe,* but to na have ye afterwards? Jesu, lass, ye'll be the death o' me."

She had no intention of not letting him have his way with her, but first, she had needs. She crawled higher, higher, until her knees passed his shoulders. His hot hands restrained her, and the headboard gave Cora something to cling to.

His finger speared into her, making her breath catch, but then his lips on her clit had her gusting that same breath out, with more to follow. "Oh, Matty."

He probed inside her, then slid in another finger and stroked. "Yer so tight."

God, having him inside her felt fantastic. "No traffic. Only you."

"Good."

His fingers found her secret spot, the one that made her bladder quiver. Her body tensed. "I'm gonna pee."

"No yer not. Ye know that."

"Feels like it."

"It always does."

True. Based on talks with her girlfriends, few guys knew how to hit a woman's G-spot, let alone make their woman ejaculate.

She was gonna squirt. Soon. "Matty...."

He licked and sucked her as his fingers inside her tickled away.

"Oh, my God, I'm gonna pee."

"No, yer not." He sucked on her clit, using his tongue to toy with her inside his mouth.

"Oh, God. Matty."

He tortured her for another long moment, her desperation to hit the bathroom or lose control battling for honors.

She bashed the headboard against the wall as she rocked back and forth against his tongue. "Take me there.

Take me there. Take me there."

The stiff brush of his chin whiskers on her clit undid her, and her body exploded as she collapsed atop the headboard. She even leaned forward so her sweating forehead could lean against the cool walls.

"Got ye there," he whispered.

"Aya," she whispered back, the crawled back down his chest to smile at him. "Your turn."

"Na if yer na ready."

"Oh, I'm loaded, and ready to be cocked." She giggled, then lowered herself to sheathe his cockstand deep inside her. "Oh, my God!" It felt so painfully good she couldn't help but cry out.

The pain must have shown on her face, because Matty said, "Jesu, lass. Ye alright?"

"Fine. Shut up." Oh, dear God, she wasn't used to the sensation anymore, and she swore Matty was bigger now than before, if that was even possible, but she hitched up and down his length, taking him slowly deeper and deeper with each stroke.

"I must be splitting ye wide open, lass. Jesu, yer tight."

"I'm fine."

"Good." He braced her hips for his thrusts, but then his hands flew to the headboard and gripped tight, his expression one of agony.

"Hold me still."

"I said ye'd be in control."

"I am. Hold me still."

He gripped her hips, and she bore down harder and harder on him, their heavy breaths turning to grunts and moans and then hopeful cries as the sensation crested. She could tell by his vocalizations that he was close to his limit, and some part of her was aware enough to prevent him ejaculating inside her, so she tried to slide off him.

He gripped harder.

She glanced down at his face; his grimace told her his orgasm crescendoed, and Cora tried to pull away before he reached it. He grabbed her waist and flipped her to her back, pinning her hands to the pillows as he mounted her and thrust harder and harder.

No! She tried to push him off, but her own body threatened another orgasm, and her mind couldn't wrap around the danger of letting him continue, not when it meant the difference between another mind-blowing orgasm and *coitus interruptus.* His thrusts ignited her, loosened her desire to maintain control. So she arched her hips into his thrusts, meeting and matching his own heated fervor.

He pushed off her and knelt between her thighs, hefting her body up to his lap. He impaled her slowly, holding her hips aloft and immobile as he brought her to the brink of her next orgasm.

Her body tumbled and crumbled as he drove her over the edge, raising a cry from her lungs that embodied all the joy and pain she had ever felt for this man. She felt her body clench and squeeze around him, milking him of everything he had.

He practically roared when he came, his liquid searing inside her, warming her deeper than anything had all week.

All month.

Hell, all year.

He collapsed beside her, pinning her with an arm and leg. He nuzzled her cheek before propping himself up on one elbow. His eyes parted open, the crystalline green capturing her as he held her gaze. "Are ye okay, lass? Did I hurt ye?"

She felt like a red-hot snowflake drifting slowly back to earth. "No. I'm fine."

"I couldna stop. I'm sorry."

The realization that he came inside her roused her

from her drunken stint. “You came in me.”

“Aya.”

Shit. When did she have her period last?

Fuck. Two weeks ago.

She tried to fling off his arm, run to the bathroom to pee out his semen, but he either anticipated her moves or was simply ready for the next round. She opened her mouth to tell him off only to have his lips land on hers.

She was gone. Done-zo.

Matty’s kisses weakened her, destroyed her thoughts, crushed her will. He mounted her and slipped inside her once more, his thrusts slower, his kisses longer.

Tears leaked from the corners of her eyes as she realized he was her single weakness. “Stop kissing me.” There. She said it.

“Stop kissing you?” He leaned back. “Where? Here?” He nuzzled her neck, then nibbled on her earlobe.

“Yes. Don’t do that anymore.”

“What about this?” He swirled his tongue in her ear, then blew on it, causing shivers to race down her spine.

“Don’t do that, either.”

“No? What about this?” He teased the corner of her mouth with his teeth and tongue, tracing the seam of her lips by brushing his own against hers so lightly that it tickled.

A soft cry escaped her. “Definitely not.”

“What else can’t I do? This?” He bent and massaged her breast, then captured her nipple in his mouth, nipping and kneading and sucking until she arched beneath him and dug her fingers into his hair, holding him flush to her chest.

She cried out and rolled on top of him, stretching out along his frame. He gripped her hair in his fists and tugged her face to his, but instead of diving headlong into passion, Cora placed her palm on his cheek to gaze at him in the reflected moonlight off the snow outside. They were always so good together, in bed and out. He knew her heart, mastered her body. Called her bluffs, like right now. He knew she wouldn't walk away from lovemaking. She was on top again, could spring off and pee him out.

She should.

She should get up and pee out his semen.

She couldn't risk getting pregnant again.

But her body had already settled onto him, accepting his heat deep into her core.

Her chest clenched as she gazed at him, his expression soft as he trailed his fingers down her arms, back up, then along her back to her waist.

Her body clenched as he slipped in and out of her.

"I love ye, Cora. I always have, and I always will."

Tears filled her eyes, and in her moment of weakness, Matty rolled on top, cradling her in his arms. His hands stroked away her tears, smoothed away her strands where they had plastered themselves to her face. His lips calmed her fears and roused her interest.

She was fucked, no matter how she looked at it.

He couldna stop himself, no matter the right or wrong of it. He should have pulled out, God knew he should have, but he hadna felt so alive all year as he had with Cora these last few hours. Her sitting on his naked lap, tossing her shirt over his head, tempting him beyond reason, all built up to this moment in time.

Having her in his arms, naked and willing, was a boon he couldna pass up.

Despite knowing the better of it, he came in her. Three times.

A buggered rat bastard yet again.

But some part of his foggy brain whispered this might be his only chance. If he got Cora pregnant, she'd be bound to him for life through their child.

A lowly move, but a desperate man took all chances as they presented themselves.

He rolled her to her side and spooned her, lifting her leg to make love from behind. Exhaustion had crept up on both of them, but he wasna done yet, couldna stop until he did his level best to keep her in his bed and arms and planted his child as deeply as possible.

He only had one chance, one chance to bind her to him, and right or wrong, she was his wife, the only one he wanted to ever mother his children.

She may hate him in the morning yet again, but with every touch, every stroke, Cora fastened herself tighter around his heart, cleaving to him like a memorable riff.

She was the music he never wanted to forget.

She clenched once more around him, milking his balls dry, then rolled to her belly, likely as exhausted as he. His hips ached from thrusting, his cock felt numb, his arms weak from spending hours braced above her upon his elbows, but he wouldna trade his fatigue for anything. "Roll in, lass."

She turned and snuggled close, resting her head on his shoulder as she flung her arm around his waist. His leg covered one of hers, his breathing slowed.

He chuckled and squeezed her. "Truth or Dare?"

"Truth."

He hesitated for a moment. "Do ye still love me, lass?"

"Truth." She looked up to meet his eyes. "I've never stopped loving you, Matty."

He nodded and crunched her closer. "Truth or Truth?"

She smiled and drew circles around one of his nipples, making his breath catch. "Truth."

He leaned back to hold both of her eyes. "Do ye forgive me?"

She wiped a tear from her cheek. Then it seemed

her nose ran, and she sniffled as she nestled her fingers into the hair on his chest. "Mostly. But I'm still a little mad at you."

Only a little? Perhaps she wouldna hate him so come morning. "I understand."

He didna miss the accusation in her tone when she said, "You stuck me with all those bills to pay."

Ah. The past rattled her more than the present. Time to come clean. "Ye probably doona know this, but I sent money every few weeks to Grandmamma, who passed it along to ye. I paid off our debts. Every penny. I know it."

He could tell by the way she swept away her gaze that she somehow already knew this. "Nana showed me the letters."

"She kept them?" At least Cora knew then that he wasna lying.

"Yes. But I don't understand one thing. You said you left me a note. Something about calling you at the airport?"

He thought back a moment. "Aya. I stopped at the hospital florist before I left. I wrote a note to send with the flowers. I told ye I'd make everything aright."

"Flowers? The note was in the flowers?"

"Aya. I had no pen or paper in yer room."

She shook her head and fondled his chest hair. "I threw those out."

"Ye did?" Well, that made perfect sense as to why she thought he'd abandoned her. "Why would ye toss out fresh flowers?"

"Really?" She heaved up to one elbow to stare at him, incredulous. "Because only you and my parents knew I was there, and they certainly didn't send them. And I couldn't believe you'd take off and think a handful of flowers would make everything better. Of course I threw them out. And I swore like a fucking sailor when I did it, too."

He could only stare at her, knowing she told him the cold, hard truth. "But that's where I explained where I was going. That I'd send ye money. And if ye didna think ma taking a chance on changing our situation was the better choice, to call me and I'd come right back. Eleven hours I waited for yer call, *mo chridhe,* and when ye never called me, I left."

She stared down at him, no anger, no hate, only contemplation. "You could have called the hospital to check on me."

"Na, lass." He shook his head. "If I heard but one peep from ye, I would have turned tail and abandoned our best chance of getting ahead."

"Your best chance, not ours."

"No. Ours."

But then she dropped back to the bed and tucked her hands under her chin—a defensive yet vulnerable position if he ever saw one. "You're never going to give up your music for me."

He shifted to better hold her eyes. "Cora, think about what yer asking me. I couldna give up ma music any sooner than I'd ask ye to give up yer love of animals. It's in yer blood, lass."

Damn it. He knew her too well. It *was* in her blood. And until this week, she'd never known a moment where she hadn't nursed something back to health. She'd spent every minute of her youth and adult life following her passion, and all it got her was unemployed.

Perhaps the alcohol loosened her tongue, or the amazing sex, or perhaps it was simply time to come clean. As she held his eyes, the teeter-totter of indecision... tipped. "I lost my job."

"You what?"

Sick of crying, of being weak and unsure, she only

traced her finger around his other nipple. "Day after Christmas."

"What happened?"

She rolled in tighter, seeking shelter in his arms, the one man who always tried to take care of her when she could no longer take care of herself. "The hospital manager, we call her the Black Widow, is a real piece of shit. Nasty, vic... vitriolic backstabber. Hate her fucking guts. She kept taking away our controlled-drug log books. I confronted her, told her that it looked like she was hiding something by keeping them locked up. That's when she fired me."

"Ye think she was? Hiding something?"

"Don't know. Doesn't matter." She shrugged. "Carla talked to Mary in HR about getting my job back, but it doesn't look very promising." She shrugged like it didn't matter, but Matty knew her too well. He wrapped her tighter in his arms and squeezed for a good two minutes.

His arms loosened. "I'm so sorry, Cora. No wonder ye were hiding in the barn. I knew something was wrong."

She glanced up at him, realizing now why he seemed so persistent in getting an answer from her. Wrong? No, more like epic.

He pressed a soft kiss on her forehead. "Nursing's in yer blood. If ye canna go back, ye'll find a better job."

"Carla was my friend."

He crunched her to his side. "She'll always be yer friend. Ye just might have to make some new ones."

"Ugh."

He inhaled a deep breath and stared at the ceiling for a moment. "Ye could come with me."

"Where?"

"On tour."

She eased back to study him. "You shittin' me?"

"No." He turned and propped himself up on the elbow that had been under her. "Why not? Take six months to spend with me. We can see the world. It's the Romance Tour coming up." He shifted closer. "There's nothing I'd like more than to have ye with me. Truth be told, I never leave ma hotel room when we travel. I've been to the most beautiful places in the world and only see them through windows." He stroked her cheek. "With you, though, it would be different. Will ye come with me, lass?"

And there it was, just like Cora feared. "I don't want to see the world, Matty. I'm happy staying home, near my family, in case they need my help."

"But it would be the chance of a lifetime. Think about it." Now he rolled atop her, pressing his point along with his weight advantage. "Even if ye get your job back, or get another job, ye could at least ask for a week or two off. Whichever city ye want to visit, we can go to. Amsterdam is beautiful, and so is France, they tell me." He looked down at her and stroked the sweaty strands from her temples. "Or ma homeland, by Edinburgh. It's so beautiful there. Greenest place in the world. Ach, I'd wander through a field of heather and imagine making love to ye, right on the hillock, no one around for miles. Nothing but the birds above and the wind in the thistles, like we did that one time." He held her eyes. "God, I'd love to take ye there." He grinned at the double meaning of their phrase. "And then I could *take ye there.*"

They had made love outdoors once before, in their youth. Their parents had been at work, high school was over, and summer had officially started. Cora was soon to report to her mom's veterinary hospital to intern prior to starting college, and Matty had off that day from his part-time job at Wegmans grocery store. They had crossed the pasture and gone into the woods, then a bit farther until they came to a clearing. There, Matty had lain her down.

They had fooled around a bit before, but that day had been their first time together.

He smiled with another thought. "Perhaps we could

stop in Italy for wine tasting. Maybe even—"

"No."

"No?"

She shoved him off. "No, Matty. This is exactly what I mean. You're choosing your music over us. Again." She rolled away, putting her back to him.

"No, I'm not. I'm trying to share it with ye, lass. Let ye see things that most people never get to experience. It's not choosing music over ye."

She looked back at him. "It's me joining you on tour, while you work. Yes, it is."

She heard him sigh as he flopped back to the mattress. "Will ye at least think about it?"

"There's nothing to think about. We've spent the last five years having this exact same conversation. Me following you means your job is more important than mine. It's not. I help save lives, Matty. I'm licensed. I'm damned good at what I do."

"I never said ye weren't."

"But giving up my career means you think yours is top priority. It's all about you. Again."

"Cora—"

"Good night." And suddenly, all the feel-good vibes she'd accumulated over the last few hours died a hasty death.

Chapter 23

By the time noon rolled around, Cora's stomach insisted she get up, even though her head throbbed, her eyes felt like shriveled little raisins, and her bladder felt like it held six gallons of urine waiting to be expelled. Her elbow had a difficult time supporting her as she tried to sit up, but she told herself it was only the low blood sugar that made her so woozy she had to drop back to the mattress. Yeah, no. Cora wasn't buying her own lie. She was as hung over as a girl could be.

Matty remained resting but awake, turning his head toward her. Without opening his eyes, he asked, "You getting up?"

She kept her eyes squinted and averted from the glint of sunlight off the snow outside the window. "Yeah. Hung over but famished. You?"

He opened his eyes, smiled, and winked at her. "Ye taxed me sorely, wife. I doona think Grandmamma has enough food in the house to make up for what ye pumped out of me last night."

She grinned and hesitated a second, not feeling an ounce of the anger she had last night. "You started it."

The tease made him startle. "Truly? Ye wish me to pan yer cousins on that one? I'm sure they'll have a far different answer."

Her face heated as a glimmer of memory stirred. Had she really tossed her shirt over his head and gyrated on his lap? "Sore loser. That's what you are."

"Sore, aya, for sure." Now his expression turned to concern. "What of ye?"

As Cora studied him, she took inventory of her body and replied with her standard medical grading system. "Apart from being hung over, I have an acute pain score of one from being rammed all night. Chronic pain?" She gripped her back and stretched. "Yeah. Everything hurts. Deep tissue kind of pain. Ow."

He grinned and indicated the bathroom with his arm. "After ye."

She rolled out of bed and braced as soon as her feet hit the floor. She grabbed her lower back and straightened, then felt the ache in every muscle from the stretch. "Ow. Maybe two of four?"

"That all? I was aiming for three."

"Bastard."

He grinned.

Her knees hurt from kneeling, her thighs from supporting her weight in a squat, her back from arching, even her neck hurt, too. As she ambled to the bathroom she smirked at him. "Was sex always this aerobic?"

"Aya, lass. Every single time."

She grinned and closed herself in the bathroom, then ran the shower. As it warmed up, she downed three glasses of water and the same amount of aspirin, the clatter of the plastic cup returning to the counter sounding almost as loud as the hiss of the shower.

This was gonna be a hell of a long day.

Matty slipped in and joined her under the spray, his company as comforting as the arms he slipped around her.

Doomed.

She was doomed to love a man who would leave her yet again.

When they dressed and headed downstairs, Nana took one look at their joined hands and beamed. Shit. Was it that obvious? More Wegmans subs lined the counters, the round tray rather picked over. She grabbed two ham sandwiches and emptied two liter bottles of pop, the orange for Matty and the cola for her. When they settled in the dining room, Jemma shared a benign smile, then her eyes narrowed. "You totally did what you said you would, didn't you?"

Damn, it *was* obvious. "Um, did what?"

But Jemma looked up and down at everyone at the table, then grinned at Jonah and cranked her head back at them. "Look at them. Totally."

Jonah's eyes swept between them. "You're right." His brows waggled. "Welcome back."

"Shut up." Cora *so* did not want to be having this conversation, but Matty braced his arm around her and tugged her close, pressing a scorching kiss to her temple.

He chuckled and told them, "I think ye have some serious competition this year."

She gasped and faced Matty. "Shut up!"

But her cousin giggled and leaned back in her chair to study them. "It's alright. I totally understand."

People now *knew*, she realized. And then she was afraid Jemma and Jonah were going to say something. "What we talked about, yesterday...."

"I won't. We won't. We promise." Jemma met Jonah's eyes, and they both nodded agreement. She faced Cora again. "We would ask the same of you."

As Cora met Matty's eyes, she realized this secret was what cut him so deeply in the first place. "We won't mention what you told us."

He held her eyes, likely waiting for her to hurt him again by demanding he hold their secret yet again, but Cora added nothing to her statement. She watched the understanding of what she *didn't* say fill him, and he lowered his chin once to nod.

As they dove into their sandwiches, Nana came up and dropped her hand on Cora's shoulder. "Someone called here an hour ago, looking for you."

"Oh? Who?"

"She said to call her Crazy Carla."

A laugh slipped out. "That's my boss. Hope you don't mind, but I invited her to the party yesterday and forgot to tell you. She had a rough week." Not that Cora hadn't, too, but no point sharing that.

"She said she tried to reach you all morning, but you didn't answer your phone."

Cora held Jemma's eyes and tried not to grin. "Must have turned my ringer off."

"Hm," Nana said, but her eyes sparkled. "Anyway, she asked for directions. They are in Syracuse for the next few hours. She said they're renting a hotel room to catch up on sleep after a long flight. She wants you to call her."

"You didn't give her directions?"

"She said her name was *Crazy* Carla. No, I did not give her directions."

Cora laughed. "Fine. I'll call her in a minute."

"If you work with her, why was it a long flight?"

"She's coming back from Key West."

"Oh. Well, that's nice."

"Carla's great. You'll love her."

"Whatever you say, dear." Then Nana turned to Matty. "I love the layout of the barn. It's really going to encourage people to mix and mingle."

"Aya. I know. That's why I set it up that way." Cora watched Matty dart a glance at her father as he grabbed a cookie from the platter in the kitchen, but her dad couldn't hear them from so far away.

"On that note, would you mind being present when the balloon vendor arrives? I'd like you to monitor where everything goes."

"Of course."

"Good. They'll be here any minute."

Foisted into work yet again, but this time, it was Matty, not Cora, being hunted down for free labor. She met his eyes and found her lips curling in a smile.

"Na a problem, Grandmamma." He wiped his mouth, then kissed Cora before standing up. "Why doona ye call Carla? Make sure she gets here aright. I'll be back when I'm done."

Cora grinned up at him. "Have fun."

"Aya. Fun. Definitely."

She finished her sandwich and grabbed their paper plates, then put them in the trash and headed upstairs, where she opened the crate to let Herbie out to play while she dialed. Carla didn't answer her phone, making Cora wonder if she was having as much fun in bed as she had. But, wait, didn't Carla say her niece, Karrolin, was with them? Having a kid in tow would definitely put the brakes on getting hot and heavy in a hotel room.

Cora couldn't wait to meet the man who revved her boss' engine. She deserved a great man in her life, and hoped she'd finally found one. At the beep, Cora left the address to her family's farm, giving detailed instructions to head to the hay barn and not the horse barn.

She flopped back into the bed, enjoying the scents of sweat and sex and Matty's cologne on the sheets. With him outside working, Cora had the bedroom to herself right now.

Today was the big day.

New Year's Eve.

The day she agreed to Matty's extortion of a kiss for helping her with the horses.

While that part was over, she still had a ton of angst about her future. When was Matty heading back to Europe? Where did that leave them? Would she ever see him again?

What if he got her pregnant last night?

She didn't want to think about that possibility now any more than she had last night.

Really, what was the difference between him leaving her pregnant a year ago to take a new job, and her insisting they have hours of unprotected sex right before he left on tour?

Fuck.

She gazed at the bedroom door, knowing she had

time to mull over her life.

She loved Matty.

She'd always loved Matty.

And he was right about two things: she never let him grieve the loss of their child, and she continually insisted he give up his passion, when he never made the same demands of her.

Realistically, this would be the perfect time to get out of Dodge, take a world tour. If Matty could afford to take her overseas, show her the world, she'd be a fool to pass it up.

But she had no desire to travel the world. She liked living home. Her family needed her, and her grandparents were in their eighties. What if something happened while she was overseas? Who would help out? Who would give Faberge his fluids and take care of the horses?

Logically, she knew her family had contingency plans.

Emotionally, Cora was always there for her family, whenever they needed her.

Right up until Matty made sure she took care of her own needs, too, and made them back off and give her a break. She loved him for that, for making sure she didn't give until empty.

But the downside to traveling was she'd probably never get to cuddle a dog or cat daily, and she certainly couldn't take Herbie with her. Who would take care of Herbie?

Speaking of....

She flopped on her stomach and peeked over the lip of the bed, searching for him. "Who's mommy's naughty boy?"

At her playful tone, Herbie disappeared around the side of the bed, then came back into view, reaching out to nibble on the wooden bed post. He looked up at her, the little stinker, knowing he was being naughty and inviting her to chase him. So Cora hopped off the bed and crawled on her hands and knees to play along. He abandoned his nibbling and kicked up his heels, racing under the bed, only to poke his head out and then race to the other side.

"Are you being naughty again?"

Nails digging into the carpet answered her question.

"Oh, so naughty," she smiled. She crawled back to his cage and pulled out one of his toys and tapped it on the floor, and he peeked out at her. After ducking in and out from the bed for a moment, he raced out, kicking up his heels, then snatched the paper tube out of her hands and flung it about two feet. He eyed her, then raced around the bed and reappeared with one of Matty's socks in his mouth.

She gasped at his audacity. "Give that back!"

He hid it under the bed.

"Stinker." She crawled to Matty's side of the bed and moved his duffle bag, accidentally tipping it over as she tried to reach his stolen sock. But some pamphlets tumbled out. She flipped through them, seeing photos of Matty in full Scottish regalia on the fronts, with *Bagpipe Barons Romance Tour* displayed across the bottom.

They were all about Matty and his traveling band.

Her eyes burned at the painful realization. Another six months without seeing him. She smeared away the tear, hating the thought of being without him again.

Hating every fucking thing about this week.

Everything but Matty.

Damn it all. She didn't want to go another six months without seeing him, so where did that leave her? His groupie? His kept woman?

Semi-annual sexual playmate?

Her hand landed on her stomach; she caressed her belly. She couldn't deal with this. Not now. Not again.

She chased Herbie around the bed a few more times, then lured him into his cage with a shaggy green carrot top. Once he munched away, Cora closed the door and headed downstairs. Bright sunlight glinted off the fresh snow outside, and the clear blue sky was a welcome sight.

"Clear and cold today," Nana announced with a smile. "No more snow for the party."

"Great. Should make parking easier." She looked around. "Where is everyone?"

"Barn."

"Okay. I'll head over, too."

As she bundled up and headed to the hay barn, she paused at the horse barn, then went inside. All the lights were on, and her Mom wielded a pitchfork as she cleaned out a stall. "Here to help?"

She wasn't, but found herself bopping a quick shrug."Why not?"

"Thank God." She pointed into the feed room. "Can you start the rations?"

She glanced at her cell. "It's one o'clock. Am I doing morning or dinner?"

"Unfortunately, morning. I had another emergency call and I just got back. You were... unavailable." The look spoke volumes.

Was that a blush heating her cheeks? But Cora rallied through it and thought, *See*? This was why she needed to be here; her mom depended on her. "Morning feedings coming up." Cora headed into the feed room and followed the whiteboard, adding mare food to some buckets, supplements to others, water into the bran for one and antibiotics into the last. She dangled three buckets from her arms as she headed stall to stall, reading the names scrawled on the buckets and ensuring the correct horse got the correct feed. Took her three trips, but she got everyone fed, then unrolled the hose and started filling water buckets.

"Can you top up their hay?"

Cora shrugged. "Sure." She went upstairs and tugged down a bale to use. The set up for her Mom's barn made hay delivery a snap. As Cora cut the twine on the hay bale, she pulled off a few square flakes, then dropped them into floor holes along the wall, where they lodged into wire racks in the upper corner of each stall for the horses to nibble. No lugging heavy bales up and down stairs, just a quick and easy drop delivery.

As she headed down the stairs, her father pulled up on the tractor, the flatbed now empty. She smiled and raised a hand in greeting. "Hey. You taking out another load?"

"Yeah." He turned off the engine and stepped out, then stopped before her. "Cora, I know I promised that boy of yours that he could—"

"He's my husband, Dad, not my child."

They locked eyes, but her father didn't seem willing to amend his speech. "—That he could stay through midnight, and I'll keep my word, but Cora." He rubbed his nape and watched her mother muck for a second. His voice dropped. "I know your mother and grandmother believe in working things out, but if you need me to help pay for the divorce, you let me know. Okay?"

Words failed her, and words normally didn't fail Cora. They usually involved profanity and blistering people's ears, but right now, silence was her arch-nemesis. Where was this offer when she struggled a year ago? When she wanted to break free of him?

And why now, when she was so torn over her immediate future?

He gripped her shoulder in a fatherly way and headed over to the wheelbarrow to dump the next load onto the flatbed, and all Cora could do was watch, struck mute by an offer she didn't want.

While her parents dragged a bale of wood chips to layer the next stall, Cora left and headed to the hay barn.

She'd let the next words out of Matty's mouth decide her future.

Chapter 24

Jesu, setting up the barn for the party was just as bad as setting stage, but Matty was fully up for the challenge. Besides, this was for the woman he loved, and her family, and he was determined to put his best foot forward. Peter labored at his side, helping the caterers haul in their hot silver trays and set them up on the serving tables. Once the last tray had been placed, Matty stood at Peter's side, watching the commotion and taking a breather. "So, tell me about this space attached to yer garage."

Peter glanced at him, then back at the bustling servers. "It's about ten by twenty, front is all windows, has its own entrance. Actually, it's got a better view of the lake than my portion, since I have a building directly across the street on my side. Why?"

"Curious, is all."

But Peter must have seen through his words. "You thinking of staying this time?"

Ouch. Word must have gotten out, despite Jemma's promise. But Sherry and Davey had pledged no troth, so the tale must have come from them. Matty darted a glance to his brother-in-law. "Never wanted to leave, bro. I messed up, but I never stopped loving yer sister. Ever."

Peter made a noise of acknowledgement. "What's this got to do with the vacant space?"

He glanced over at him again before resuming their shoulder-to-shoulder stance. "I'll need a space to build ma pipes. And they're loud when I test them." He crooked a smile at Peter. "Think the windows will break when I strike in the drones?"

His question made Peter grin. "If revving a 1972 'Cuda with dual exhaust hasn't done it, nothing will."

The image of seeing some nice MOPAR cars

parked out front, as well as Peter's comment, made Matty chuckle. "Fair enough."

But Peter leaned back against a nearby table, addressing Matty even though he studied his shoes. "Don't do this if you aren't going to stay. Cora's my sister, man. I'll have to beat you up if you pretend to do this and then jet out on her again."

"I won't. I promise."

Peter locked eyes with him.

"Will it help if I pay ye three years in advance?"

Now Peter's lips curled, and the skin around his eyes softened a wee bit. "You don't even know what my rental fee is."

"Pissingly small. I've heard yer Ma say how loud that place is, what with ye revving those dual exhaust engines all day."

They chuckled, and Peter rocked back to his feet, standing tall. Matty squared up with him, and they both shook hands. Peter looked around for a second. "Does Cora know?"

Matty shook his head as they released their grips. "I didna even know until a moment ago." But he smiled. "Feels good and right though, doesn't it?"

"It does." Then Peter seemed to have a weight lifted off of him, and his whole body relaxed. "It really does." He lifted his hand, and they bumped fists. "Thanks, man."

"Thank *ye*."

Now Peter looked at his attire. "I should get inside, get showered. Can't show up to a formal event in grease and jeans; Mom will wring my neck."

"Aya." Matty realized he was equally grungy. "Time to face the music."

Chapter 25

As Cora trudged her way to the hay barn, she saw the caterer's vans pull out, the scent of roasted beef trailing after them. Damn, she was still hungry after her exertions last night. Hungry and hung over. She tugged open the barn door and inhaled the delicious scents of beef and ham and turkey, of potatoes au gratin and veggie casseroles, of simmering chocolate sauce and freshly baked apple pies.

Ahead, Matty and Peter were talking, and then they bumped fists and smiled. Well, that seemed like a good sign.

Still, she'd let Matty's next words guide their future. A stupid way to decide, but no worse than flipping a coin or playing *eenie meenie minie moe.* He looked over as if he sensed her and a giant grin split Matty's face. He stepped near and drew her to his side, facing her brother as she peeled off her coat. "Here she is, ma beautiful wife, come to tell me what a great job I've done." He winked down at her and took her coat to hang. "Right, wife?"

Well, that was fifty/fifty. Half compliment, half dredging for compliments. Still, she looked around to see what he'd accomplished and caught her breath. The helium balloons were clear but sparkled against the white tarps pinned overhead, and their placement around the paper lanterns almost lent a disco-ball effect on the ground. Large Mylar balloons with the new date blazed across them were the centerpieces on each table, tables which she now saw were covered with alternating rows of black and silver tablecloths. In the clear space between the dance floor and the tables, a screen had been erected along the wall, and mounted to an overhead beam was the projector, most likely to televise the ball dropping at midnight. And on the wall behind the bandstand, two giant banners hung, one with an old man, and one with a new baby.

Out with the old, in with the new.

Across from those, over the door she just came in, hung another banner labeled, *Auld Lang Syne,* a subtle reminder to those leaving to go with happy tidings.

"Wow, Matty."

"Screw you, sis."

She grinned at her brother, then frowned in play. "But, nothing here has an engine. How could you have possibly helped?"

He gave her two middle fingers in reply, making her laugh. To both of them she said, "It looks amazing. Smells even better." And she lifted her nose and sniffed in appreciation.

"I hope ye like it," Matty said, his voice low and earnest. "I want to make sure yer family's happy with this year's first party in the barn."

Knowing Matty like she did, she knew his actions stemmed from love, and she felt that same emotion crest in her at his efforts. "They will. It's amazing."

Her confident claim made him smile. "Grandmamma says we can all have our meals out here once we're dressed. That way, we'll all be available to greet our guests as they come."

"Our guests. I like the sound of that."

The door opened, letting a blast of cold air in, and when Cora turned, she couldn't believe her eyes. "Carla!" Carla stood beside a super hunky new dude who was leading Carla's niece, Karrolin, by the hand. A beautiful Belgian Tervuren limped at Carla's side, his front leg wrapped in a medical Velpeau sling.

"Hey!" Carla beamed. Absolutely beamed as they removed and hung their coats. But then she looked around and said, "Or, since it's a barn, should I have said *hay?"*

Cora moaned at the bad joke and rolled her eyes like usual. The sex must be great, she realized with something akin to glee as she scrutinized her former boss' glow, along with the mandatory pun. "It's definitely hey, not hay. So glad you made it. Hey, Karrolin!" Cora grinned as Karrolin broke free and raced over, crashing into her for a hug. She knelt down and gathered her close.

Carla placed her hand on her guy's shoulder and faced Cora. "Cora, my amazingly awesome technician of four years, this is Gunner, a stray I found on Flight 647 who followed me home." She grinned at Gunner, but then gave him a querulous expression. "Or should I introduce you as Agent Fitz?"

He grinned and scrubbed the dog's shaggy neck as he looked at Cora. "Call me Gunner. This is Kuba, my drug dog." He reached out and they shook hands.

"Nice to meet you." She indicated Kuba's sling with her chin. "What happened to him?"

"Long story." Carla raised her palms in the air and shook her head like she didn't want to get into it.

"He's a hero dog!" Karrolin practically bumped into Cora's jaw when she bounced with her unbridled excitement.

The motion brought a slight scent to Cora's nose. She stood and looked from the child's muted orange hair and back to Carla. "Why does she smell like Betadine?"

"Aunt Carla dyed my hair with it!" Karrolin tugged on her short strands to show her while Carla rolled her eyes, clearly upset by the occurrence.

"I'll tell you all about it, later. Much, much later."

"It's not a story for the faint of heart," Gunner added, rubbing Carla's shoulder as he smiled down at her. "But it was worth every second."

Boy, she looked exhausted, even though Carla smiled with adoration at the comment. Matty and Peter came up for introductions, and Cora noticed how Matty and Gunner assessed each other, two alpha males vying for space. Peter, non-alpha, excused himself to get ready for the party. Kuba, the dog, another non-neutered male, contented himself to curl up at Gunner's feet with a sleepy moan.

"Man, that smells good." Carla eyed the catering table with envy while Karrolin busied herself trying to jump up and catch all the balloons.

"Why wait?" Matty grinned and assessed them all. "Shouldna ye test the food for the guests? Make sure it willna kill a body?" He winked at Cora as he said it.

"Whoa." Carla leaned back. "Hot accent, Matty. Newly adopted?"

"Aya, I'm fresh back from Scotland, touring with ma cousin. He's got the thicker of it."

Carla glanced at Gunner with a teasing smile. "A Scottish cousin, huh? Maybe I should have held out."

Her man chuckled and met Carla's tease with his own. "Yeah. You're so good at holding back."

She gasped and swatted him as Cora burst out laughing. Not only did this new guy speak and crack jokes, but he had locked in on Carla's personality in *days*. She nodded approval to Carla when Gunner wasn't looking. Then she added two thumbs up, making Carla grin. They headed towards the catering tables, leaving the men to follow in their wake while Karrolin sat on the floor with Kuba's head draped across her lap. Cora scanned her boss up and down. "Nice catch."

"You, too."

The comment made Cora suck in her lower lip with doubt. "You think?"

"Absolutely. You two look good together. Better, actually, than before." Not fishing, not daring a reply, just a flat-out objective observation.

She didn't know how to respond. She focused on picking up her plate and holding it out for the servers to carve and dole out the meats. "What makes you think we're back together?"

Carla juggled two plates, filling one with tiny portions before filling her own. "Really? Fine. You laughed. Out loud. I can't remember the last time you laughed, even at my awesomely funny jokes."

She snorted. "*Gunner's* funny, you're not." Carla's glare was met and matched by Cora's sour look. "Getting back with Matty would be stupid. I'd be right back where I started from."

"He's different now, and so are you."

"No, he's not."

That comment made Carla scoff. "You're kidding, right? Look at him." They peered over their shoulders at the guys as they ogled the meats at the start of the line. "He's confident now. Where's Karrolin?"

Cora turned around and searched, then pointed. "Sitting on a hay bale. Kuba's with her."

"Okay. Good."

Cora picked up the thread of their conversation. "Matty was always driven."

"But now he's confident. That comes with maturity, success. He's not taking any of Gunner's guff, but giving out plenty of his own. If he were a dog, I'd suggest neutering."

Cora chuckled. "That's the problem, isn't it? Matty and I were always good together that way. It's everything else that's fucked up."

"No, you were always good together in every way. The sex was ancillary."

Cora fully faced Carla and curled her lip in disbelief. "Who the hell are you, and what have you done with my *toss-the-bastard-to-the-curb* friend?"

But Carla only smiled serenely and doled some steamed veggies onto both plates, looking back to monitor Karrolin and Kuba every few seconds. "It's new knowledge to me, too, but it's true. I'm standing by it." She eyed Cora over the silver ladle of fried rice in her hands. "I know you're thinking the same thing, but don't want to admit it. It's okay; I can see it in you."

"You see nothing beyond your rosy pink glasses."

"Kiss my ass. Your body language is relaxed for the first time in forever. You have color in your cheeks and little stars in your eyes." She braved a grin. "Bottom line, you're BAR."

Bright, alert, responsive. The comment made Cora scowl. "I'm not your patient." She started scooping into the silver serving trays, loading her plate with the best assortment of side dishes money could buy.

"Signs are all there."

"Doesn't change the fact that he's leaving again."

"Is he?"

"He travels abroad. That's what he does for a living."

"That's what he *did.* Is it still what he's doing?"

"He hasn't said he's not."

"But has he said he is?"

They held eyes, and Cora felt a tiny bit of hope bloom. "I don't know."

"Then ask. You'll never get ahead if you don't."

The solid advice made heat sizzle in Cora's chest. She angled to face Carla, but she indicated Gunner with her chin. "And you? Did you *ask?* For *that?*"

"Damn straight." Carla waggled her brows as she grinned. "And I followed your advice, literally down to the letter."

Cora recalled texting Carla to bang a hot stranger before considering marriage to their coworker, a nice guy who doubled as a statue. The fact Carla did as advised made Cora chuckle. "So I give good advice?"

"Yeah. Holy moly." Carla scanned the litany of trays before them like she just realized how many more food options she still had. "Your family does this every year?"

"Yup. This is the first time we've set up in the barn, though. Wow, I don't know about you, but I'm running out of room on my plate."

"Yeah. Me, too."

They got settled at a table to chat, the men boasting about their sports teams while she and Carla waved Karrolin over to join them for dinner. After a few minutes of idle chatter, Carla said, "By the way, you can totally thank Gunner. In fact, I think you should just thank him, like, now."

"Um, okay." She looked at Gunner, who stopped chewing long enough to share a mischievous grin. "Thank you." He nodded and resumed chewing. Then she turned back to Carla. "Because?"

"He singlehandedly got your job back."

"He did?" She looked at him. "You did? How? Why not you?" She ping-ponged her glance between them as she fired off her questions. "What happened? What did Mary say?"

But Gunner pointed his fork at Kuba. "Thank the dog. He did all the heavy lifting."

"That's right." Carla gave a decisive nod, but her eyes danced with her tease. "You were simply a spectator."

He grinned at her like they shared some great secret, and Cora felt a pang of envy.

The news made Matty laugh and wrap his arm around Cora's shoulders. "That's great! I'm sure yer relieved." Then his smile softened. "Although I canna say I wasna happy to have ye to maself all week for a change." He sent a mock glare to Carla. "Ye've been a wee bit possessive of ma wife these last years. Ye canna have her all to yerself, ye know."

"But you can?" Carla charged, raising a daunting brow as she regarded him.

"Aya. Bought and paid for, she is."

Gunner chuckled when Cora jabbed her husband

playfully in the ribs.

Carla wiped her mouth with a linen napkin. "Yeah, well, I may never get another Christmas off after this one. Right now, I'm technically out with hazard pay."

"Hazard pay?" Cora sat up straighter. "What happened?"

"Bullet wound." She raised one shoulder in a shrug.

"Bullet wound! Oh, my God, Carla!"

"I'm fine, but the pain meds make me sleepy."

"And then she ropes me into babysitting." Gunner gave a theatrical eye roll, then winked at Karrolin. "Do you know how hard it is to spar with that kid? She's a friggin' ninja."

Karrolin giggled and raised two fists, making Gunner cringe in mock fear.

Cora grinned at the exchange, then leaned over the table to Carla. "I can really go back? When?"

"January 2nd. Midnight to eight, like usual. And I, well, Gunner, really, hinted that you might sue for wrongful termination, so Mary had no problem shelling out back pay." Carla and Gunner grinned at each other with their accomplishment.

Cora found her eyes closing in relief, and her head dropped. She smeared her hand down her face. "Thank you. Thank God."

"My pleasure. We're a team, Cor. You know that."

God, it would be so good to get back to work with Carla again, find out all the details of her week off with the hot new beau.

She'd probably be forced to share her own details, too, of her week with Matty.

As she turned to watch Matty and Gunner talking, she realized that wasn't such a bad thing. Her cell dinged, and Cora gasped. "Oh, crap. We have to get ready." She looked to Matty. "That was my timer to come get you if you weren't done out here." Then she realized something awful and covered her mouth. She looked at the girls. “Do you have a gown? Either of you?”

Both Carla and Karrolin shook their heads. “Stores were all closed by the time we got into Syracuse, and honestly, I was too tired to even attempt to go shopping.”

“Okay.” Cora stood and collected plates, already thinking two steps ahead of the problem. “I think you can fit into one of my Mom’s gowns, and Karrolin,” she assessed the child, “I think will fit into one of my second cousin’s dresses. Come on, let’s go.”

“What about me?” Gunner stood and pointed at himself. “Do I need a tux?”

Matty scanned the other male. “No, but Davey has a suit that may fit ye. He and I will be fine and resplendent in our dress kilts tonight.”

“Really?”

“Aya. We’re playing for ye poor sods.”

They all laughed, but then Gunner patted his chest and faced Carla. “How would I look in a kilt?”

Matty cocked his head and scrutinized Gunner. “Ye think yer man enough for a kilt?”

Carla and Cora held eyes, then burst into laughter as they reached for their coats.

Chaos reigned supreme inside the farmhouse. The downstairs had all the males in varying states of undress, and Cora grinned as Carla covered Karrolin’s eyes. Cora ushered the ladies to the stairs. “Men downstairs, women up. Come on.”

It was even more chaotic upstairs, with half-naked ladies racing to and fro, crying for makeup, curlers, fresh stockings and safety pins. The bay windows had the drapes all drawn, with bright lamps spilling into the hallway for better visibility as they took turns applying makeup in front of the three standing mirrors that had been dragged into the hall. Cora waved Carla into her grandmother’s dressing room, where the walk-in closet held years of gowns in enough colors to make a rainbow quiver with envy.

"It's where bridesmaids' gowns go to die," Carla breathed.

Cora scoffed and shoved her playfully into the closet, where she took a baby blue gown off its hook. "I recall Mom saying this one was too long for her. You like?"

"Yeah. What're you wearing?"

She went into her bedroom and came back with the only dress she owned. Not a gown, but red silk, and Matty had always loved it. She hadn't even thought of that when she grabbed it, but now it seemed so appropriate. She brought it into Nana's room and held it up for Carla to see. "It's all I got."

"It's beautiful."

"Now, on to Karrolin." She took the child's hand and went up and down the hallway, asking everyone if they had another gown to spare. After a fruitless search, Cora ended up back in Nana's bedroom to rethink her attack. She shuffled through the dresses until she came to a pink sheath dress. "I wonder." She took it down and held it up to Karrolin. "What do you think?"

It came down almost to her ankles. "It's a grownup's dress."

"Not done yet." She opened drawer after drawer until she found a delicate white crocheted shawl. "We'll have to use a lot of pins, but I think this may work. Try on the dress."

Carla moved methodically, undressing Karrolin and helping her into the sheath dress. Nana stepped in and saw what they were doing, and came back a moment later with a container of safety pins. "Put the dress on inside out."

Cora grinned, knowing what Nana was up to, but Karrolin frowned. "Really?"

"Follow orders, Private," Carla said, and Karrolin snapped to attention and wriggled free, then inverted the material to put on again.

"Hold still." Nana pinched the material at both side hems until it was uniform. "I'm going to hem it to fit."

"Oh."

They pinned her and got the dress to properly fit, then wrapped the shawl around her as an overlay. Nana left and came back a few minutes later with white ribbon, which she pinned as straps across Karrolin's shoulders to keep the shawl from sliding down. Then she bunched the material into a decorative knot and wove the ribbon through it to hold it in place as an overlay.

"Well," Nana said as she heaved herself off the floor, "my handiwork won't win any awards at the beauty pageants, but you look beautiful."

Karrolin ran out the door to the mirrors in the bay windows and spun around. Then she gasped. "I love it! Thank you, Cora and Nana!" Then she ran back and launched herself into Cora's arms.

Cora couldn't help but laugh and kiss that little orange head. "You're very welcome." Karrolin hugged Nana, then jumped into Carla's arms, too.

Cora smiled at the child's exuberance. "Now, our turn to get ready, okay?" Cora managed to beg a pair of stockings for Carla, and as soon as they were all dressed, Jemma curled and styled their hair. Carla had strappy sandals with her from her trip, and Cora donned a pair of black shoes. Karrolin made a new friend with one of Cora's second cousins and got to borrow a pair of glittery pink princess slippers for the evening.

By the time the clock bonged seven times, most of the guests had managed to wrap up and head to the barn. As they descended the stairs, Cora faltered when she saw Matty smiling up at her. His Scottish regalia looked even better from this angle, or maybe it was that Cora simply appreciated him more today than when she first arrived. Everything he wore was the same, but today, he looked glorious. Beside him, Gunner smiled up at Carla, and her cousin Randy kind of grumbled as he waited for them.

"Ma favorite dress on ye," Matty said when she stepped close. He kissed her softly and held her eyes. "I'm so glad ye brought it."

She didn't want to tell him she only had this one, so she smiled at him. "Thanks."

Gunner tugged his suit into place and shifted. He sent an apologetic look to both Carla and Cora. "It's just a little snug in the shoulders. I'll deal."

That only left Randy. When she turned her gaze on him, Matty grinned and thumped her cousin on the back. "Seeing as how it's Karrolin's first time at a fancy party, yer cousin here thought he'd man up and lead the wee thing in. Isna that kind of him?"

Judging by Randy's less-than-enthusiastic expression, Cora knew where the idea had originated. Still, she gave him her best smile. "That is so amazingly kind of you, Randy. Karrolin's a good kid."

He grunted, but Cora ignored his response and hunched over for Karrolin. "For this event, it's customary for a man to lead a woman into the party. This is my cousin, Randy, and he'll lead you in with us, okay?"

Karrolin wouldn't make eye contact, and she chewed her nail and hid behind Carla.

Interesting.

With fresh eyes, Cora looked at Randy. He was twice Karrolin's age, young enough to be obnoxious but technically old enough to be a man. Did Karrolin have a crush on him? "Honey?"

She met Cora's eyes for a second before stepping behind Carla again to dig the toes of her sparkly shoe into the carpet.

Carla caught a little breath and pulled away. "What's wrong, Imp?"

Instead of answering, Karrolin shook her head and

grabbed Gunner's arm with both of her hands. "Can't Gunner lead me in?"

Carla tipped her head towards Randy, indicating him as the source of Karrolin's angst, and they both fought back little smiles. In a confident voice, Carla said, "I'm sure Gunner won't mind if this strapping young buck leads me to the dance."

The thought of having a beautiful woman on his arm and not a child visibly relieved Randy, who said, "Sure. I'll lead you in."

But Gunner's eyes went wide with mock fear. "What if Karrolin goes all ninja on me? Who'll protect me?"

"I *won't.* I *promise.*" Karrolin tugged at his arm, trying to lead Gunner away from Randy, then hid behind Gunner when Randy caught her eyes.

It was so adorable, Cora couldn't help but grin. Maybe she could talk Randy into dancing with Karrolin this evening, just once.

A battery of angry barks caught their attention, and Cora and Carla raced into the den, where the sound came from, the guys following right behind. They all stopped in the doorway to see Kuba postured menacingly over Randy's crazy Lab, the yellow doofus belly-up on the floor, groin exposed, throat exposed, eyes averted and tail thumping feebly.

Gunner kind of laughed. "I told Randy his dog was going to get put in his place if he didn't calm down. Kuba's too well socialized to tolerate that kind of behavior." Even fifteen pounds lighter and walking on three legs, the Tervuren had tumbled Dozer into a submissive position.

Randy stepped up and motioned for his dog. "Come here, Dozer."

The dog eyed him, then Kuba. When Kuba relaxed and stepped away from his domineering position, Dozer got up and sat submissively at Randy's side, all ego and oomph gone.

But Gunner looked between the two dogs. “Do you show Dozer? Work him? Compete with him?”

Randy shook his head.

The admission made Gunner frown. “Working dogs don’t get neutered until after retirement, so why haven’t you gotten him fixed?”

Cora threw out her hands to Randy, showing she had nothing to do with Gunner’s statement, as she burst out laughing.

Chapter 26

The guests seemed to be having a great time, and Cora had to admit that Matty did a fantastic job of setting up the place. Those still dining seemed relaxed, while those on the dance floor clapped and cheered and jumped with glee. The band cranked out a great assortment of songs, and the bartender scrambled to keep up with everyone's orders. As she stood there along the wall, watching the kids dance in the area between the tables and the wooden dance floor, a tap to her shoulder made her turn.

"May I have this dance?" Matty remained bowed, his hand outstretched to hers, his eyes glittering in the strobe-like effects of the sparkly balloons.

Her heart raced at the thought of being in his arms again. "Do you still remember how?"

"Aya, lass. Occasionally, they make me dance on stage." The statement made her frown, but Matty pulled her into him and drew her close. "They never give me such a lovely partner, though."

She smiled and looked down.

"Doona look away, lass." His warm finger tipped up her chin until their eyes met. "I've na danced with ye in years."

"Not since Jemma's wedding."

"Let's show them we've still got it." He pressed her tight to his chest, his cologne almost overwhelming her in such close proximity. His hand held hers, and she moved in tandem with him to the music. He smiled down at her. "Ye look lovely as a vision."

She smiled. "Thank you. You look good, too."

He grinned and tucked her under his chin, inhaling a deep breath as he held her. "Tell me what ye want, lass. I'll do anything to keep ye in ma arms."

She shook her head and leaned back. "My answer hasn't changed."

"How can it na? We love each other. We made love all night long."

She was glad the music was loud enough that nobody overheard him, but Cora still felt the awkwardness of the conversation. "Are you leaving again?"

"It's ma job, lass. But I'll try to only be gone about three months if yer na coming with me."

"Well, my job's here. In Long Island. I'll be leaving tomorrow for my shift."

She watched something like fear, or a realization, sweep his features. "Bugger," he whispered. His eyes locked on hers again. "But you doona have to work. I can support ye."

"But I want to work. Why can't you understand that?"

"But we're young. We should travel and experience the world while we can enjoy it, na when we're too old to run about."

Cora shook her head and looked down. It was as she feared. Nothing had changed. The music ebbed, and Cora shrugged off Matty's arms and huffed towards the tables where Sherry sat. Davey stood beside her, dressed in full regalia, practicing *Skye Boat* on his chanter to Sherry's obvious delight. Cora dropped down hard into a vacant chair, and Sherry took one look at her and said, "Oh, no. What happened?"

Instead of answering, Cora focused on Davey, who looked more and more like Matty every day, especially when she was so pissed. The fact he kept playing didn't help. "So, when are you and Matty toddling back off to Europe?"

He ended the line of music before answering. "Next week, I think. Why?" Then he continued right where he left off.

She turned in her chair to fully face him and felt the heat of her anger claw its way up her back. “Are we just distractions to you? Are the Foote-Steppe kids easy targets or something?”

Sherry gasped and swatted her. “*Cora*!”

Davey frowned at her as he lowered his chanter. “What are ye yammering about, lass?”

Cora crossed her arms and sulked in her chair, so pissed at the MacKenzie men she couldn’t stand it.

“There you are.” Cora looked up as Carla dropped down beside her and frowned out over the dance floor. She waved her hand at all the people dancing. “What the hell’s going on out there?”

All looked normal. “What do you mean?”

“Did you say something?”

“About what?” Cora had no idea what Carla was getting at.

“What’s this about needing a new vet in town?”

She thought for a second. “Oh. My mom’s boss needs to retire. Like, ten years ago. She said the hospital’s been looking for a managing vet to take over. Why?”

“I introduced myself to three people, and now everyone’s asking me if I’m the new vet in town.” Carla looked up and smiled as Gunner touched her shoulder and handed her a mixed drink, and he sat beside her, nursing a beer.

Cora pointed to her sister and turned to her friend. “Carla, this is my sister, Sherry. Sherry, my boss, Carla.” Then she introduced Gunner and Davey.

Sherry’s smile was warm and genuine. “So nice to meet you. I don’t get to meet many other doctors in town, especially ones as crazy as I am.”

“My reputation has preceded me, I see.”

“Yup,” Cora answered.

Sherry smiled and leaned over the table. “You ever consider running your own business?”

"Not until ten minutes ago."

The comment made Gunner nudge her with his elbow. "It would be a great adventure."

"No more adventures."

"A *safe* adventure."

"Startups require money. Lots of it. Opposite of *safe*."

He held her eyes as he swigged his beer. "If it clears federal regs, we might be getting it. *Lots* of it."

Cora watched something register in Carla's eyes as she and Gunner silently conversed. Then to Cora she said, "I could look into it."

One of the neighbors came up to Cora, excited. "Cora! I couldn't believe it when your mom said you were here. Is it true?"

"Is what true?"

Instead of answering, the woman looked at Carla. "Are you the new vet? And Cora's your tech?"

"Cora's been my tech for four years. On Long Island. Where we work."

"But you're coming here, right? With Cora? We love her and her mother. Do you treat dogs? What about cats? Mine needs a dental, but I don't have a nearby doctor I trust, and Dr. Foote only does farm animals. Is it true you worked emergency? They say you're really good under pressure. You seem nice. Do you have your calendar on you? Can I schedule an appointment?"

Cora and Carla exchanged looks for a second before Carla looked up at the woman and smiled. "Thank you, that's very sweet. And I'm sorry, but I'm not allowed to discuss matters surrounding the hospital while negotiation is underway."

"Oh. Oh! I understand. So nice to meet you. Love the dress." She bustled off, waving three of her friends with her. Cora watched them all duck their heads to gossip.

"You lied to her."

But Carla and Gunner held some kind of silent conversation, searching each others' eyes. Finally Carla asked him, "Should we?"

"We could. We'll probably get the cash."

"Nice, small town."

"You could choose your own practice manager," he pointed out.

She rolled her eyes and nodded. "Great schools."

"Days, like me, not nights." Then Gunner's eyes darted to Cora's. "And Cora's family's all here."

"Wait." Cora held out her hands between them. "Are you seriously thinking about this? Buying the hospital?"

Carla met Gunner's eyes and shrugged before answering her question. "Bottom line, I don't really want to go back home. Ever. And I know Karrolin doesn't either. Gunner will be transferring to Syracuse anyway, which is only twenty minutes away from here." Now she faced Cora. "You married to Long Island? Your studio?"

"Um, no and hell no." Another seed of hope tumbled inside her. It would be great to be so close to her family again. But it still didn't answer the question of what to do with Matty.

Chapter 27

Aya, he'd disappointed his wife yet again. As Cora shrugged off his arms and made her way off the dance floor, Matty reached to stop her, but a familiar jingle told him of an incoming call. He fished into his sporran for it and saw his boss was ringing him. "Hello?" He plugged his finger into his free ear and stepped towards the door, away from the band.

"Matteu, great news! We've added on to the Romance Tour. We've sold out in every venue, with waiting lists for cancellations that are long enough to support another full show. We're booking each city for another two days. We'll just have to crunch getting the band from venue to venue, but we can do it."

Matty looked over at Cora, who was sitting with her sister, boss, and a neighbor woman he recognized, all deep in conversation. He hated that he'd have to tell her he was leaving again after their last conversation, but this was his job. He told himself he'd make more money this way, more money to support his wife, who really needed to understand he did this for her. "That's great."

"I got more. We've added on six more cities, too. We're going into USSR, India, and Hong Kong, and negotiating for eight more venues after that. At this rate, we'll be booked solid for almost eighteen months!"

"What?"

"I know, I know. You can thank me later."

Cora stood up and spun in a circle, then laughed and hugged Carla. Damn it. She was so happy right now, and this would crush her. "Why didna ye tell me sooner?"

"Surprise. Isn't it great?"

Great? "Yeah."

"You don't seem very happy about it."

"No, no. I am. Look, I'm playing for ma in-laws in a minute, so I've got to go. I'll see ye next week."

"No, I need you back tomorrow. We're doing something new with the show, and we all need to rehearse. I've got your tickets waiting for you in Syracuse. Your flight's at seven AM, connecting in Toronto."

He glanced at his phone. Not even ten, but he was used to brutal tour schedules. "Alright, alright. See ye in Edinburgh." He hung up and looked over to Cora.

She was looking at him.

Buggered. He kept his expression neutral and tucked his phone back into his sporran. He looked up and saw her heading his way, and he smiled despite the feeling of dread that churned inside his gut. He'd locked himself into a three-year deal with Peter for a rental property he'd never see. And it hadna dawned on him at the time that Cora would wish to return to Long Island, so having a shop in Skaneateles would be a waste of resources.

Impulsive. He should have waited until he'd given notice, or resigned. He shouldna have jumped at an offer of rental space, especially since no one else had seen the merit in it.

He didna wish to spoil her night with bad news and poor choices, but he didna wish to hide the fact he was leaving on the morrow. When she drew close, he said, "Seems like Carla made ye right jolly."

She grinned. "She's seriously considering buying the veterinary hospital. Wouldn't that be awesome?"

As sure as he stood there, Matty dared brave he heard rightly. "She'd leave Long Island?"

She nodded. "And be working days. Gunner's transferring to Syracuse, and the schools are great here, so Karrolin would be set."

He forced the hopeful words to his maw. "And ye'd be her tech, I'm guessing?"

Now he could see her excitement. "Yeah. I'd be

able to see my family every day."

Matty knew how much she loved her family and spared a soft smile that grew. His wee wife would do anything for them, and Matty needed to be there to help set boundaries. Could this be a sign of Divine intervention? "It would be just as ye want it."

"Yeah. If she can swing it. I guess she and Gunner are coming into some money, so it's a distinct possibility."

Something akin to his chest ripping open made Matty look away. It would be a good month or two to get the shop set up, even longer to gain steady clientele, both impossible if he couldna get home to even finalize paperwork. He should finish this tour, request replacement by the end. But if he'd gotten Cora pregnant, that would leave her alone through her pregnancy and the delivery. He couldna do that to her. He wouldna. But he forced a smile. "That would be great, provided ye doona run yerself into the ground, helping every minute yer here."

She shrugged like her health didna matter in the least. "I've spent my entire life working here, helping the animals. It's what I do."

"Ye doona need to do it every waking minute, lass."

"Well, you were the only one to ever keep me from overexerting myself. If you're not here...." She locked his eyes, daring him to refute her comment.

Buggered. He loved her family, truly, but they didna know when to lean back, when to let her have a day to herself. If he wasna here for her, she'd look a day shy of the grave by the time he returned. His chest squeezed in on him, made it difficult to take a breath, but he stepped close and cupped her cheek in his hand, warming her chilled flesh as he stroked her. "I told ye I'd be here for ye, and I meant it."

She angled her head to eye him. "So... you're staying?"

His chest squeezed out what little air he held. "I

want to."

"But... you're not."

Damn, she read him like a book. "I want to, Cora."

She glanced down to his sporran. "Who called?"

Buggered yet again. "Ma boss."

"And?"

He ripped his fingers through his hair as he scanned the people dancing, happy and oblivious to the pain tearing into him. "He added onto the tour."

She studied him. "That's great."

He couldna meet her eyes. "Aya, would be the most money I'd ever made."

"How long?"

He didna want to tell her.

"How long, Matty?"

He dragged his eyes to hers, but the latent pain he saw there made him look away. "Almost eighteen months."

"I see."

He was sure she did. He couldna find his tongue.

He heard her draw in a long breath. "I wonder if I can get a Morning After pill on New Year's Eve?"

His hand lashed out to grip her elbow. "No, lass. Doona do this. I canna lose another child."

"Why not?" She yanked her arm out of his grasp. "So one day I can prop our kid in front of the television and say, 'Look, there's your father. Don't blink or change the channel, might be the last time you ever see him?'"

The reality of losing a second child, this one to scorn, dragged tears to his eyes. "Let me figure this out, Cora. Please."

"There's nothing to figure out. I'll always be your second. You've just made sure of it."

"That's na true."

"Safe travels," she tossed over her shoulder as she walked away.

Chapter 28

Her words chewed at him as he unfolded his pipes. Gnawed away. Burrowed holes from gullet to gizzard. He didna want to go, to leave. He didna want to risk losing Cora, *again*, to prove himself. Hadna he already showed the world the type of man he'd become? Hadna he earned accolades and adulation galore wherever he inflated his bag?

Aya, he had. He felt no desire to step back on that plane, but perhaps, if he pretended to try, at least for another week or two, he'd be able to bow out, to resign, with a clear conscience. Beside him, Davey unfolded his own pipes, assembling the bass drone as they readied for their turn this evening.

Across the barn, in the wee farthest corner by the bar, Cora nursed a cola, her arms tight about her, her sister and boss flanking. And as people moved about, he saw her mom, and Nana. And as he draped his drones along his shoulder, her Da looked up, accusing eyes boring into his.

Buggered. Matty didna need to know that his welcome would expire in one hour. The band was wrapping up, and he and Davey were to play the next half hour. Then, from eleven-thirty to midnight, the projection TV would simulcast the festivities in NYC.

The ball was in his court.

The ball was also dropping.

So were his chances of making this aright.

He and Davey were dressed in full regalia, the only difference the colors of their plaids. Matty wore the pattern created especially for the Bagpipe Barons, while Davey wore clan MacKenzie colors.

Matty missed his home plaid.

He adjusted the colorful tassels and ribbons on his

pipes, his set far more flashy than Davey's, and not just because his cost one thousand dollars more. His belonged to the Barons, and as Master Piper, Matty's set stood out.

Davey leaned toward him. "Starting with *Kilworth Hills?"*

"Aya, as planned. Then *Scotland the Brave* and *Skye Boat.*" He eyed Davey as he fidgeted with his pipes. "Nervous?"

"Na at all. I love playing for the gathered masses."

The admission made Matty snap his head around. "Aya?"

"Aya. Tell the band to stop their yammering already; I'm ready to take stage."

It was then Matty recalled a clause in his contract, one that might be the answer to his prayers this day. Warmth welled inside him as the resolution to his problems presented itself to him. He grinned with his thoughts and waited while the band vacated the platform. When clear, Matty headed toward the mike. "Hello, everyone, and welcome to the Foote-Steppe annual New Year's Eve ball. I'm Matteu MacKenzie, of the Bagpipe Barons, and—"

The audience went plum barmy, and he had to wait a full minute 'til he could speak above them. "And this here is ma cousin, Davey MacKenzie. For those who doona know, that lovely lass in the corner, Cora, is ma beautiful wife."

Cora flashed a perfunctory smile and raised a hand, then went back to sulking. Matty didna mistake the way her Da rested a heavy hand about her shoulders, one intended to keep her there.

Away from the likes of him.

He met Davey's eyes, and together they struck in their drones, playing *Kilworth Hills* and marching in place in perfect tandem. And although he scanned the audience as trained, his eyes drifted continually to Cora and her family. Now, both her parents hovered about her, their postures bordering on intimidation. Were they talking her out of his arms?

He couldna do this. He couldna play his routine as if naught were amiss. He let the last note die out before he crunched his pipes to his side to make them whine, earning a smart glance from Davey for breaking protocol. He stepped towards the mike again. "I've something special for ye this evening. Cora, would ye come here, lass? Right up front. Come now. Ye can do it. I won' bite."

He noticed a lot of the ladies hoped he *would* bite, but Matty focused his attention on his wife as she shrugged off her parents' hands and wove through the parting audience.

She looked haggard, torn, and once more Matty knew he'd done this to her. She looked as gaunt as the moment she walked into Nana's house last week, with all the weight of the world atop her shoulders, bearing down. He held her eyes and fished into his sporran. He tugged out two sheets of paper and handed the one with the music notes on it to Davey. "Will ye play this on yer chanter for me?"

He glanced at it. "Sure." But confusion lingered in Davey's gaze as he stepped off the stage and pulled his chanter from his pipe case and returned with the smaller instrument raised to play. Then he motioned to Sherry, who stepped forth and held the paper aloft for him to read it.

Nerves shot through Matty, and not just because he was deviating from the plan. He studied Cora as she stood inches away from him, eyes hard but hurting, arms crossed but not to the point of looking pissed, only awkward as she stood front and center, called there by a man who broke her heart.

Again.

He knew what Cora wanted, knew what it would take to win her back, and with Papa Bear ready to toss him out on his arse, and a manager waiting for him in

Edinburgh in barely eight hours, he had no time for leisure. He held her eyes, then addressed the crowd. "I'd like to share a song that ma wife helped me write."

He watched the confusion play about her features, and he smiled down at her. "Aya, ye did, and ye didna know it. But I wrote it for ye, lass. Months ago, but I kept getting stuck. It took yer help to finish it. This song is for ye, Cora, in so many ways." With racing heart and damp palms, Matty nodded once to Davey, who raised the practice chanter to his lips to play. Matty held the mike in his hands and locked eyes with his wife. As soon as his cue came, Matty licked his dry lips and sang.

I've journeyed all around this world
I've seen love in every land.
In India, the men walk ahead
The French kiss their lady's hand.

English men court their ladies by rules
The Spaniards make women swoon,
Italians toast their lovers with wine
The Celts make love under the moon.

While all of these are pleasant indeed
None of them mention their hearts
I canna live without ye, ma dear.
My life has been torn apart.

Ma love is strong, ma heart's been wrung.
The errors I've made, I've flung.
Mo chridhe, mon coeur,mi corazón,
You're ma heart in every tongue.
You're ma heart in every tongue.

Tears filled her eyes as she watched him sing, and her sister lowered the sheaves of paper to stare at her. The crowd clapped and cheered, but for once Matty cared naught for it. With baited breath, he waited for Cora's reply.

She blinked again, then dashed a tear away.

Nodded once to him and turned away, worrying her lip all the while.

He'd granted one of her four requests, yet it did nothing.

His chest tightened; he looked at Davey, inflated his bag, and once Davey had his own pipes inflated and ready, they moved on to *Scotland the Brave,* playing a rousing march when Matty's soul desperately cried for a retreat.

Chapter 29

Despite the tears leaking from her eyes, despite the soulful gaze of her sister and the hardened one of her Dad, all Cora could think was *he sang to me.* She had been drunk, but she distinctly recalled telling him she'd forgive him if he ever got up on stage and sang to her.

And he did. For her. For the first time in his life.

In front of everyone she knew.

She shrugged off Sherry's gentle hand on her shoulder and slipped through the crowd and their curious expressions. She didn't want to make eye contact. Didn't want to see their elation at witnessing a serenade, or concern at her tepid reaction to being the recipient of one. She headed to the dessert table and stared at the cookies, cakes, fondue, cupcakes and pies, all picked over.

Her stomach clenched.

Scotland the Brave filled the air, and a few discordant notes pulled her attention.

Matty missed a few notes.

Matty never missed notes.

Her heart tugged her back to the stage, but fear kept her rooted.

More tears came, harder to stop, harder to hide. She picked up two cookies and set them on her plate, not having an appetite but needing to be away from the crowd. As she considered which pie she should slice into, someone joined her side.

Carla.

"I'm pretty sure I'd strap any man who serenaded me to my bed and ride him 'til I couldn't stand."

Cora resorted to their old banter rather than face the truth. "Slut."

"Beeotch."

"Skank."

"Cocktease."

That comment made Cora look up. "Am I?"

"Don't know. Are you?"

Cora set down her plate, the sight of food nauseating her. It hurt to swallow, but she had to in order to keep down her stomach contents. "He asked for three things."

"What three things?"

A deep breath. "Three things that would guarantee his forgiveness."

"Let me guess: serenading you was one."

"I added a fourth."

Carla glanced back at the stage. "Was that it?"

She nodded. "Yeah."

"So, he's working backwards. Okay. And I'm guessing it's working, or you wouldn't be standing here, all alone and actually crying. You. Crying."

"Fuck you."

Carla chuckled, then leaned her hip on the table to face her. "I'm not the one who's fucked."

Cora sensed the smile, even though she didn't look up to see it.

"Seriously, he left you bleeding in a hospital room, and all you got was pissed. For an entire year. Now, the thought of him coming back does this to you? Not for nothing, but...."

Cora stared at her plate of cookies, mute to reply.

"So, what's next?"

Cora glanced down the long line of caterer's tables to dry her eyes. "Today, Dad told me he'd pay for my divorce."

"Today? Seriously?"

One nod. "And Mom wants me to move back home. I guess word got out that I lost my job, so now she wants to hire me to take care of the horses."

"You have a job. With me. It's still yours, Cora, and you know there's no one I'd rather share deep moments over rotten bowels with than you."

She felt a smile bubble up. "I know."

"But you want to be with Matty."

She turned to meet Carla's eyes. "I've never stopped loving him, Carla. Ever."

"Which is why you never had any interest in dating anyone, even the hot drug rep who always asked for you."

"He was gay."

"He was definitely not gay." Carla grabbed a cookie off Cora's plate and bit into it. "Mm. So, again, what's next?"

Might as well spill it. She pushed the plate closer to Carla, then ticked them off on her fingers. "I asked him to pay back all the debt he stuck me with, which was like, eighteen grand. And to choose me over his music. For once and for all."

"That's only two. What's the third?"

Now she felt her cheeks prickle with heat. "Hypnotize me into forgetting everything."

Carla lowered her cookie. "You didn't."

"I was mad, okay?"

Carla tugged out her cell and looked at the time. "Well, unless a hypnotist shows up in the next forty minutes, I don't see that one happening."

"Or the others." Now she felt more tears brewing. "And he's leaving. For eighteen months this time."

"Really?"

"Yeah."

"Ouch."

"Still think he's worth it?"

Now Carla's expression softened. "Doesn't matter what I think; it's what your heart thinks that matters. And I'm guessing your answer is yes."

The astute comment made Cora touch her belly.

"What if I'm pregnant?"

They locked eyes for a long moment. "Are you asking me to spay you?"

Cora smiled and looked down. "No."

"Good."

After another long moment, Cora asked, "So what should I do?"

"Waste not, want not," Carla said as she took the remaining cookie from Cora's plate and bit into it with relish, and Cora wasn't sure if that was supposed to be her advice or not. But then Carla swallowed and met her eyes to continue, and Cora was surprised to see the glisten of tears. "I almost lost everyone dear to me this week. Life is short. Nothing is guaranteed. I know how much he means to you, and you to him. Give him a chance."

"Another chance?"

"Do you have a choice?"

"According to Dad, yes."

Carla opened her mouth to reply, but turned when Gunner rested his hand on her shoulder. He asked her to dance, and Carla shared a warm smile with him. As he pulled her to the dance floor, Carla tossed a concerned look over her shoulder to Cora. "It's not up to him."

No. It wasn't. It didn't matter, though. No one could make this decision but her.

Chapter 30

When the last note played on his pipes, Matty lifted his elbow from the bag and did his best to share an appreciative smile with the audience, but truly his thoughts were for Cora. Where had his wife gone off to? Last he'd seen her, she been puttering about the dessert table with her boss, but one Double D later, she was gone to his gaze.

Victory shone in her Da's eyes, but that only strengthened Matty's resolve to make things aright with his wife. He pressed the air from his bag, the whine annoying now as never it had been. He disassembled his bass drone and tucked his instrument back into its case. Though people tried to stop him, clap him upon the back, beg for autographs, he excused himself best he could and pushed past, scanning for Cora. "Have ye seen ma wife?" he asked all, to no avail.

No one knew where she'd gone off to.

That meant, most likely, the horse barn.

He rifled through the hanging coats and didna see hers, so he donned his own and marched into the bracing air, his path as sure as the crunch of his soles against the snow. He tugged open the barn door, only to be greeted by pitch darkness.

No light, anywhere.

He listened, but not a keening to be heard, not a breath not belonging to a horse stirred the air.

Raucous noise from the hay barn made him turn in time to see her Da emerging, and by the stance of him, Matty knew he meant to kick him out on his arse, twenty minutes too early to prove his intent and accomplishment. He tugged the barn door closed and headed to the house, his steps faster, his intent purer than that of her Da.

Matty stomped off at the entrance, shaking the mire

from his boots, then dashed up the stairs as silently as possible to their room.

Dark.

Her duffle and Herbie remained as they had been.

She wasna packing up as yet, then.

He raced downstairs as silently as his boots would allow, not wishing to wake the wee children tucked away in their sacks in the windowed corner of the hallway. He looked through the front door window and saw her car still parked, a foot of snow atop it. Her Da exited the horse barn and turned to the house, making Matty duck away from the glass lest he see. Matty glanced about himself, then called her name in a hushed whisper, receiving only silence in reply.

He hastened to the backdoor and saw a clear path through the fresh snow, the doorknob unlocked. He followed the path with his eyes and knew where she journeyed.

The clearing in the woods.

The place they first made love.

He tucked out the door and tugged it closed in his wake, the snow tumbling over the tops of his boots. As it spilled into the gaps and melted along his socks, Matty feared that Cora had journeyed this way in naught but her dress shoes. Concern for her welfare sped his path, shoving through the snow faster until both his knees and thighs braced from the chill of it.

Scotsman or no, no man in a kilt wished to travel thus. He grimaced with worry and marshaled on. He broke into a stuttering jog, trying to catch up to her. As he crested a hillock, he caught the barest glance of movement, a dark shadow against shadows. He wished he had brought a torch— flashlight, he corrected— but perhaps stealing up on her would be best.

She wouldna run if she didna knew he pursued her.

There. He spied her dark coat, the flash of her red

dress, and he redoubled his pace.

The crunch of snow must have carried to her, because she turned then to face him.

"Cora."

"Matty, don't."

"Cora, stop."

She did, bless her heart, and he raced to her side. Her frigid hands he collected in hers. "Lass, it's beyond freezing out here. What're ye doing?"

With feeble effort, she tried to pull away. "I needed to be alone."

"Aya, I know. But I canna let ye. Na here, na at night. Na in those clothes." But he leaned closer and breathed heat onto her hands. "But it warms me to think ye were headed to our spot."

"How did you know?"

"Seriously?"

She blinked and looked away.

He couldna lose her, na again. He collected her hand tighter in his own. "Come, lass. While we're here, I wish to show ye something."

"I thought you didn't want me outside."

"I don't. But what's one more minute if we're both to die of hypothermia, eh?"

She huffed out a breath, the gray pillow of it hanging in the air.

Emboldened, Matty turned to face fresh snow and marched perpendicular to where Cora had headed, across the top of the hillock instead of beyond it, gritting his teeth as more snow tumbled into his boots. He went one more hill and stopped, turning her to overlook Skaneateles Lake.

"This is Moses' land."

He smiled at the childhood name they used to describe the old man who owned this land. "Aya. But na for long."

"What do you mean?"

He hadna yet earned the fullness of her forgiveness, but perhaps this would tip her favorably in his direction. He dropped his aching fingers to the clasp on his sporran and met her eyes. “Remember I told ye I wanted to show ye a piece of paper?”

“Yeah?”

“I know ye doona yet forgive me, and now I’ve gone ma new touring schedule has gone and blundered things worse than before, but I want ye to know what I’ve been about.” He fished into his sporran until he found the paper he had folded over and over, then pulled it out. A sliver of moon above offered little light, but he did have his cell on him. Once he managed to open the paper to its fullness, he shone the light upon it.

“What is this?”

“Preapproval from the bank. Ye asked me to pay back ma debts.”

“You did that. Through Nana.”

“Aya. And I’ve made money enough I can offer ye a home, Cora.”

He watched a small furrow appear on her uncovered head. “So, why are we on Moses’ land?”

“Because I’ve been in correspondence with him over these last few months. He’s willing to sell us a wee bit of his property. Property which I can afford to build on, according to this slip of paper. Say the word, lass, and I’ll make it happen.”

She looked up at him in stark disbelief. “Here? Lakeview property? Us?”

He nodded. “Right near yer family. We can even keep our wee clearing right as it is. If ye’ll take me back.”

She sucked in a breath and looked away, teeth chattering. “I’m freezing.”

Too much, too fast, and Matty felt as deflated as his pipes in their case, but he knew he’d ticked off two of her four requests. “Aya, lass. Let’s get ye inside.” He claimed her hand in his and tugged her to his wake, plowing his way back to the house and taking the brunt of the frosted hillocks into his boots.

The door opened easily, and they shucked their footwear inside and padded their wet feet across the floor. Matty listened intently but heard no sign of her Da. Perhaps he'd gone to his own home for the night, a wistful thought tickled inside his brain. Emboldened, hope thick in his voice, he asked, "Fireplace?"

"No. I might be frostbitten. Let's get upstairs."

No one had come back from the hay barn yet, but Cora didn't even care. Her feet stumbled up the steps, her teeth chattered, her fingers clenched both the handrail and her soggy skirts without sensation. Stupid. Fucking stupid move, running outside into the field in a dress. What the fuck was she thinking?

She hadn't been thinking; she'd been worrying. About losing Matty, saying goodbye. As usual, Matty rescued her from herself, her blindness to her own actions when she became this overwhelmed. They entered the bedroom, and Cora headed straight to the tub and ran tepid water, taking a minute to plug it to fill up a few inches. She unzipped her dress and let it puddle on the cold tiles, not caring about it or her near nudity right now, only caring about getting warm. She folded a thick bath towel and laid it along the edge, but leaned over and slurped the water with her mouth to test the temperature, since her hands and feet were all numb.

"Thirsty, lass?"

"Checking temp." She spat it out and got up. Then Cora took two hand towels from the cupboard and handed one to Matty before stepping into the tub and sitting on the folded towel. She dipped the small one in the water to hold. Matty peeled off his flashes and tall socks and joined her on the towel, hissing when his feet met the water.

"It's too hot."

Her teeth still chattered. "It's actually cold. Let me know when you feel it." She reached over and turned off the spout. Four inches was plenty deep to stave off imminent damage.

He dipped his small towel to hold, too, wrapping it around his hands. "Plum barmy, lass, running off like that."

She didn't look at him, even though he waited for her to face him.

"You could have died."

"You, too."

"Nah," he chuckled. "I'm a Scotsman."

She noticed he still wore his kilt, though the edges were far darker from the melting snow. "Gonna take that off?"

"You saucy little vixen," he said as he winked. "I figured ye were only luring me out of doors to get me good and naked."

She thought her face might crack with smiling, but she braved one. "Wrong again."

"Holy Mother of God," Matty said as he shot to his feet. He danced his way out of the tub. "It's bloody freezing!"

Sensation hadn't returned to Cora's extremities, but she managed an envious look to Matty. "Told you so."

"Ye, lass? Nothing yet?"

She shook her head and dipped her towel again, then bent and wrapped her fingers around her toes. She could feel the pressure but not the temperature. So she pinched them and felt the pain. "I can feel deep pain, so I think it's returning."

"Hot cocoa, lass?"

She looked back at him. "How about broth?"

He nodded and headed downstairs. Within a minute of him leaving, Cora's numbness had subsided, the frigid temperature drawing an equally vocal curse from her lips. She drained the tub of the cold water and started filling it for a nice, warm bath. When Matty stepped into the tiled room with two steaming mugs, he grinned. "Seduction it is, I see." He placed the mugs on the sink counter and braced her arms, testing her skin for heat.

"Let me guess: two degrees shy of the grave?"

He grinned. "Na, lass, but mebbe ten." He glanced at the tub, then raised an eyebrow at her. "We have the whole house to ourselves."

She nodded, too cold to even think about seduction. She shucked her panties and bra and hissed as she stepped into the tub. She shimmied down into the soapy water, bracing as the heat sizzled against her skin. "Holy shit."

"Why'd you make it so hot, then?" Matty undid his kilt and yanked off his dress shirt, then grabbed the mugs and stepped into the tub behind her.

"It's not. It just feels it."

"Drinking to test the temp again?"

She grinned, then leaned back against his warm chest. She accepted the mug he handed her and let the heavenly aroma of home fill her nose. She heard Matty sip his own mug, then rest it on the corner of the tub. "We havena done this in years."

"I know. Standup showers suck."

"Never again." He wrapped his arms around her middle and drew her close, burying his nose in her hair. "Ye smell good enough to eat."

"That's the chicken broth."

"It's na the chicken broth."

She smiled. "The caterer's food, then. Chocolate sauce." She took another sip, then closed her eyes, settling against Matty's chest. Soon his hands cupped water on her arms and shoulders, trying to warm her. "Comfy, lass?"

She nodded, eyes still closed, but she perched her mug on the tub and settled back.

He cupped more water on her shoulders, trailing his fingers down along her erect nipples before cupping more water onto her again. His motions became automatic: scoop, splash, tease. Scoop, splash, tease. She relaxed against the feel of his hands tickling her breasts, his deep breath stirring her hair, his strong legs bracketing her own.

Comfort. That's what Matty brought out of her, to her. Comfort.

Though she tried, she couldn't remember a moment all year when her mind turned blissfully off, enjoying nothing grander than a long soak and a hot mug.

His fingers tweaked her nipples, and the slow curl of heat deep in her belly awakened. Eyes still closed, Cora guided one of Matty's hands lower, under the water, until he found her thatch of curls. She heard his low chuckle as he slid one of his fingers along her seam.

She sighed and relaxed further into his chest, her shoulders dropping back, her knees parting to his touch.

God, he made her feel so good. She tipped her head back, and Matty stroked his whiskers along her neck, drawing her hair away to expose her throat to him. He pressed a hot kiss there, long, slow, and she felt his mouth work her skin long enough she knew he'd leave a mark.

Cheers carried from outside, noisemakers blaring, and the familiar *Auld Lang Syne* could be heard being sung by a hundred ebullient drunks. As Matty snuggled her tighter to his chest, one hand buried in her thighs, the other thumbing her nipple, she whispered, "Happy New Year."

His lips never left her throat, but he murmured, "Happy New Year, *mo chridhe.*"

She never wanted this moment to end. "What's next?"

His fingers slipped in and out of her, slowly, tantalizingly slow. "What do ye mean?"

What did she mean? She rallied her thoughts. "I'm leaving in the morning. What about you? Are you staying here with your parents?"

"I'll be seeing them soon enough. The bigger question is: what do *ye* want me to do?"

A simple question she could have answered easily a few days ago laced with snark and bitterness, but now, after all he'd shown her tonight, asking him to stay— to not return to his job— seemed downright selfish. Her throat tightened, and the words *stay with me* hovered on her tongue, but despite giving a grand fight, she swallowed them.

Hard.

Her fingers stroked up the dark hair on his forearms, loving the feel of his skin under hers. God, how she wanted him to stay! Again and again he came to her rescue, saving her from everything that distressed her—everything but himself. Bottom line, Cora loved him too much to keep fighting him on this. "I want you to do what makes you happy."

He chuckled and released her to stand. "Easy enough." He grabbed her arm and drew her to her feet, then snatched the bath sheet and wrapped it about her, drying her so thoroughly and slowly that heat made her skin tingle with his touch.

He wrapped her tight in the towel and scrubbed himself dry with his own, then scooped her into his arms and carried her to the bed. He shucked the covers and lay her down, then peeled back the towel to gaze on her nakedness. A crooked grin warmed his eyes. "Doing *ye* will make me verra happy."

It hurt to smile, but Cora welcomed him into her embrace.

Chapter 31

Aya, her sweet words took a grand toll on her, in truth, for Matty could see the angst in her eyes, but now he knew he had one final card to play, one last swan song to make his wee wife understand the depths to which he had gone and would go for her.

Their joining this time was slow, rocking. She was the most precious thing to come into his life, and he wansa about to lose her when his alarm struck in the next few hours. He gathered her close in his arms, drawing her fair off the mattress, wanting their bodies to have nary a pocket of air betwixt or between them.

Dampness from the tub soon morphed into slick sweat as he rocked into and against her. He took his time, not needing to rush any of these wondrous moments granted to them by a kinder God than any he could imagine. His mouth rarely left hers, his hands wished only to cleave to her, his heart wished to pound itself straight from his chest fair into her own.

Her heels locked about his thighs, and she angled her hips to his, but he didna want to rush this. He smoothed the damp hair from her forehead and nuzzled her jaw, and she shivered out a breath. “Whiskers.”

He smiled and brushed his rough jaw along the width of her shoulders, making her sigh. He continued to slip up and down atop her, rubbing along her clit, stimulating her without thrusting. She bared her throat to him, breathing faster and faster, and her arousal undid him. When her body clenched and squeezed his, Matty gave in, letting his soul pour into her.

He rested his forehead against her own, their panting in perfect tandem.

Her body folded underneath his, spent and tiny in

his arms.

"I love you, Matty."

He pressed his lips to her earlobe to kiss. "*Mo chridhe,* I love ye with all ma heart."

When his alarm beeped a scant two hours later, Matty startled, pushing off from Cora as he reached for his cell to silence it. She sucked in a sleepy breath and faced him. "It's 4 AM. Why the alarm?"

He hadna told her, but he thought what he had planned would be better shown. He peeled away from her body, feeling the icy brace of air against skin that had been plastered together all the night. He kissed her swollen lips and stood. Turned on the lamp. "Plane leaves at seven."

She blinked against the stab of light and squinted up at him. "What?"

He sat beside her and cupped her cheek, stilling her to face him. He held her eyes for a long moment. "I need ye to trust me, Cora. Trust me as never ye've done. Can ye do that?"

He watched the war in her eyes, and her voice squeaked. "So you're going? Leaving?"

"Yes or no, Cora? Will ye trust me on this? Trust in us?"

Her lips twisted as tears welled in her eyes. "Eighteen months, Matty?"

"Cora," he warned, then he softened his expression. "I've shown ye a year's worth of good intentions in the last twelve hours. Will ye no let me finish ma plan?"

He watched her suck in her bottom lip and turn into his palm, away from his fathoming eyes. He waited, breath held, for a yea or nay from her. "Nana says I need more faith."

"Now is a prime time for ye to spare me a wee bit. Will ye, lass?"

With a long pause leading to a little hiccup, she nodded.

"Aright, then. I'll na let ye down, wife. Get dressed. I'll need ye to take us to the airport, if ye will."

He heard the sniffle and turned his back on her. All for the greater good, he told himself, fighting his better urge to comfort her against his actions yet again. But he forced his feet to carry him into the bathroom, where he cupped water over his unruly topknot and toweled off.

He looked a wretched sight, but he didna want to linger overlong on it. If all went aright, he'd prove his full intent to Cora for end and for good.

He rummaged through his duffle and tugged on jeans and a sweater. Cora had donned similar attire and bent to gather Herbie's belongings. She didna face him but asked, "Syracuse airport, I'm guessing?"

"Aya."

She inhaled a shaky breath and nodded once. "Carla's expecting me to be at work at midnight, so I might as well head home."

He said nothing to contradict her.

He carried her bag and Herbie's supplies, and Cora slung Herbie's carrier strap over her shoulder. As they slipped down the darkened stairs, the light at the front door was on. Davey and Sherry were there, one packed and dressed for travel, one in sweats.

Matty took charge. "Cora's driving us to the airport. Ready, coz?"

Davey nodded and collected his belongings. "Aya. It'll be good to get home." Then he looked to Sherry. "Although, I've gotten a bit of thirst for travel, I'll admit."

Sherry smiled and looked down, then up at him through lowered lids. Then she faced Cora. "You leaving, too?"

Cora nodded. "Back to work at midnight."

"Yuck. I mean, that's great."

She inhaled a deep breath and nodded but said naught.

Before anyone could spoil his intentions, Matty stretched his arms for Sherry, who stepped into his embrace. "Great seeing ye, sis."

"You, too, Matty." She gripped him tight. "Safe travels."

"Aya, ye too, if ye head into Africa again, Glory knows why."

She laughed and pulled away, then turned her gaze to Davey. Matty watched as they stared at each other for what seemed to him an awkward moment, then Davey tugged her to his chest and squeezed.

No words passed between them, and both seemed hesitant to meet the other's gaze as they parted. He would have devoted more energy to their status had Cora not shuffled. He tugged on his coat and pulled Cora's off the hook for her. "Off we go."

Sherry and Cora gripped tightly to one another, and Matty let them be as he scooped up their belongings with full intent and met his wife's gaze. She gasped and darted off to the back room, then returned a moment later with their footwear from last night dangling in grocery bags. "Almost forgot." Then she looked back to the kitchen. "Left a note for Nana, too."

"Aya, good thinking. Thank ye."

They donned their winter gear and slipped out into the bracing air, pillows of fog puffing from their lips as they trudged to her car.

"You want to drive?" Cora dangled her keys at him.

"No, lass. I'll let ye be in control of the driving this time." He didna want a repeat of the worst day of his life. Too much was at stake.

"Great," she muttered, but Matty paid her no heed, na wishing any conflict on this of all days. He and Davey brushed off her car while Cora warmed it up, then Matty joined her upfront as Davey took to the back. They headed east on 175, the traffic nonexistent this morning. "Will I see you again?"

"Of course."

"When?"

"Sooner than ye'd like, I wager."

She parted him a beleaguered glance, but Matty tugged off a glove and slipped his hand around her nape. He gave her a gentle squeeze that turned into a soothing massage. "Trust me, *mo chridhe*. Please."

He could tell by the way she bit her lip that she wished mightily to argue but didna, which made Matty love her all the more. Whether from having a witness to their conversation in the car, or beholden to her own vow to trust him, he cared naught, only grateful she granted him this quiet opportunity free of accusation.

Davey, bless his soul, broke the tension. "I hopped on the Barons' website last night. Do ye know they're looking for a step-in?"

He nodded. "Aya. Siobhán's babe is due mid-February. Already it presses up on her lungs. She willna be able to play much longer." He turned to meet Davey's eyes. "Ye're a right fine player, coz." He winked and grinned. "For a green Highland lad."

An indignant gasp met his taunt. "I'm na a green Highland lad. I could teach ye a fine thing or two about pipes."

They chuckled.

The majority of the trip passed in silence, Matty focusing on the thoughts that must be tumbling in Cora's mind as she focused on the plowed roads. Soon enough they took the airport exit. Cora veered towards drop-off, but Matty pointed to short-term parking. "I'll cover the fees."

"But Herbie's in the car."

"I'll carry him in." He met her eyes. "Come in with me, lass."

He watched her blink fast and swallow, then turn

into the parking garage and pull into a vacant slot. The guys carried their luggage, and Matty slung Herbie to his shoulder as well. They dashed across the asphalt into the elevator and headed to the main gate, where Matty drew Cora into line with them.

"Wait." She balked and looked at him. "You can't possibly think I'm going overseas with you, right? I don't even have a passport. And Herbie's carrier's not airline approved!"

He granted her a quelling look, complete with raised eyebrow, and he watched Cora nod and settle. Aya, a right fine prick he was being, but he didna want her to fuss so close to the finish line. As they got to the main counter, Matty presented his ticket and passport to the woman in a smart suit, then pointed to his cousin. "I'm in a wee bit of a quandary," he told the ticketing agent as he faced his wife. "I canna leave ma pregnant wife, but I'm a member of the Bagpipe Barons, and I need to send ma verra talented cousin in ma stead." He pointed to Davey.

Cora snapped her gaze to him.

The agent's eyes lit up in recognition. "Oh, my God." Then she composed herself and smiled. "I saw you when you played in Paris. I was on my honeymoon." And she granted a warm smile to all of them, and to Cora said, "Congratulations."

Cora smiled back, then turned curious eyes to Matty.

He turned back to business. "I need to give up ma seat, but make sure ma cousin gets it. The troop is meeting in Edinburgh today. Can ye help a Scotsman out?"

She grinned. "Let me see what I can do."

While she tapped away at her keyboard, Matty held Cora's eyes. His wife battled between smiling and crying, worrying away at her bottom lip until all he could think about was nibbling on it instead of letting her do honors.

"There," the agent proclaimed. "I just need ID," she

said and turned to Davey.

"Aya," he grinned, smiling bright eyes on Matty. "It's about time the world got a fine view of Davey MacKenzie."

"Ye'll always fall second to Matteu," he joked. "But ye look close enough that the hopeful will think yer me up there."

"I can tell the difference," the agent said, making Matty grin. She glanced around and shoved a slip of paper at him. "Autograph?" she whispered.

"Ma pleasure." He glanced at her nametag and wrote her name, then signed his with a giant *Thank Ye* on it, making her beam. She quickly washed away her glee and settled a bright but professional smile upon Davey. "Please place your luggage on the scale."

"Wait." Matty opened his pipe case and stared at the plaid made especially for the Bagpipe Barons. The fancy tassels. The last fourteen months of his life. "Ye'll need these, lad."

Davey caught his breath. "I get the master's pipes?"

"Ye'll need it to lead them."

"I won't be a step-in?"

"Na from the front."

But Davey frowned, cocked his head. "Won't I need to audition?"

"Na, lad. I remembered a clause in ma contract last night. It says I can choose ma own replacement, should the need arise. Yer born to this, Davey. Ye'll knock 'em all dead."

Davey stood taller, his eyes bright. They clasped hands, then leaned shoulder to shoulder and thumped each other heartily on the back.

"Safe travels, Davey. I'm taking the MacKenzie pipes." He grinned and snatched Davey's case, daring his cousin to stop him.

"Best plaid in the world."

"Aya. I know." He held the case to his chest and patted it.

They nodded goodbye, and Davey set his luggage on the scale as Matty drew Cora out of the line. They watched Davey raise his hand in parting as he headed for TSA screening, and before they left the lobby, Cora pulled Matty to a halt.

"You did it." Now the tears fell swift from her eyes. "You chose me over your music."

"Us. Aya. I begged ye to trust me, and ye did. I'll never do ye wrong again."

But now she shook her head. "But you'll never get your house now. The bank won't grant a loan if you're unemployed."

"Our house," he chided, tapping her chin. "And the Barons provided but one source of ma income."

"I don't understand."

"Ye know I write bagpipe tunes, which is faster income than touring. And I repair pipes, as well." He grinned at her. "I'm renting the space from Peter."

"You are?"

"Aya."

She frowned. "But my job's in Long Island."

"Aya. I didna think of that at the time. I saw how happy ye were and wanted to show ye I meant to stay." He licked his own lips as his tone turned doubtful. "Ye think Carla will buy the hospital?"

"I don't know. She's definitely considering it."

He braced her hips and drew her flush to him. "Wherever ye wish to be, Cora, I'll be at yer side."

She fast blinked again. "Thank you. You don't know how much that means to me." But then she looked down. "But you were right; I've always asked you to give up your passion, but never once did you ask me to do the same."

"Na, lass, ye were right to—"

"No, I wasn't." He watched her take a fortifying breath. "I'll take two weeks off. Maybe in the spring or summer. Wherever you want to go, we'll go."

Hope swelled in him, making him lean back. "Truly?"

She seemed nervous, but managed a nod. "I've never flown. I never wanted to leave home, only to be with you. But if you want to take us someplace— maybe a belated honeymoon?— I'll be happy to go, as long as you're with me."

His chest tightened and his vision swam with the sweet words his wife offered. He stabbed his fingers into her mess of hair and locked his lips to hers. Everything he ever felt for her crested in him, every battle, every tender touch, spilled from his heart into his kiss.

People parted around them, crowds came and went, but all Matty cared for was the woman in his arms. When he finally pulled back, her eyes remained closed. He thought of the four things she asked of him, how he had granted three of them to her satisfaction. "All that's left now is to erase your memory of the last year."

Cora's eyes were slow to part, but when she focused on him, she smiled, then looked around, a tease in her eyes. "Why are we at the airport?"

He laughed and kissed her yet again.

This time, when they parted, Cora unzipped her coat. "Is it hot in here, or just me?"

Matty looked at the crowds gathering, the harried travelers, the tearful goodbyes, and felt his heart near to bursting. He flicked open Davey's pipes and stared down at the instrument clothed in his home plaid, feeling connected in a way he hadna since adolescence. He pulled out the pipes and assembled the bass drone, then hefted it to his shoulder. He grinned at her and puffed up his bag, and then struck in the drones.

The soulful retreat reverberated through the chamber, deep and rich, bringing tears to Cora's eyes. People stopped in their hustling to stare openmouthed in awe and reverence, young children plugged their ears, women tugged their men to a stop as they either recognized or were in awe of her husband playing.

Playing a tune that meant the world to her.

Their tune.

He had sung it once, but she couldn't forget the tune that she herself helped create. As she watched and listened, waves of love filled her; the very notes Matty played were filled with his joy, exuberance. It was then she realized: he was serenading her. He'd always been serenading her, just not in the traditional way. Matty filled his bag with love and released it into the air every time his fingers danced on the chanter.

Effortlessly, seamlessly, he flowed into the next tune, a lively march, and Cora stood straighter, holding his eyes, blinking to keep the tears at bay from both her epiphany and Matty's choice of music.

His eyes sparkled at her and his heels lifted and settled, one after the other, marching, stepping in place, keeping the beat, keeping time.

A couple stopped beside her, wanting to face the man whose playing moved people to their core.

"Pretty song," the woman said.

"Tune," Cora corrected automatically, watching Matty as his talented fingers danced.

The woman nodded, her head moving in time to the music. "Wonder what's it called?"

Without tearing her eyes from Matty's, Cora smiled. "*When the Battle is Over.*"

Epilogue

Matty draped his arm across Cora's shoulders and she watched as he stared, openmouthed with mock horror at the dreary, vacant little space before him. "I gave up touring the world for *this?"*

Cora laughed and shoved him off, and Peter crossed his arms over his chest and glared. "You paid me three months' rent and never touched the place. Not that I minded your absence...."

Cora laughed and jabbed her brother in the arm, feeling a happy need to knock both these males around a bit. "Be nice. We've been a little busy. And, unlike Matty, I'm not used to time travel."

He chuckled. "I think ye mean time *zones*, wife."

"Whatever. By the time we got to Paris, I felt like I spent a week in the air."

"That's only because ye insisted on watching the longest movies known to man."

"Anyway," Peter interrupted and relaxed his pose, sensing Cora wasn't going to swat him again, "I swept it out, but the rest is up to you two."

"What color should I paint it?" Matty looked expectantly to her.

"Plaid, of course."

He rolled his eyes.

"You choose whatever color you want. I have no intention of lifting another paintbrush ever again."

"Ye'll have to when they build our house."

"You've got two hands," she retorted.

He laughed and crunched her to his side.

"Besides," she continued, "I'm sick of smelling paint. I just spent a week painting the hospital."

"Better that than old man smell, is what ye told

me."

"True. But still, it's killing my brain cells."

"I'd never notice," Peter teased.

"Fuck you very much." And she added his personal favorite— two raised middle fingers— making her brother chuckle.

Peter turned his gaze to Matty. "I'll let you pay me three more months in advance if you promise to leave again." He cracked a grin.

Matty laughed at the taunt. "Afraid ye'll turn into ma biggest fan? Or that I'll sway yer customers to abandon their ungodly muscle cars in favor of something that truly catches a woman's notice?"

"No, and no."

"Wait." Cora grabbed Matty's arm. "Are you saying you only play the pipes to get women's attention?"

He smiled down at her. "One woman, and I've claimed her heart long, long ago."

He was nothing but steadfast, Cora had to admit as she returned his warmth. Even with her brother goading him, Matty never faltered in his devotion to her.

"Disgusting." Peter rolled his eyes and turned away.

"If you'd leave your garage once in a while, you might find someone, too."

"No one wants a grease monkey." He dug black chunks from under his nails as he said this, avoiding their gaze.

"Grease monkeys are allowed to be happy, too, you know."

He met her gaze for a moment, then turned to Matty. "You've got the key. Let me know if you need anything."

They shook hands. "Thanks, man." Then Matty looked down at his palm in mock horror. "Is this *grease?*"

Peter scowled at Matty in lieu of words, met Cora's eyes, then left.

The March air spilled through the door when he opened it, making Cora shiver. "Poor Peter." She frowned and watched him slide into his own shop next door. "I know he's lonely, but he never leaves the garage."

"Aya." Matty stepped close and wrapped her tight in her arms. "Not yer problem, wife. He'll find a woman when he's good and ready."

"You mean, when he's not looking."

"Aya. That."

She grinned, then turned when the door opened again. Carla stepped in. "Knew I'd find you here." She looked around the bare room. "*Love* what you've done with the place."

Matty narrowed his eyes as Cora laughed and told Carla, "I volunteered you to paint here, too."

"I'm done painting."

"That's what I said."

"Is the smell gone?" Matty asked.

"Finally. Thank God for primer." Then she dug dried paint from under a nail.

Cora turned to face her, feeling the excitement. "We set to open soon?"

Carla nodded, then turned when Gunner entered, bearing four coffees in a tray. They dove in, eager for warmth. "You're the best. Thank you. April fourth, if all goes well. We're already booked for the day."

"Mom's spreading the word," Cora said. "She's so happy you took the plunge."

"We are, too."

Gunner sipped his coffee and looked at Cora, but his words were for Carla. "Did you tell her?"

"Oh." Carla lowered her coffee. "Hope you don't mind, but you're not going to be exactly a tech."

"What?" Fear surged in her. She loved being a tech! Her brain rattled off a dozen scenarios, from receptionist to supply ordering to kennels, all demotions. "What do you mean?"

She shared a conspiratorial glance with Gunner before facing Cora again. "I thought you might prefer to be *head* tech instead."

Relief washed through her. "That implies staff."

"Yeah. Two techs from our old hospital are moving here."

"Tell me Phil's not one of them."

Gunner chuckled at that. "Phil is *definitely* not one of them."

Cora didn't mean to throw Carla's old beau in Gunner's face, and she felt herself grimace at the faux pas. "Sorry. Just slipped out."

"I'm crazy, but not that crazy." She grinned at Cora. "They work days, so you might not know them. You'll like them, though. They're good. Smart. Sarcastic."

"Perfect."

"I'd like you to manage them."

"Okay."

But Carla pressed her like she argued the offer. "You'd get better hours."

"I said okay."

"Fine. And a pay raise."

Cora laughed. "Alright, already!"

Carla smiled. "This way, you can work right up until your due date."

Openmouthed, Cora faced Matty. "You told her?"

"Aya. And I don't regret it."

After what they'd been through, Cora couldn't fault him. "I wanted to share the news."

"What news?" Carla asked, her eyes bright with mock innocence.

So Cora spared a narrowed gaze to Matty, who only returned a cheeky grin, then she faced Carla. Suddenly the reality of saying words she'd never once gotten to speak made her heart race. She looked at everyone, took a deep breath, and spilled it. "I'm pregnant."

Carla squealed with joy and pulled her in to hug. "That's it; you're not allowed to take x-rays. Damn it, or anesthetize. You trying to kill me before we even open?"

"Hardly. And I know, I know." She pulled away and touched her hand to her stomach. "I was going to tell you."

"I'm not sweating it; it's why I hired the other two techs. Does your family know?"

"Not yet."

Matty picked up her hand and drew her to face him. "You're twelve weeks along. Let's stop in to see both our families."

She watched his fingers stroke and dance along hers, mesmerized by the gentle strength they held. "We'll have the first grandchild."

"Aya. And he'll be a right fine lad."

"Lass."

"Lass?"

She nodded. "Lass."

Wonder filled Matty's eyes. "A wee lass." He smiled down at her. "Guess I'll have to say *mo chridhe* twice as often now."

She shared a secret grin. "Unless I'm having twins."

His eyes locked on hers. "Are ye?"

She shrugged. "Maybe?"

"Twins. Wee little lasses."

He looked so proud in that moment that Cora hoped the feelings she had of what was growing inside her truly came to pass.

Now he beamed as he met her eyes. He gathered her close but addressed everyone. "And that, dear friends, is the first of the American Clan MacKenzie."

Tears of joy slipped from her eyes as Matty drew her in to kiss. When he pulled back, she smiled up at him. "I love you."

He grinned down at her, love shining bright and clear in his crystalline green depths. “And I’ve loved ye ever since.”

The End

Did you like this story? Help spread the word! Please leave a review on the website where you bought it, or on Goodreads.com. Even something as short as “I liked it” is a tremendous help and completely appreciated. Leaving a review not only helps readers find books that others like, but it helps authors gain free advertising and promotions. Bottom line, the more reviews a book gets, the easier it is for others to find it. Thank you in advance for your review.

ABOUT THE AUTHOR

Dorothy Callahan is one of those authors who annoys other authors by refusing to be tied down to one genre. If a tale demands to be told—even if she's never read a single story like it—she'll find a way to write the book of her heart. This is the only way to quiet those demanding characters begging to be heard.

She lives in New York with her wonderful husband, a pride of demanding cats, and two loyal dogs, all rescued from shelters (well, not the husband). Her love of both animals and writing prompted her to start READ AND RESCUE, an organization where animal-loving authors and readers can find one another. The unique aspect to this group is that each author pledges a portion of proceeds to his/her favorite animal cause.

When Dorothy is not writing, she and her husband enjoy shopping for antiques and renovating their pre-Civil War house. If you are interested in learning more about Dorothy or how to help other animals in need, please visit her at dorothycallahan.com, dorothycallahanauthor@gmail.com, Facebook at Dorothy Callahan Author, or Twitter under Dorothy Callahan@Callahanauthor.

Interested in other books by Dorothy Callahan?

Here they are, in order of (original) release:

Taming the Stallion **ISBN-10:** 1440563454
Loving Out of Time **ISBN-10**: 1512022268
Third Eye's a Charm **ISBN-10:** 1440580146
A Decade for Darius **ISBN-10**: 1499399448
Nominated by Sweet 'n Sassy Bookaholics as "Best of the Best Reads of 2015"

Impenetrable: Let No One In **ISBN-10**:1516932102
To Catch a Star **ISBN-10**:1532986513
Crazy Little Fling **ISBN-10**:1539438228

Thank you for your interest, and may all your days be filled with happiness.